HER
FATHER'S
SECRET

HER FATHER'S SECRET

SARA BLAEDEL

TRANSLATED BY

MARK KLINE

GRAND CENTRAL
PUBLISHING

New York   Boston

Copyright © 2019 by Sara Blaedel
Translation copyright © 2017 by Sara Blaedel
Translated by Mark Kline
Cover design by Elizabeth Connor
Cover copyright © 2019 by Hachette Book Group

Originally published as *Ilkas Arv* in 2017 by People's Press in Denmark.

Grand Central Publishing
Hachette Book Group
1290 Avenue of the Americas
New York, NY 10104
Hachettebookgroup.com

First Edition: March 2019

Grand Central Publishing is a division of Hachette Book Group, Inc.
The Grand Central Publishing name and logo is a trademark of Hachette Book Group, Inc.

The Hachette Speakers Bureau provides a wide range of authors for speaking events. To find out more, go to www.hachettespeakersbureau.com or call (866) 376-6591.

The publisher is not responsible for websites (or their content) that are not owned by the publisher.

Library of Congress Cataloging-in-Publication Data

Names: Blaedel, Sara, author. | Kline, Mark, 1952– translator.
Title: Her father's secret / Sara Blaedel ; translated by Mark Kline.
Other titles: Ilkas arv. English
Description: First edition. | New York : Grand Central Publishing, 2019.
Identifiers: LCCN 2018036326| ISBN 9781538763254 (hardcover) | ISBN 9781549170829 (audio download) | ISBN 9781538763278 (ebook)
Subjects: | GSAFD: Mystery fiction.
Classification: LCC PT8177.12.L33 I4513 2019 | DDC 839.813/8—dc23
LC record available at https://lccn.loc.gov/2018036326

Printed in the United States of America

LSC-C

10 9 8 7 6 5 4 3 2 1

To my friend Preben,
who told me about Racine

HER FATHER'S SECRET

If she'd known what was about to happen, she probably would have just leaned back and enjoyed the show. Instead, Ilka stared anxiously over at the house, steeling herself to walk up and knock on the door. The coffee in the paper cup was cold, but she drank it anyway, hoping it would help. She clutched the five letters in her lap. It was hard to see the most recent one as anything other than a threat.

"You have a week to pay, otherwise, the truth will come out. Maggie."

It had been lying on the reception desk yesterday, inside an envelope at the bottom of a stack of mail. Immediately Ilka had recognized the feminine handwriting. Several days after arriving in Racine she'd discovered the first four letters in an upstairs room at her father's funeral home, bound together by a brittle rubber band, all from 1997–98, with Maggie's signature on them. The envelopes had no stamps or return addresses.

Nothing in the letters hinted at what her father could have been trying to conceal. But honestly, Ilka had plenty on her plate without having to deal with this mystery. She'd recently inherited his Wisconsin funeral home, despite the fact that she and her mother hadn't heard from him, not a single peep, since he'd abandoned them thirty-three years ago.

The first letter was dated June 1997.

Dear Paul,

Your wife is having an affair with my husband.

Maggie

Ilka read the short message again. Her fingers were frozen, and the car's windows were fogged up, further blurring the hazy residential street. The sun was trying to peek through, but the gray morning mist still covered Racine.

She had no idea who this Maggie was, but if anyone were being blackmailed, surely it must be the two people accused in the letter. After a few cups of morning coffee, she'd driven her father's silver-gray Chevrolet over to give the letters to his second wife, Mary Ann. On the way, though, she'd begun to consider her motives. To throw some light on her father's life since he left Denmark? That's what she wanted to think. But more likely it was to pay Mary Ann back for how she'd treated Ilka when they first met.

She glanced up at the house again. Mary Ann and her daughters had practically thrown her off their porch. All she'd done was bring them some drawings her two half sisters had made when they were kids. Ilka had found the drawings while cleaning her father's room, along with a clay figure and some photos she'd also taken along. They'd given her an excuse to meet the family her father had started after leaving Denmark. And to be shunned, as it turned out. Later that evening, when she'd returned to the funeral home, the younger sister had been waiting for her in the dark in her father's room.

"Don't come by the house again," Amber had said. "It's not good for Mom. It's not good for anything."

Amber's mother had been in a car accident years ago and was confined to a wheelchair, but Ilka couldn't understand why getting to know her half sisters could harm Mary Ann.

She turned back to the letters. The next one was from March 1998.

Dear Paul,

I came home this morning and found your wife and my husband in our bedroom! He says he wants to leave me. You have to make them end it.

Maggie

And two months later:

Dear Paul,

Finally! My husband is heartbroken, but I'm sure we can find what we once had together.

Maggie

These first letters had troubled Ilka when she found them,

but the fourth, from June 1998, was the one most difficult for her to give Mary Ann.

Dear Paul,

I hear your wife is paralyzed from the waist down. And that it's a miracle you walked away from the accident without a scratch.

Maggie

Ilka emptied the paper cup. As she was about to crush it down in the cup holder, her phone pinged—she had a match on Tinder. Shortly after arriving in Racine, she'd created a profile, to have something that could distract her from the funeral home, which already had become her responsibility. She grabbed the phone. The photo of the smiling blond man interested in her showed him holding hands with two young children. Ilka deleted him at once and looked up. Two black four-wheel-drive vehicles were parked in front of the house—how could she have missed them driving up?

She laid down her phone and watched six men in dark suits climb out and gather on the sidewalk. Moments later a monster of a moving van drove in and blocked the driveway. The quiet street where her father had lived was suddenly a traffic jam.

She leaned forward to get a better look at the man approaching the front door. He knocked and rang the doorbell several times, but no one answered, though Ilka noticed a curtain moving to the left of the door. He knocked one last time and waited before rejoining the others.

The door finally opened when the rear cargo door of the

moving van began folding down. It took Ilka a while to spot
Mary Ann's wheelchair behind a long wicker sofa on the
porch. Her blond hair was pinned up, and a thin shawl covered
her bare shoulders. Then Ilka shot up in her seat: The woman
was holding a rifle on her blanket-covered lap. Slowly she
rolled toward the steps, picked up the rifle, pointed it at the
dark-suited men, and yelled something at them. Ilka nearly
jumped out of her skin when the woman pointed the rifle in
the air and pulled the trigger. All six men immediately pulled
out handguns, which startled her even more.

Mary Ann's older daughter, Leslie, hurried out onto the
porch. She wore a short-sleeved flowered dress, and her hair
was wet. Insignificant details, given the situation, yet they
caught Ilka's eye before the next shot rang out. This time a bullet smacked into the side of the moving van.

Mary Ann planted her elbow on her wheelchair's armrest
and kept the rifle aimed at the van, where the men had taken
cover, though they still held their guns. Ilka opened the car
door and froze; she was scared, but she couldn't just sit there
and do nothing either. A deep voice ordered Mary Ann to put
the rifle down.

The sun had briefly broken through the clouds, and its rays
in the side mirror blinded Ilka when she finally worked up
the courage to get out. Mary Ann concentrated on reloading
as Leslie dragged her back to the door, and when she started
shooting again Ilka hit the asphalt behind the car. The sight of
the small, frail woman handling a lethal weapon was simply
too surreal; it made no sense at all. None of this did.

Mary Ann managed to fire one more shot before disappear-
ing inside the door. Immediately the six men started shooting
back, then they spread out and surrounded the large wooden

house. One of them ran up on the porch and pointed his gun at the front door, yelling for Mary Ann and Leslie to come out with their hands up. The others ducked around back.

Desperate now, Ilka peered over the low hedges of the neighbors' houses, but she saw no sign of anyone calling the police or doing anything to help the two women.

The door opened slowly, and Leslie walked out with one hand over her head, the other pushing the wheelchair. Mary Ann held her thin arms straight in the air. The man ordered them over to the far end of the porch, then signaled to the moving van. Ilka stared in bewilderment as a small army of broad-shouldered, muscular men poured out of the van and entered the house. A few moments later they began carrying furniture out. While they quickly filled the van, another man changed the front door lock, then picked up his tools and walked around back.

A car turned onto the street, and the driver honked in irritation at the blockade of vehicles in front of the house. Before he could get out, one of the black-suited men trotted over to him. Ilka was back in her car and out of earshot, but she got the drift of the conversation. A moment later the driver whipped his car around and drove off.

The whole episode seemed utterly insane to Ilka. For a split second she wondered if it was some sort of hidden camera show, or a scene in an action film. Then she noticed her half sister covering her mouth with both hands, fighting to hold back her tears.

Suddenly it was over. They shut and locked the front door, and the furniture movers climbed into the van. When it began backing up, the two black SUVs made U-turns on the street, and before she knew it they were gone. Once again, the street was quiet and deserted. Neighbors cautiously ventured out on their porches, though none of them dared walk over to Mary Ann's house. Ilka sat for a moment, wondering how long it had lasted, but she'd lost all sense of time.

Leslie stepped down off the porch, as if she were thinking of chasing the men who had taken everything from them. She was crying now, her head bowed as she wiped the tears from her cheeks. Then she noticed Ilka. Or maybe it was her father's car she recognized, because she looked startled when she met Ilka's eyes. She rushed back up the steps to her mother.

Ilka had just turned forty, and she guessed that Leslie was about ten years younger. Maybe in her late twenties. It was hard to tell. Her cardigan sweater and wavy blond permanent made her look like a middle-aged woman in an ad for a floor cleaner, but earlier Ilka had noticed her smooth, silky skin. It was hard to imagine her half sister had ever been young. After nursing school, she'd taken over the care of her mother.

Ilka sat for a few moments before getting out of the car and walking to the house. She left the letters from Maggie on the front seat.

She stopped at the front steps. "What on earth happened? I hope neither of you were hurt?" She tried to sound calm, though she wasn't. At all.

Leslie didn't react when Ilka stepped onto the porch, but Mary Ann abruptly turned to her. "What do you want?" she snarled. It began raining; heavy drops pounded the porch roof. "Leave us alone."

"But somebody just emptied your house! And it doesn't exactly look like you hired them to. You both could have been killed, have you called the police?" She gestured toward the neighbors. "Surely somebody has!"

"We don't want the police out here, and anyway it's all over."

Mary Ann's thin shawl was already soaked from the rain, and Ilka started to pull her farther under the roof, but the woman waved her away and rolled her wheelchair back herself.

Leslie didn't budge an inch.

Ilka had to lean in close to hear Mary Ann. "Leave us alone. This is none of your business, keep out of it."

Ilka seldom cried, but now she could barely hold back the tears. She'd been about to offer them her phone to call for help or suggest they all go to the funeral home and talk about what to do.

Without a word she turned and walked to the car.

She was still quivering with rage when she stopped at a filling station for ten dollars of gas. She slammed the car door shut, counted the coins in her small coin purse, and decided to buy a pack of cigarettes. She longed to fill her lungs with smoke, hold it in until she felt dizzy. Something was stirring in her chest, a vague emotion, an uneasiness she couldn't put her finger on, though she was certain it had nothing to do with the humiliating rejection her father's second family had put her through again.

You never really know someone you live with before you're seven, she thought. *You're not old enough to see him as he really is. You're just with him, and you feel safe. Until one day he suddenly disappears, and you're panic-stricken when you understand you've been abandoned.*

She still remembered that feeling of being around her father, how much she loved him, counted on him. But she didn't know him. And why should she suddenly spend time getting to know his idiotic second family? They meant nothing to her.

Ilka glanced around when she realized she was talking to herself. Her pack of cigarettes was open, and she was about to light one when she noticed the gas pump close by. It reminded her of something embarrassing back when she'd just gotten her driver's license. She'd been smoking a cigarette while filling up. An older man yelled at her, but several days passed before it came to her why. Luckily nothing had happened, but that was the moment she gave up cigarettes. At least until now, after moving to Racine had interrupted her stable Copenhagen life.

She stuffed the cigarettes into her pocket and got in the car.

It had stopped raining, and now patches of blue sky began peeping out from behind white clouds. A glossy sheen covered the asphalt. Ilka let a pickup pass before pulling out and heading for the main drag. She drove by several empty stores on the way back to the funeral home; few businesses were left in West Racine, where her father had lived. Many of the neglected facades looked as if they'd been closed for years. She stopped for a red light at one five-way intersection and noticed firewood and bottled gas stacked up outside a convenience store on one corner.

When the light turned green she took off, but in the middle of the intersection she flashed on what had been nagging at her earlier. An image of herself popped up: a little girl with much-too-long front bangs, standing in the living room in her pajamas. She must have been three or four years old. The doorbell had rung, and several people stood outside. A bailiff, a policeman, a locksmith, and a woman from their district, her mother had explained to her later.

Ilka hit the emergency lights and managed to pull over to

the corner, where she scraped against the high curb. She'd forgotten the incident, but now the memories of the small apartment overwhelmed her. The sweet aromas from the bakery; her bed by the living room window. The black-and-white checkerboard linoleum in the kitchen. They'd had to take the back stairs down to pee.

The memories were only flashes, fragments from deep in her subconscious, repressed but now brought up to the surface by what she had witnessed earlier. It *had* happened. She remembered being thrown out, losing all their possessions. Ilka had hidden behind the sofa, but the woman from the district had grabbed her and dragged her away.

Now she saw herself as a little girl crying down in the courtyard, alone with the woman holding a few bags filled with Ilka's clothes. But none of her toys. After they left the apartment, her father argued with the strange men.

When her mother finally came down and joined them in the courtyard, she was crying too, though in a different way. And later her father left. Back then Ilka thought he was gone for a long, long time, but now she wasn't so sure. She'd been so young and had missed him so much.

She lit a cigarette, and slowly the car filled up with smoke. How could the memory of something so dramatic vanish, only to pop up again so many years later? And where had they lived after that? She couldn't remember. Up until now, her only memories had been from the house in Brønshøj she'd thought of as her childhood home.

She rolled the window down to get rid of the smoke, and after crushing out her third cigarette in the tiny ashtray she felt clearheaded enough to drive again. She wanted to call her mother, but instead she slowly pulled away from the curb.

* * *

She turned into the parking lot behind the funeral home and parked beside Artie's black pickup. He sat on the back steps with a cup in his hand and a cigarette hanging from his mouth, watching her. His weird longish hair was knotted up in a bun, and he wore a Hawaiian shirt. All in all he looked a bit quirky, yet for a moment she was tempted to sit down and cuddle up to him, hold him, let him cheer her up. Though not just because of all the forgotten childhood memories suddenly returning; as she began loosening up after the wild episode at her father's house, a sort of delayed shock set in.

Artie Sorvino had worked for her father for eighteen years. He was the closest thing she had in Racine to a friend she could confide in, though that wasn't saying much, because she still couldn't figure him out. Most of the time he backed her up, but occasionally he acted like he wanted nothing to do with her. At least their relationship at work hadn't suffered after the night she'd seduced him; he seemed to be okay with it as just a one-night stand.

Without a word she sat beside him and fished out her pack of cigarettes. He watched her reach for the lighter lying on the steps.

Finally she said, "She could have mowed them all down." She took a drag and blew the smoke out. "Okay, she shot above their heads first, but then she aimed right at them. It's a miracle nobody was hit."

"Who are we talking about here?" He turned to her and leaned closer to the doorway.

"Mary Ann, that's who! She and Leslie were thrown out of their house, I was there when it happened. A bunch of men came and emptied the place. They took everything away in a

11

big moving van. But before that she shot at them with a rifle. The woman's crazy!"

"Sounds like she was trying to defend her property," Artie said.

"But they hadn't done anything to her! She rolls out onto the porch with a gun on her lap, nobody says a word, and she starts shooting. It was absolutely insane! She shot right out into the street! Somebody could have been walking by! Then one of the men started shooting back, and nobody did anything to help, not even call the police. What's wrong with everybody?"

"Maybe you should just be happy you Danes don't have to defend yourselves that way over there. People don't buy guns here just for fun. In Wisconsin, nobody needs a special license to keep a gun in their home, as long as it's for defending yourself, for hunting, or for anything else legal."

He ticked that off as if it was something every single person in the state knew by heart.

"Listen," she said. "The men weren't even close to the house when she started shooting. You can't say you're defending yourself before someone threatens you or does something."

"They were on her property. I understand it's different in Denmark. You're so busy having fun, or whatever that *hygge* of yours means, that no one has time to shoot at people. Your father told me about the Danish police, all the time they spend helping mother ducks and their little ducklings across the street. Well, guess what, the cops over here have other things to do. We're prepared to defend ourselves. We have to be."

She ignored his attempt at humor. "That's not true. It's just that in Denmark it's not legal to have a gun on the table beside your bed."

He shook his head at her, but he added that there must have

been a reason why Mary Ann felt threatened. "I mean, we don't just start shooting at people who happen to stop by."

She stared at him for a moment, then he shook his head again and smiled. "No, I don't own a gun. But I do have a fishing knife, if it came down to that. Why don't I get you a cup of coffee, then you can tell me exactly what happened out there."

Before he could stand up, Ilka said, "No thanks, I've already had three cups. Another thing, in Denmark the person who takes over someone's property doesn't show up carrying a gun."

He looked at her in surprise. "The bailiff?"

"If that's what he's called, yes. Six men in fact, plus the ones who emptied the house. Mary Ann and Leslie didn't hire them, that's for sure."

"It couldn't have been the bailiff."

"Well, they were put out on the street, anyway. I saw the man changing the locks."

"That sounds strange." Artie swung his legs to the side so Sister Eileen could get out the door. Her gray habit grazed Ilka's shoulder. She was associated with a parish outside town, and for the past twelve years she had worked as an unpaid volunteer for Ilka's father, though she did accept donations for her church. Yet she was often the first to show up for work in the mornings, and she knew the most about managing the funeral home. Her small apartment was next to the coffin storage room, and it seemed that Ilka had inherited her along with the business.

She stepped past them and turned around. "Who's been put out on the street?"

"Mary Ann and Leslie were thrown out of their house," Artie said. "But the law didn't do it, I'm sure of that. It's got to be somebody else."

"It was so humiliating for them, standing out on the porch, watching them drive away with everything they owned," Ilka said. "They didn't even get to keep their coats and bags."

"You don't need to feel sorry for them," Sister Eileen said without blinking an eye. "They probably went right out to Mary Ann's father. He lives very comfortably, and his daughter and granddaughters will too."

Ilka raised her eyebrows.

"Raymond Fletcher is one of the richest men in Wisconsin," Artie said. "And one of the most powerful. He owns a stable and breeds these insanely expensive trotters on his ranch."

Ilka's heart skipped a beat when he mentioned trotters. And a stable. Now it made more sense why her father's financial situation had collapsed, why he'd left everything in a big mess. Not that it changed anything. She hadn't forgiven him for dragging her into it. Just thinking about it made her angry, and suddenly she felt no sympathy at all for the two women. Apparently, they had no money worries, yet obviously they weren't going to help her, even though legally they were Paul Jensen's nearest family.

She pulled Maggie's letters out of her bag and handed them to the nun. "Do you know anything about these? The reason I drove over to Mary Ann's house was to give them to her. Honestly, I don't care anymore about anything that comes out."

The nun skimmed the five letters, then folded them up again and handed them back.

"Who's Maggie?" Ilka said. She looked at Sister Eileen, then at Artie, who stood up and shrugged. He held out his hand when Ilka started to rise. "The name doesn't ring any bells." He dumped the rest of his coffee on the ground.

Sister Eileen shook her head and turned to go to her apartment, but Ilka stopped her and asked them to come into the office to discuss the future of the funeral home.

"I've been going over the books," she began after they sat down around her father's desk. "We have an agreed overdraft in our bank account of almost two hundred thousand dollars. Besides that, we haven't paid several suppliers; that adds up to over forty thousand of debt. The two hundred thousand comes from withdrawals this spring. If I close the funeral home and go home now, I'll be paying off this debt the rest of my life. So I have to talk to my bank before I make any decision."

Ilka had thought about how to say this so it didn't sound as if she was abandoning them, yet that's what it came down to. Her father had been broke, and when he died he left the business deeply in debt. The past several days she'd gone through all the books for the past five years. She had no choice: She had to shut down.

"If they even let you leave the States with a debt like this," Artie said. She knew he might be right. Her mother had warned her about that before Ilka flew over to Wisconsin. Her ears began ringing.

"Right now we don't have the money for the funeral tomorrow. It's not prepaid; we'll have to wait for the family to pay the bill. Luckily, it's not one of the more expensive funerals. We just have to deliver the body to the church. But we're still responsible for the flowers and decorations."

"I'll take care of the flowers," Artie said.

Ilka knew he had stolen flowers from the common grave for an earlier funeral, but decided not to say anything. She saw no alternative. "What about embalming supplies?"

"I think we have enough for five or six more jobs."

"The biggest problem is the coffins," Sister Eileen said. "The suppliers have shut us down because of what we owe them. There's only one white coffin left, and then there's the light-blue used one out back, waiting to be hauled away."

"When we need more coffins, I'll order them online from Costco. We'll just have to say we can't trust our regular suppliers. I don't feel bad at all for blaming them, it's their fault for not giving me a chance to get the business back on its feet."

Artie and Sister Eileen stared at her.

"Really, though, we don't need to tell anybody where the coffins come from," she added.

Most people wouldn't even notice if the white coffin in the catalog was different from the one they got, she thought.

Sister Eileen spoke sharply. "But will you charge them the catalog prices?"

"We'll see." Ilka asked if they'd eaten lunch, if she should bring them something when she went out to shop.

Artie offered to make her a sandwich from what he had in the refrigerator, but Ilka politely declined. Her father's partner had already sunk a great deal of money into the bottomless pit of the funeral home's debt by paying back taxes that would have shut them down. At the time they'd believed they could sell the business to another undertaker in town, and Artie's dream was to start up an embalming business and freelance for other funeral home directors in the region. That way he could avoid all the pickups, conferences with families, and services themselves. Unfortunately, it didn't happen. Golden Slumbers Funeral Home had been bought out by a large chain, American Funeral Group, which almost certainly wouldn't make use of Artie's special talents. The chain had also been interested in Ilka's business, but she'd played her cards all wrong. At best Artie would be left with the funeral home building, and his dream of freelancing would probably remain just that—a dream.

Abruptly she stood up. "I have to go out anyway, there's something I have to take care of." She grabbed her coat and umbrella and started down to Oh Dennis!, a local pub that also served as a hangout for people in Racine who had run into hard times. A week earlier she'd been standing in front of a one-armed bandit in back, unable to stop pouring coins in it. She was hoping he was working today—the young bartender who had finally refused to break more bills for her. She wanted to thank him.

He was off work. A younger woman with colorful tattoos on her brawny forearms stood behind the bar. Ilka scanned the menu prices and ordered the cheapest lunch without even looking at what it was. She felt dirt-poor, down and out. She remembered back when she was a kid, on Children's Aid Day at the Triangle in Copenhagen with her friends. A small carnival had been set up, and Ilka had emptied her piggy bank and coaxed a little extra out of her mother. She'd spent most of the money on a one-armed bandit, the rest on a scratch ticket at the hot dog stand while her friends ordered hot dogs and chocolate milk.

Ilka paid for the lunch and was about to sit down when she noticed Larry out on the sidewalk. Less than a week earlier, she'd met him in a bar and screwed him behind a shed down by the canal, and a few days later he stopped by the funeral home and invited her out. She explained she wasn't looking for any sort of relationship, that it had only been a physical thing, and though she'd tried to put it nicely, she felt she'd made it clear she wasn't interested in seeing him again.

She turned quickly, but it was too late; he'd spotted her. He was on his way to the door, and to avoid him she hurried to the back of the pub, where the only other person in the place sat at a table against the wall. A small man in a light-blue windbreaker. He'd been sitting at the same table the evening she'd lost it. She didn't know him, but she pulled a chair out and asked if she could sit down. "Would you do me a favor and pretend you're talking to me?"

"Who are we hiding from?" He was old, and from his rusty voice she guessed it wasn't often people sat down wanting his company.

Suddenly Larry was standing at their table. Ilka smiled politely up at him.

"Hi!" Larry unzipped his jacket and told her he'd been trying to get in touch with her. Ilka glanced at the elderly man out of the corner of her eye and nodded as Larry rambled on about a visiting delegation from a European architectural school they were going to show around their headquarters.

Ilka had no idea what he was talking about, and before she could react he pulled a chair out and sat down beside her. Then she remembered he worked for Johnson Wax, which was in Racine.

"It's a historical building," he continued, as if Ilka had begged him to describe Racine's architectural wonders. "In fact, the administration building and the research tower were designed by Frank Lloyd Wright."

He scooted over so his leg grazed against hers. Ilka moved her leg away; forcing this spectacle onto a stranger enjoying his afternoon coffee was embarrassing. Her food arrived, but before the waitress could ask if Larry was ready to order, the man leaned over the table.

"Excuse me, I hope you don't mind, but I've been looking forward to this lunch with the daughter of my deceased friend from Denmark."

Ilka and Larry were both surprised. Larry because he likely couldn't imagine her having lunch with an old bum, and Ilka because the man knew who she was. And apparently had known her father.

Larry regrouped and stood up slowly. He held Ilka's eye, as if to give her a final chance to reconsider.

She watched him walk off. He was in good shape, and he did have a nice ass, but she turned and instantly forgot about him.

"Your father and I were colleagues," the man said. He explained that he'd been a funeral home director in town before her father had arrived. "But that was years ago. I had to give up my business. He was a fine man. It's hard knowing he's not around anymore."

Suddenly the memories seemed to overwhelm him, and he fell silent. Ilka ate her chicken wings. After she'd gnawed the last bone clean, she tore open a tiny plastic sack, pulled out a damp napkin, and wiped off her fingers. "Did you see much of each other? You and my father?"

"We did a betting game, a weekly lottery where you paid to keep the same numbers year after year, and for a long time we went together to the track, harness racing, but the track went bankrupt. And it wouldn't be the same without him anyway."

Ilka pushed her plate away. Of course her father had kept betting over here. She was about to mention that weakness in her father's character when the man nodded, as if he were reading her mind. "It wasn't always easy for Paul to control his gambling—it was in his blood—but he tried. And there were

21

long stretches when he stayed away from the track. In the end he wasn't out there at all. He paid the price for his habit, we knew that. His friends. By the way, did you know he bought a horse for you, not long after he came here?"

Ilka nodded slowly. She'd read it in one of the letters she found in his desk. A packet of letters he never sent. But it touched her that he'd told his friend about her.

"The pony died just a few years ago. At a ripe old age, very ripe. Toward the end it didn't even want to leave its stall. But it had a good life, and the kids loved it."

Ilka stared down at the table. When she was a kid she would have given her right arm—both arms—to have a horse. It was strange to think she'd actually had one waiting for her over here.

"Another friend of your father's, Frank Conaway, boarded it at his family's stable. Occasionally Paul drove out and checked on it. Sometimes I rode along. It's a nice drive, and we'd known Frank for many years. When the pony wasn't out in the pasture, your father walked it in the woods behind the stables. Like he was walking a dog."

He looked away while the tattooed waitress picked up Ilka's plate and asked if they wanted coffee. Ilka shook her head, but he held up his cup.

"I haven't heard about Frank Conaway," she said. "I'm sorry, but what's your name?"

"Gregg." He put his cup down and held his hand out. "Gregg Turner, and your name is Ilka Nichols. Your father told me. Back then I had no idea I'd ever meet you. But word gets around when strangers come to town."

"Please excuse me if I'm being nosy, but are you the one who sold your funeral home to the American Funeral Group?"

Artie had told her about a funeral director who made a deal with the large chain, and as soon as he signed, things went downhill. And not only for the man Artie described as a shadow of himself: The funeral home was abandoned. Now it was boarded up, the Old Glory out front in tatters. No one had been inside since the sale. American Funeral Group had only been interested in wiping out one more competitor, which sent a message to all nearby funeral homes.

His smile disappeared as he nodded. "The past is dead and gone, you can't change it. I was naïve. I thought they'd keep their word, but they just wanted to crush me. It was my uncle's old business, and I figured they'd keep me on. I was out of work before the ink on the contract dried."

They sat for a moment in silence.

"Is Frank Conaway one of his friends from the racetrack?" Ilka asked. She imagined her father had hung out with others interested in horses, just as he had in Denmark. Several times she'd gone along to the stables, where he visited the sulky drivers he knew. While the grown-ups talked, or while he watched the horses being trained, she was allowed to run around in the stables. Once in a while she'd even ridden in a sulky.

He nodded. "They had a long friendship. They met back when Paul first came over. Frank was young, he was a groom in the stable your father worked for. Over the years they grew close—it's like he was almost a son to Paul. And Paul was the godfather of Frank's older daughter. Later on, when Frank had his own stable, your father boarded the pony with him."

Ilka was overwhelmed at learning he'd taken on responsibility for someone else's child as a godfather, had considered this

Frank to be his son. She felt split: She wanted to know more, yet it scared her. It was all too much.

But a moment later, without considering the consequences, she pushed on. "Where does he live? Do you think it would be okay for me to go out there? It would be fun to hear about the pony."

He didn't hesitate. "I'm absolutely sure Karen would be very happy if you stopped by. She's his wife. It's not far away, an hour's drive, maybe a little over."

Ilka wrote the name down and waited while Gregg brought out a notepad from his inside coat pocket and gave her a phone number. "If you look the number up, I'm sure you'll find the address. I'm so glad I got to meet you."

His rusty voice had livened up during their conversation, and when Ilka scooted her chair back to leave, he smiled. "Anytime you need to be rescued from some other young man, just let me know."

She smiled back and turned to go, but then thought of something. "Do you happen to know if my father knew a woman called Maggie?"

After a few moments he shook his head. "Don't believe so. Not that I recall."

Ilka had borrowed twenty dollars from Artie for gas. She'd also asked him what he knew about his father's friend, but Artie had only met Frank Conaway a few times, and he made no secret of his fear of horses. He wouldn't dream of setting foot in a stable.

She punched in the address on the GPS and turned on the radio as she left Racine. The highway ran straight as a string, all the way to the horizon, and she gripped the wheel to fend off the occasional gusts of wind. It didn't take long to see this stretch wasn't going to be a nice little Sunday drive. At least she wouldn't get lost.

As she neared the Conaways', she and the car behind her had the highway to themselves. Farmhouses were spread out, some close to the highway and others set back, hidden by windbreaks. Fenced-in pastures and hay barns were frequent reminders that she was in horse country now. She noticed several training tracks beside pastures, horse trailers parked by driveways.

Two gigantic round hay bales were stacked up beside the gravel drive leading to the Conaway family's farm; a hand-painted sign with their address stood in front. Ilka slowed down and double-checked the address before heading up the driveway. She spotted the woods behind the buildings, then the trail leading from the broad barn. She didn't at all consider herself sentimental, but the thought of her father leading the pony down that trail moved her.

"Stop it!" she snapped at herself. As if him taking care of a horse was some great thing, when he hadn't so much as sent her a single birthday card.

Gravel crunched under the tires, and a small black-and-white dachshund raced around the house and started yapping. Before Ilka shut the motor off, the farmhouse door opened and a middle-aged woman stepped out. A little girl clinging to her from behind stared wide-eyed at the stranger.

Earlier Ilka had called to ask if she could stop by. "But Frank's not here!" Karen Conaway had said. Ilka suggested she could come later that week if it was more convenient, but that it didn't matter if Frank was there or not. She just thought it would be nice to see where the pony had lived.

"Of course, I understand, sure," Conaway's wife had said. "And I know my daughter would love to show you our stable. You're more than welcome to come. I'd love to meet Paul's Danish daughter too. We've heard the stories about you charming the pants off everyone at the track, after your father said you were named after a Derby winner."

Ilka had offered to bring along some kringles from Racine, even though the pastry wasn't at all like what she was used to at home. But Karen told her it wasn't necessary, that she'd baked some Danish cookies and she'd like Ilka to taste them.

They greeted each other at the door before going inside. The dog hid under a kitchen chair while Karen handed Ilka the coffee cups. Her young daughter was shy, but she followed them into the kitchen and sat down at the far end of the table. Soon she was absorbed in coloring in a page in a coloring book, though every so often she glanced up at Ilka in obvious curiosity.

Karen poured coffee. "My husband knew your dad most of his adult life. In fact, Frank was the one they sent to pick Paul up at the airport, when he flew in from Denmark."

Ilka sat down at the plank table. Karen placed in front of her an old-fashioned cookie tin covered with elves and gold hearts, similar to the ones Ilka's grandmother had.

"Your father bought this at the museum. Have you seen it yet? They have tons of Danish things, and occasionally they hold a bazaar."

She offered Ilka a vanilla cookie. It was a bit odd for Ilka to see what to her was a Christmas cookie in late September. She laid it on her saucer and waited for Karen to serve her daughter juice and a cookie and sit down herself.

"Paul gave me the recipe. I also make the flat brown cookies. But Lily and I like these the best."

"I didn't know my father could bake Christmas cookies."

"They're not Christmas cookies to us," Karen said. "They're just Danish cookies. Or like your dad said, Danish *smo-kay-ger*, right?"

Ilka smiled. "*Smah-kay-uh.*"

"I don't think he baked either. He just handed me the recipe and said if I got bored, he'd be happy to taste them. He was a charmer, that dad of yours! He gave me the cookie tin too."

"How long did my father and your husband work together before he went into the funeral home business?"

"It was before I met Frank, so I don't really know. At first I got the feeling something had happened that kept Paul away from the stable. I thought it was weird Frank was friends with an undertaker! I got used to it, though."

She smiled sheepishly. "When Paul married Mary Ann, Frank and I were invited to the wedding. After that, he started showing up at the stable here and there."

Ilka hadn't touched her coffee or the cookie. "What happened?"

Immediately she regretted asking; Karen looked uneasy, as if she wanted to ignore the question, but then she straightened up and focused on what to say. "Well, I don't know all the details. It wasn't something people talked about. But when someone struggles with an addiction, they can lose control, the devil gets the upper hand. That's what happened with your dad."

"He gambled?" Ilka said, to help her along.

Karen nodded. "Frank said that when he came over, the plan was that he'd make a big investment in the stable he'd been hired to manage. Several other investors were involved too. And private people also put up some of the money. They aimed to establish one of the most successful trotter stables in North America. And the way I understood it, your dad's job was to hire the best sulky drivers and get on the good side of the best breeders, so the stable would get first dibs on the new foals. That's how he met Mary Ann. Her dad owned the stable."

She paused and gazed out the window.

"But he couldn't stop himself. The bets were small at first, but he also gambled when he traveled around visiting racetracks, scouting the sulky drivers and horses. My husband thinks it got serious when he tried to cover losses by upping his bets. It ended up with him losing it all."

Karen peered at Ilka for a moment. Checking to see if she could handle the rest, Ilka thought. Lily had stopped drawing and was staring at them.

"So besides losing all the money he'd brought with him, nearly two hundred thousand dollars, he also gambled away the investors' money. Frank called it a fever Paul couldn't shake. He was deep in debt, and it was a disaster for everyone involved. Frank can give you more details. I remember once they talked about Paul leaving it all behind, going back to Denmark. But he knew he couldn't just run, it would catch up to him. Things didn't settle down until he got married."

"But what about all the money he owed?" Ilka asked.

"His father-in-law covered the debt. Mary Ann was expecting their first child, so I'm guessing Raymond Fletcher wanted the scandal to go away."

"When did my father meet Mary Ann?"

"They were married a year or two after he came. It all happened pretty fast."

"I guess so," Ilka mumbled. Lucky that she and her mother hadn't known, she thought. "And that's when he started the funeral home?"

Karen nodded. "He needed a job to support his family. More coffee?"

"No thanks." Her stomach ached from what Karen had told her. She pushed the half-full cup away.

They listened to the girl's crayons scratching in the silence that followed.

"I'm looking forward to meeting your husband." Ilka didn't know what else to say. And she needed to get up, move around.

She kept jiggling her cup, until the teaspoon inside hopped out and clattered on the table.

"Things are a bit difficult at the moment." Karen looked away. "But I'll have him call you."

"It wouldn't have to take long," Ilka hurried to say. "I just want to talk to the people close to my father in the years after he left. There's so much I don't know. Maybe all I really want to know is how he felt, if he was happy. And if your husband doesn't have time to meet with me, a phone conversation is okay."

"I understand, and of course Frank will talk to you. How long are you staying in Racine?"

"I don't know yet."

Karen stood up, and Ilka carried her cup over to the sink.

"Don't bother with that, just leave it," Karen said. She asked her daughter if she wanted to show Ilka Benjamin's old stall.

"Yay!" The girl jumped up.

Ilka slipped her jacket on out in the hallway and peeked into the living room at the high ceiling, heavy furniture, empty walls. Several rows of shiny trophies stood on shelves of dark wood.

"Frank isn't a sulky driver, of course, but sometimes trophies are handed out to an entire team when a driver wins a race. And it means a lot to my husband to be appreciated that way. If it was up to me, I might decide they don't all have to be here in the living room."

She smiled, then walked over and opened the door. The mood was lighter now, and the little girl was already headed to the stable. Ilka asked Karen if she'd heard her father mention a woman named Maggie. She frowned in thought, then shook her head.

"Is it someone he met at the racetrack?"

Ilka shrugged. Of course, that was a possibility. "It's just that she wrote a letter to him, and I'm trying to track her down."

"Sorry I can't help."

Ilka held out her hand and thanked the woman for letting her come on such short notice. Suddenly the situation felt awkward: A handshake seemed too little, a hug too much. Ilka smiled at her and walked over to the girl waiting at the stable door. She took a deep breath and closed her eyes a moment before stepping inside.

The stable was cool and dark. Lily chattered happily as they walked down the row of empty stalls, but Ilka wasn't really listening. The smell of horses was so intense that she guessed they'd just been let out to pasture. A handmade plaque hung from the last stall; the crooked letters spelled out BENJAMIN. The pony's stall was smaller than the others, and it was filled with food buckets and other things for the horses. It led to a room where a harness hung from a hook up by the ceiling.

"I did that." The girl pointed to a drawing, a whirlwind of dark colors. "My big sister did all the others, but she's in school."

Ilka nodded. She was touched by the hearts and small, finely detailed horse heads surrounding the pony's name. Obviously, the Conaway girls had loved him.

"I can show you where his saddle was," the girl said, eager to move on. Her mouth suddenly turned down. "It's just hard to open the door."

Ilka smiled at her, even though her mind was elsewhere.

"Maybe your father can help you fix it." She followed Lily to a low wooden door she had to jerk open; inside there was more tack and a saddle stand with a pony blanket.

"Mommy says he won't be home for a long time." Lily had lost interest in the saddle and the room, so Ilka closed and latched the door.

They walked back along the stalls in silence, and when they stepped outside the little girl ran off.

On the way home Ilka's thoughts were on what Karen had told her. Which was why she first noticed the dark car when she pulled out to pass a truck. She kept an eye on the car in the rearview mirror. It looked like the one she'd seen on her way out to the Conaways', though she wasn't sure. But it was following her on the long, straight stretch of highway. When she slowed, the car didn't pass her.

A gas station appeared up ahead. She slowed down again, but she waited to signal until she turned in. The dark car drove on. It must be the Conaways' stable, she thought, that explained why her heart was hammering, why she was so emotional. She watched the car disappear.

She parked between two rows of gas pumps and gathered her thoughts. Should she have gone back and asked Karen what Lily meant when she said her dad wouldn't be home for a long time? But she hardly knew the woman, and if they were breaking up...No, she couldn't go down that road.

The truck she'd passed earlier stopped beside the diesel pump farthest to the right. The driver jumped down out of the cab. His full beard covered most of his face, and his cap was turned backward. He looked like one of the men she'd seen at the bar the evening she met Larry.

Suddenly she felt lonesome. It wasn't that she had a lot of friends back in Copenhagen, but she missed running into people she knew, seeing a familiar face at the bakery or when she stopped by a café for coffee. She didn't have a network of friends in Racine, people she felt connected to. She was alone, a stranger, and that was fine for a while, but it wasn't going to work in the long run. Definitely not with the way things had gone. She closed her eyes; yes, she missed her apartment, her daily walk in Østre Anlæg, the old Copenhagen park. When she got home, she was going to get a cat!

Stop it, she mumbled to herself, looking around as if she'd just woken up. *Now, wouldn't that be lovely, Ilka the crazy cat woman. Christ!*

A car behind her honked, and Ilka pulled over to a marked space and shut the engine off. She scanned the matches that had come in on Tinder. Quick dates. No obligations. Possibly ending with sex, possibly not, but at any rate a human being to be with. She wrote to a blond man, Jeff, and suggested they meet for a drink. *Sounds good*, he wrote back. He asked if she was new in town. *Yes*, she wrote. He offered to pick her up and take her to a bar north of Racine on Lake Michigan that was built into the bluffs along the shore, like a grotto. But she wrote that she'd rather stay in town, so she could walk home. They agreed to meet at a bar beside the old jazz club, which Ilka thought must have closed decades ago. She'd passed by there a few times on the way to the pub.

She dropped her phone in her bag and pulled out of the filling station. The white center stripes flickered by on the deserted highway. Suddenly she remembered that she hadn't emptied the refrigerator back home in Copenhagen before she left. Or the trash. That would be loads of fun to come home to, that and all her dead plants. She'd have to ask someone to go over there. Mom.

For the past several days Ilka had avoided returning her mother's calls. She was going to go crazy when she heard Ilka was bringing home a debt of a few million kroner, exactly as she'd predicted. It would haunt Ilka the rest of her life, limit her in so many ways that all she'd be able to do would be to try to keep her head above water.

It wasn't the first time she'd cussed her father out. "Thanks for absolutely nothing except all the shit you've dumped on my head!"

She yelled in anger, felt like crying, screaming even louder. And in this hurricane of emotions, Ilka had no idea what to do about everything. Or what to do with herself, for that matter.

Traffic picked up as she approached Racine. She noticed the dark car again, several cars back. She stopped at a red light, but when it turned green she didn't move. The drivers behind leaned on their horns, and she turned on the emergency flashers. Gradually they began driving around her. She waited for the dark car to pass so she could see the driver, but it stopped directly behind her. When she turned and headed into Racine, the car followed.

She still wasn't sure it was the car that had followed her to the Conaways', but she was convinced it was the one that had driven on when she'd stopped at the filling station. She sped up, and the rest of the way home she avoided looking in the rearview mirror.

When she walked in, Ilka recognized Jeff from his profile photo. Which was easy to do, because he was the only customer in the place. He was leaning over the bar, talking to a girl drying glasses, and they turned and looked at her. For a moment the situation was awkward; the girl clearly was aware that though they didn't know each other, they were there to meet each other. Ilka noticed the look they exchanged before he turned to her and smiled. She walked up and said hello to him and nodded at the bartender, who asked what she'd like to drink.

"Why don't we go for a walk instead," she said, even though he had a full glass of beer in front of him.

He hesitated a moment before nodding and laying a few dollars on the bar. He held the door for her on the way out.

Outside in the evening light, she sized him up. He was short-legged and muscular, and good-looking, though with a serious, somewhat stubborn expression. The air was cool but not cold. She'd been told that Wisconsin could get a hard frost in late September. Or it could be eighty degrees all the way into October. Right now it was somewhere in between.

Ilka smoothed her hair back, tried to make it behave, but the wind kept blowing it into her face. Her hair was thin and a bit sad-looking to begin with.

They walked down toward the marina. "How long have you lived here?" she asked. Was he using Tinder just for sex, no strings attached, or was he the dating type? While walking he told her a lot about the town but very little about himself. By the time they reached the pier and passed by the hotel, she realized he hadn't answered her question. At least now she knew the population of Racine was just under eighty thousand.

He stopped so their shoulders were touching. They were the same height, but either he didn't notice she was a beanpole, or else he didn't care. He didn't seem to be reacting to her physically, and she wondered if he might just be lonely and in need of company. Then he pointed out along the pier, and she felt his hand on the small of her back.

"My boat's over there, you want to see it?" His voice was lower now, with a different feel to it.

She smiled and nodded. The only other person on the pier was a man coming from the parking lot, carrying a small bag.

On the way to the boat, she wrapped her arm around his waist to make things a little easier. It was a fine-looking motorboat, brimming with features that anyone interested in boats would notice, but Ilka was only interested in the man glued to her, stirring her body. She felt his back muscles clenching under his sweater as they walked in unison to the boat. Jeff jumped down and lifted the short gangplank into place, then held his hand out and helped her over. A real gentleman.

When he let go of her hand, Ilka swayed for a moment.

She'd never been much of a seagoer, and even the mild rocking did something to her sense of balance. She was afraid of getting seasick if she lay down. Which meant they'd just have to stay on their feet. And really, there was no reason to drag things out. He didn't seem all that interested either.

She followed him to the small cabin hatch and ducked her head as she squeezed her way down the short steps. There wasn't much room below. A few empty beer cans and a pizza box lay on the countertop at the bottom of the steps. The narrow opening toward the front, too tight to be called a doorway, led to another room with an unmade bed. She wasn't about to crawl in there; she already felt claustrophobic. Maybe she should find some excuse and get out of there, but he seemed like a decent guy. When he brought two beers over to the table, she reached for him and pulled his shirttail out. He looked surprised as he set the beers down.

Darkness was falling outside, and the small portholes didn't let much light in anyway. Maybe she was just paranoid from the episode with the car, but several times she had the feeling someone was walking on the deck above. She pulled off his shirt, and he unzipped his pants. Before she could react, he pushed her head down and shoved his cock in her mouth. She almost said something; she was the one who'd started all this, it seemed like she ought to have some say in the matter. But when he unbuttoned her blouse, she squirmed out of it and unhooked her bra and threw it on the floor. He began moaning, then he pulled out of her mouth and lifted her up. She winced as he began kissing her breasts; they were small, embarrassingly so to her. His focus, though, centered on his throbbing erection. His eyes shone, his hands were all over her, and his heavy breathing felt hot on her neck. Finally, he yanked down her pants. Ilka was dripping with sweat as she laid her hand on his chest and felt his heart pounding. She surrendered to the heat of his body, trembled as the hair on his arm brushed against her naked skin. He turned her around and pushed her against the table, then he pulled her panties down with his finger and entered her.

Ilka rarely felt uneasy even when with a man she didn't know. She'd never experienced anyone wanting more than she did, and this was no different. She was totally into it, into his violent thrusts; her thoughts and worries about the future were in another world. She came with a scream, her anger joining the spasms running through her body. A moment later he gripped her hips tightly and came with a final thrust, then he collapsed onto the table as they caught their breath. She pulled away and turned to him. No kissing, no signs of affection. This had been a release, nothing more.

As she gathered her clothes, they heard footsteps crossing the deck and onto the gangplank. She turned to the steps, and Jeff pulled on his pants and raced up the steps and outside. Ilka banged her head on one of the beams when she stood up. "Shit!" She rubbed the back of her head.

Jeff peeked down through the hatch. "You all right?"

"Is someone there?"

Jeff shook his head. She didn't ask more. He'd reacted, and that was all that mattered. Someone had been there. She hadn't even considered whether he was married, but if he got caught, that was his problem. He'd served his purpose.

He hopped back down into the cabin. "You want a beer?"

She noticed the boat's toilet beside the small kitchen, and another bedroom behind with more headroom. It didn't matter, though; the table had been fine. Her body felt relaxed and

light, refreshed. She almost thanked him, but she caught herself. The silence felt a bit strained, as if he was wondering if he
ought to invite her out, so Ilka quickly said she needed to get
going.

He handed her a can of beer as a final friendly gesture, but
when she said she was meeting someone, he lowered his arm.
He looked relieved.

The funeral is at the Lutheran church in West Racine at twelve thirty," Sister Eileen said when Ilka walked into the kitchenette the next morning. She'd had a long, dreamless sleep, interrupted only by her alarm clock ringing, and when she woke up she'd felt rested and ready to go. And a bit disoriented; she'd been uncertain about where she was, though the sound of Sister Eileen rustling around below quickly reminded her.

"The body is on a stretcher in the cold room," the nun continued. "The family approved the white wooden coffin, so that's taken care of, but we still need flowers to decorate it and the rows of chairs in the church. The family didn't say what flowers they wanted, only that they be in autumn colors."

Ilka put down the carafe of coffee. The other day she'd made it clear they had no money for flowers. She'd already emptied her own account to keep the funeral home going, and the fact that they were losing money made it impossible to ask the bank for a loan.

"Artie's taking care of the flowers," Sister Eileen added.

It seemed as though Sister Eileen enjoyed watching her face turn white. Like now, as Ilka pictured him walking around the cemetery, gathering up wreaths and bouquets. But she saw no other solution. "What if he gets caught?"

"Then we'll have one more problem on our hands." Sister Eileen walked back to her office in the reception.

Ilka closed her eyes and leaned her head against the doorframe. Might as well be bars on all the windows and doors, she thought. She felt trapped, with no way out of the mess her father had put her in. She'd never dreamed of being an undertaker, had never wanted to live in a small city like Racine either. When she was younger, she would have given anything to have even occasional contact with her father, but right now she wished he'd completely forgotten his daughter from his first marriage and instead let lovely Leslie and awkward Amber and their sharpshooter mother deal with his mess.

But he'd left the business to her, and no matter how much she struggled or how hopeless the situation seemed, that meant something to her.

Artie barreled in from the parking lot. "Can you give me a hand here?" He threw an armful of orange and yellow chrysanthemums on the floor. "There's more outside."

Ilka stared at the mound of flowers, not wreaths or bouquets, but cut flowers, fresh. She followed him out. "Where have you been, a greenhouse?"

He grabbed another armful from the pickup bed. "You could say that. I got ahold of some greenery too. You any good at binding flowers?"

Ilka shrugged. She'd never done it, but just like her job as a school photographer in Denmark, it wasn't anything she couldn't learn. She'd taught herself photography, and that had worked out okay when she took over the business after Flemming's death. So, what the hell; surely she could learn to tie flowers together too. She waited for Artie to gather up the last of them.

"Where have you been?" she asked when he shut the tailgate. "Out at the common grave?"

He stopped and looked up at her a moment before shaking his head. "I drove by, I admit that, but a family was there in mourning, so I didn't stop."

"So where *have* you been?"

He walked past her without answering. "I think there's string and wire in the flower room." He nodded at a door beside the trash container.

Ilka picked up the flowers on the floor inside and carefully laid them on the table in the flower room. Artie tossed down the greenery. "You've got an hour, then I have to drive them over to the church."

"What do I make, wreaths or bouquets?" she yelled. But he was already gone, so she went to look for the funeral contract Sister Eileen had laid somewhere. She was hoping to find some videos on YouTube explaining how to tie up wreaths and flowers, because the only time she'd ever tried it was in seventh grade, during a "vocational evening" when students could check out various workshops. All they'd made back then, though, was a table arrangement. How to arrange flowers in a vase to make it somewhat symmetrical. They'd never gotten to bouquets like this. Ilka went upstairs for her iPad and grabbed a pair of scissors in the office, then she yelled to the two others that she'd be in the flower room.

* * *

45

Twenty-four small sprigs of chrysanthemums. The wrong flower, because their blooms were too large for the small vases at the end of each row of pews. Ilka gave up on a casket spray; it was too difficult to make the flowers stand up in the middle and lie down at the ends of the coffin. Instead she'd made a type of table arrangement directly on the coffin, though without a vase. Then she'd placed cut flowers and greenery loosely on top of the coffin lid, her own variation of a tied bouquet. More modern. The question was if they would stay put when they lifted the coffin. Several times she'd almost thrown in the towel, but finally she fetched a roll of tape in the office and taped the flowers to the lid, with the next flower covering each piece of tape. It ended up looking like vines surrounding the flower arrangement.

When Artie was ready to leave, she said, "We need to be very careful when we carry the coffin."

He made no comments on the alternative decoration, though she thought it looked really nice. At least from a distance. She helped him carry the coffin to the hearse, but before they reached the parking lot, the tape started falling off. They set the coffin down, and Ilka ran back for the tape, but when she returned Artie was already wielding a staple gun; each sharp crack signaled another flower fastened to the coffin. When he was finished, he claimed they could turn the coffin upside down without the flowers falling off.

Ilka watched him drive away. She felt leaden, all the way down to her feet. She couldn't handle this, she was incompetent, and besides, she was broke. Not only economically, but mentally. She couldn't even do this last funeral without ad-libbing. Cheating.

After lunch they sat down in the office. Ilka had made coffee and tea and set a bowl of small chocolates on the table, along with a large notepad. "Forget about me," she said. "This is about finding the best way I can help you two, because my decision is definitely going to change your plans for the future."

Sister Eileen stared out the window. Not demonstratively as she sometimes did when Ilka spoke. This time she looked resigned. Which was exactly how Ilka felt. She was ashamed of herself for giving up, but there was nothing to do about it. Besides, she barely knew these people, and it wasn't her fault their futures were threatened.

And yet…maybe it really was her fault. If only the memories of a father who'd abandoned her hadn't been so disruptive when she'd arrived in Racine, if only she'd kept her head and trusted Artie Sorvino to do what was best for the funeral home and her by selling it to Golden Slumbers, none of them would be in this mess. She'd been thinking about that since

47

she watched Artie drive off with the coffin. She'd reached rock bottom and dragged them down with her. Now she had to find out what she could save. For their sakes.

"I've called the American Funeral Group, and they've agreed to meet with me today. But before I talk to them, I need to know everything we want included in a contract."

Neither of them spoke, so she turned to Artie. "Are you still interested in taking over the house? I can say that's part of the agreement, that you do the embalming and re-construction work for them. So you'll have work, but as a freelancer."

"It would be great if you can get that into the contract. I'd hate to not have a job when they take over."

Ilka thought of his house out by Lake Michigan. It couldn't be cheap. "Then that will be a condition."

She turned to the nun. "How about you, would you like me to see if they'll keep you on, move you over to their offices, or…"

Finally the nun turned to her. "Don't think about me, I'm not an employee."

"Of course I'm thinking about you; you live here, you're part of the business. Or I can also make it a condition that you con-tinue living in your apartment."

She had no idea about the rules the nuns had regarding their volunteer work. She didn't even know if Sister Eileen wanted to stay, now that her father was gone. A lot of the time she didn't seem to want to be here. Or maybe she just didn't want to be around Ilka.

"Just let me know when they take over, and I'll be out by then."

Artie had lit a cigarette without her noticing. She was about to say something, but if they were all on their way out anyway, what difference did it make if he smoked inside?

"I'd really like you to stay," he said, blowing smoke to the side as he looked at Sister Eileen. "'Course we don't know if I'll get any work, but if I do I need someone to run the office."

Her father had always taken good care of Sister Eileen, Artie had told her. Now she felt guilty, as if she wasn't living up to her obligations, but she didn't see what more she could do. "I'll tell them you have to stay in the apartment."

"But what about you?" Artie asked. "You have any idea how much you need to get out of debt?"

Ilka nodded. Apart from the $60,000 Artie had chipped in to pay back taxes, which could be seen as a down payment on the house, she owed just under $240,000. Surely that wasn't an unreasonable amount for them to pay, though in fact she had no idea what the funeral home was worth. The deal with Golden Slumbers she had scuttled included them taking over her father's customers and the large bank account consisting of payments for prepaid funerals. Though money was freed up only after a funeral was held, it did represent significant value. Or at least that's what she kept telling herself. It might not be cash right here and now, but it was guaranteed revenue. Luckily the account was inaccessible, which meant the money hadn't disappeared into the hole her father had dug.

Ilka had been shocked to learn how expensive funerals were in the United States, often twice or three times as much as in Denmark. No wonder people made arrangements—so their children and grandchildren wouldn't have to go into debt. And yet it seemed a bit morbid to her that so many young Americans paid into burial accounts.

"Surely they're interested in taking over the prepaid funerals," she said. "It's money in their pockets."

Artie nodded.

"Not unless some of the people who have paid do in fact die," Sister Eileen said.

Ilka studied her a moment before standing up. "I have to be there in twenty minutes, and I need to change."

She probably should have asked their advice before contacting the funeral home chain, but she'd hit the wall. And she was the one heavily in debt, not them; no matter how much she wanted to help them, she had to think of her own situation. Which was what kept stirring in the back of her head. If she couldn't sell the funeral home, her future back home in Denmark was a big question mark, because her photography business was rapidly going down the drain.

She stopped at the door and turned to them. "I wish we could go out and celebrate when I get back, but I can't even afford a full tank of gas. So you'll have to wait until everything's taken care of."

That wasn't entirely true; she did have sixty-eight dollars. But that was it. She had no more money, anywhere.

Sister Eileen didn't look all that disappointed as she stood up. "I truly hope you know what you're doing." She left the room.

"Don't you think it's better I do this?" Artie said. "It didn't turn out so great the last time you locked horns with them."

Ilka shook her head. He was right, though; her last meeting with the American Funeral Group had not been a success, to put it mildly. At the time, Ilka thought she'd already had the business sold, and she'd been less than hospitable when two men showed up and practically bullied their way into the funeral home. Finally, Ilka got so mad that she almost shoved them out the door.

Fortunately, the episode hadn't been mentioned when she called them before lunch to set up a meeting. And they asked her to come that very day—a good sign, she thought.

Ilka parked behind what until recently had been the Oldhams' funeral home. The family had owned it for several generations, until a sudden tragedy forced them to sell the business almost overnight. Ilka had heard that the funeral home chain planned on running the business the Oldhams' way, so the change in ownership would be less obvious.

They must have changed their minds, Ilka thought as she walked in. The row of family portraits of former owners hanging in the long hallway had been taken down, the wallpaper torn off, the floor covered with plastic, and the walls puttied and primed. The portraits lay scattered in a pile among strips of wallpaper and metal buckets.

Ilka shook her head and trotted up the few steps to where the nun working for the Oldhams once received visitors. She was gone now, replaced by a young, blond woman behind a glass window who asked Ilka if she had an appointment.

Ilka gave her name, and the woman told her to take a seat. She was five minutes early. *Don't look too nervous*, she told herself. She politely refused an offer of coffee and brought out the list of her demands in connection with the sale. Sister Eileen was to be allowed to stay in the apartment rent-free for as long as she wished, the same agreement as existed now. Then there was Artie. If the American Funeral Group couldn't guarantee him work, he might not get anything out of taking over the house, she thought. In his will her father had specified that Artie and Sister Eileen had first refusal rights to it if she decided to sell, which was fine with Ilka. All she cared about right now was breaking even on what she had inherited.

Her final condition was that all her father's personal belongings would remain in her possession. She was thinking of everything up in his room, where she now slept. Some of it she'd managed to look through, but there were still several boxes she hadn't opened.

She checked the time on her phone. Twenty minutes she'd been waiting now, without a word from them. At last a door opened, and the arrogant bastard she'd almost kicked out of the funeral home approached her. His aftershave smelled sweet and slightly nauseating. He greeted her curtly and handed her what looked to be a long standard contract. All they needed was her signature, he told her.

Ilka hesitated before taking it. She was about to stand up to follow him into the office, to discuss her conditions and have them added to the contract, but when he reached into his suit pocket and brought out a pen, she realized the negotiations would take place there in the reception.

She sat with her notes on her lap and read through the contract to find where her conditions could be inserted.

"As you can see on the first page, we're offering you an immediate takeover." He jerked the contract out of her hand, leafed back to the first page, and pointed to a date.

Ilka nodded. She was relieved, knowing it would all be over this week. She grabbed the pen he was holding out. "About my two colleagues, Artie Sorvino and Sister Eileen O'Connor, I've written down the conditions of their employment after the transfer. Of course, that can be negotiated, depending on if the funeral home will be run as it is or if the two funeral homes will be merged."

Before she could mention Sister Eileen's apartment, he said, "It's going to be shut down. We'll take over your portfolio. Your employees will not be needed."

After a quick glance over at him, she steadied herself without him noticing her clutching the paper in her lap. In short, concise sentences he explained to her that the American Funeral Group would take over her prepaid funerals, including the obligations concerning them. And they would also take over all their customers.

"So the buildings aren't included in the deal?"

He cut her off before she could mention Artie's plans for embalming and reconstruction. "No."

Ilka had a good feeling about this. It seemed like the perfect arrangement. She would be rid of her debt, and Artie and Sister Eileen could do what they'd planned to do all along. This was close to the deal she had said no to earlier. She relaxed and smiled up at the man.

He grabbed the papers again and turned to the next page, where he pointed at a number. Forty thousand. His hand covered the rest of the text. With a down payment of forty thousand dollars, she could pay off all their suppliers. That would leave her with the two hundred thousand dollars she owed the bank.

"When will the rest be paid?"

He didn't even look at her when he said that forty thousand dollars was the entire amount.

Ilka fell back in her chair. The population of Racine was approximately eighty thousand. Three hundred eighty-six people had an agreement with the Paul Jensen Funeral Home covering their final journey. Most people had deposited $7,000 to $10,000 in the account, and the last time she'd checked the balance was $2,272,000. The amount grew every month, even though money was withdrawn when people died.

The man stood waiting; Ilka was nearly gagging from the smell of his aftershave. She obviously hadn't expected to be paid the entire two-million-plus, but she'd thought they would pay at least ten percent. That's what the agreement with Golden Slumbers would have given her.

She stood up slowly, folded the paper, and walked off. During the time she'd sat in the reception, half of the long hallway had been painted eggshell white. Loud music seeped out of the painter's headphones, and he didn't even glance at her when she stooped down and grabbed the portraits of Phyllis Oldham and her husband. She'd have Artie drive them over to her.

Ilka laid the portraits in the trunk of the car and slammed the lid. Her phone rang.

"We've got a pickup," Artie said. A woman in the morgue. And he needed her help.

She sighed. There'd been no time to think about how to say it. "We're going to have to shut down." Immediately she felt like a coward for not telling him face-to-face. "This is it, you'll have to call another funeral home to do the pickup. Just not the American Funeral Group," she added, holding back her anger.

"Would you cut this shit out! We're leaving in five minutes!"

Later, in the hearse with Artie, she felt her life was in free fall. She had no idea what would happen now. On one hand, she felt ashamed about not even trying to haggle with the guy; that was childish of her. On the other hand, her neck tingled with rage and humiliation. "It didn't work out, at all, not even close."

The bastard had crushed her, and she was absolutely sure

he'd enjoyed it. On the way back to the funeral home, she'd realized that was the reason they'd agreed to a meeting so quickly. Of course! They hadn't needed time to prepare, hadn't needed lawyers, because all they cared about was destroying her. And savoring every minute of it. She could still smell that sickening, nauseating aftershave.

"They didn't go along with any of your demands; not even one?" Artie said.

She stared straight ahead and explained that she hadn't been given the chance to present them.

"Listen," he said, "they'll be back. He just wants to see if he can intimidate you. If it works, it works, and they save a little money. What did you tell him?"

"Nothing. I just left. Unfortunately, I don't think you're right, he's not interested in us. They run over everybody, and they don't need us or our business."

"Maybe they don't need us, but they want our customers. He'll be back."

Ilka shook her head. She doubted that. And she had the feeling the national funeral home chain had been one step ahead of her at every turn. "He knows we'll have to close if I don't find another funeral home to take over. And we'll have to return all the money in the burial account. It will be a lot of work, and it'll be expensive too; I'm sure the bank will charge for every person we pay back. The hole we're in will be that much deeper. And believe me, he'll welcome them with open arms when they need a new place to go. We mean nothing to him, and he doesn't need our business."

"Anyway, let's see how it goes. They know their offer is an insult. He's set his trap, he just wants to see if you fall in it."

The hearse creaked as it pulled into the morgue's parking

lot. Before they got out, she turned to him. "He won't be back. He's going to the bank to open a new account, for all the customers we're going to lose. It will be one fucking great start for them here in town. I'm closing the business and going home."

Artie leaned over and put his arm around her. For a moment she appreciated his sympathy, but then she remembered she was the one who would be left with the debt. The only one.

She got out to help him with the stretcher. They pushed it up the ramp to the rear entrance, and she held the door for him. The walls inside were damp, and the air smelled musty. Ilka shivered as the stretcher rattled over the concrete floor.

The automatic double doors slowly opened. "Who are we picking up?"

"Female, fifty-four years old, gunshot victim." They walked into a hallway with cobalt-blue walls. Farther down a guard sat reading a paper beside a small reception counter.

"We're here to pick up Margaret Graham," Artie said when the guard looked up. A sign on the wall said they needed to show an ID, but Artie had been there so many times that it wasn't necessary. He signed and jotted down the time. Ilka stood by the stretcher and nodded at the guard when he gestured for them to continue down the hallway. All the doors along the way had frosted glass. Another automatic door opened, and after rounding a corner Artie parked the stretcher along the wall and locked the wheels.

A man approached rolling a steel table with the woman's body, which was covered by a white sheet. He smiled at Artie. "Hey, man." He looked in curiosity at Ilka, and she nodded politely. She was freezing in her too-thin jacket. Artie introduced them. She regretted coming along; she hated to be reminded that she'd taken over Paul Jensen's funeral home.

And it wasn't worth it, now that she was done with the business. She stepped back while Artie signed again for the deceased and her identification papers.

"This one was shot in her home early yesterday evening," the man said. "They did the autopsy this morning, the cops are finished with the body. Thanks for coming in so quick, we're full up right now. The husband wanted us to contact you guys, by the way."

Artie unlocked the wheels and pushed the stretcher away from the wall. "Is he the one who shot her?"

"That I can't answer. He was a free man when we talked to him, anyway. He asked if he ought to be here when she was picked up. We got lucky on that one, it's a hassle when family shows up and gets in the way. Like we don't have enough to do anyway."

"How did it happen?" Ilka asked. She didn't care for his annoyance with families. The three of them lifted the woman's body over onto the stretcher without the white sheet slipping off.

"Can't tell you that either, ma'am." The man didn't even glance at her. "Down here we just bring 'em in and send 'em out when they're done upstairs. All we know is what's on the ID papers and the note telling us who gets the body."

She nodded, and Artie started pushing the stretcher back down the hallway. She walked beside it. Out on the ramp she grabbed the front end, and they carefully rolled it down. She lifted the sheet a bit to keep it away from the wheels, but when they stopped at the hearse, the sheet fell off to the side. She stared into the body's face.

The woman looked younger than fifty-four. Her face already had the waxy, unnatural color Ilka was slowly getting

58

used to, but her skin was smooth. The bullet hole was about an inch above the nose. A modest hole. When Ilka noticed the bloody mass that once had been the back of her head, though, she turned away.

She was reminded of the day before, the shock she'd felt when Mary Ann suddenly started shooting. For a moment she felt homesick; in Denmark it was still breaking news when someone fired a gun. And thank God for that, she thought. It was hard to imagine shooting homicides as every-day fare.

"Do you know her?" she asked as Artie grabbed the other side of the stretcher to roll it in.

He glanced at the woman's face, then shook his head and covered her up. Ilka assumed it had become so routine for him that he didn't think about the person a deceased had been. His sole concern was making bodies look presentable if the family wanted to see them.

She turned and got in the front seat, leaving him to shut the door in back.

"You could talk to Paul's father-in-law," Artie said as he pulled out onto the highway. "He might help if you explain our situation."

He told her that Raymond Fletcher had paid for a local school's new swimming pool, and he'd also sponsored the mosaics in the church down by the harbor.

"But the family doesn't want anything to do with me, remember?"

He glanced over at her. "He helped Paul without Mary Ann knowing about it. Maybe he'd help you too. She doesn't need to know."

"But from what Karen Conaway told me, my father owed him quite a bit of money. It seems like a lot to ask him."

Artie slowed and parked the hearse on the side of the road, then turned to her. "I still have some money left. I think we can get the business back on track, and I'm willing to invest what I have to make it happen."

"Are you crazy? It could be years before the funeral home makes a profit. You've already put sixty thousand dollars of your own into it. Surely that's more than enough."

"I believe in it. And in all the years I worked for Paul, I spent my money on fishhooks and cigarettes and not a whole lot else."

Ilka knew that was a lie. He had expenses with his Lake Michigan house, even though he'd inherited it from his father. Property taxes, heat, electricity, water. And back in the office she'd seen in his eyes how having a job was important to him. His offer touched her, and she felt even more ashamed that she hadn't even tried to work out a deal.

She nodded; after all, what did she have to lose? "I'll try."

"Paul's debt is a drop in the bucket to Fletcher. He wouldn't even notice it was gone. We could start off by asking for a smaller loan, just to buy some time while we make plans."

"While we wait for the American Funeral Group to come crawling on their knees!"

He smiled at her. "Or more so we're not forced into making hasty decisions." He offered to meet with Fletcher. "Not that I know him really well, but I have met him a few times. And I don't mind at all having a talk with him."

"No, I have to do it, it's my family and my problem."

Not that she wanted to run into Mary Ann and Leslie when

she showed up with hat in hand, but she wasn't going to be a coward and send Artie out there.

Ilka grabbed a half-full bag of peanuts from between the seats and began stuffing them into her mouth. Artie pulled back onto the highway. They drove home in silence. Nor did they say a whole lot while they pulled the dead woman out of the hearse and laid her on a shelf in the cold room.

Artie folded the white sheet and pushed the stretcher up against the wall. "Is it okay if I run home now?"

Ilka nodded. A few minutes later he caught her on the way to her father's office and handed her Raymond Fletcher's address.

She wavered again as she watched him walk away, but then decided to leave at once. What did she have to lose, other than her dignity. And what difference would that make? She'd lost so much already in her short time in Racine.

She opened the refrigerator and made herself a sandwich from what Artie had left behind. After eating she grabbed the keys to her father's car. Hopefully there was enough gas. She didn't want to think about being stranded out in the sticks.

After Ilka turned off the highway, the roads kept getting narrower. The flatlands stretching out on both sides were broken up by horse pastures with white fences. She drove fast, as if that could keep her from regretting what she was about to do.

Right after a curve that according to the GPS was close to her destination, a horse trailer pulled by a truck appeared, headed in her direction, followed by a black four-wheel-drive with tinted windows. The same kind of vehicle that had driven up to Mary Ann's house. When the truck was only seconds from her, Ilka realized it wasn't going to slow down or give an inch on the narrow road. She jerked the wheel and slid over into the ditch, and as it thundered by, she shut her eyes. As Flemming would have said, it missed her by a whisker. She yelled and gave the driver the finger, but he was already long gone. Only the man driving the black SUV noticed.

Her hands gripped the wheel, her heart hammering as she

sank in her seat; she could have been killed! But as the shock faded and she wondered what to do, she realized she had to go on. Persuading her father's second family to assume his debt certainly made more sense than watching Artie ruin his future by throwing away his money. On the way out here, she'd put together a plan. To begin with she would try to borrow the sixty thousand Artie had paid to cover her father's back taxes. And when he got his money back, she could close up shop in good conscience. Artie could either freelance as he'd planned or get out of the undertaker business. The $240,000 she owed was another thing.

When she'd finally recovered enough to drive again, the car wouldn't budge from the ditch. Clumps of dirt and grass shot up and clipped the side window. She pounded the wheel; just what she needed, walking up to Fletcher's place and having to ask to be pulled out of the ditch. After cooling off a few seconds, she put the car in reverse and began rocking it free. A minute later she was back on the road.

After taking two more curves she drove up to the broad drive leading to the ranch. The white gate stood open, and a large, impressive house loomed behind several low white stables. It looked as big as a Danish manor house. And grandiose, Ilka thought. Something like Dragsholm Castle, where she and Flemming had stayed once.

The place distracted her so much that she'd almost reached the house before noticing the spooked horses running around loose. She slammed on the brakes and pulled over. Seven or eight horses, it looked like. An old man leaned against the house, maybe catching his breath. Old, or even elderly, seen from a distance. An undershirt hung down over his thin, sunken body, and his arms were pencil-thin. When she saw him struggling to kneel beside a curled-up figure at one end of the house, she jumped out of the car and started running over to them. Though dark hair covered the figure's face, Ilka was sure it was Amber, her younger half sister.

The old man apparently hadn't heard her coming. He was trying to slip his wadded-up shirt under Amber's head. Ilka had never been afraid of horses, but she stopped in her tracks when a dark-brown thoroughbred reared up in front of her.

Two cars flew down the driveway to the house, which frightened the horses even more; they ran by the stables and out into the pasture behind. The old man staggered to his feet when four armed men jumped out of the cars. The front door opened, and a blond, well-dressed young man appeared with a jacket and white shirt on a hanger slung over his arm. He walked past the armed men with hardly a glance, and moments later he began helping the old man with his clothes. Ilka was about to return to the car when she recognized one of the men: Jeff, her Tinder date. They formed a ring around Raymond Fletcher as he finished dressing.

"They've been keeping an eye on the ranch," Fletcher said. His firm voice belied his age, and he seemed transformed. It wasn't just that his sorry undershirt was hidden now; he looked taller and no longer helpless, with an authority he wore like a jacket. One of the men handed him a gun, and he checked it before casually sticking it in his pocket. "They must have known you just left."

"How many horses did they make off with?" the man closest to Ilka asked. He was blocking her from Jeff's sight.

Fletcher's security guards, she thought. Had she said anything about her father on the boat, something that should have made Jeff acknowledge that he knew her father's family? Or at least that he worked for the family? She couldn't remember. Had they even talked about anything?

"Five or six. And we have to find them, now." Fletcher pointed at the man standing in front of Ilka. "Get inside and send a message to everyone, to start looking for the horses."

Two men trotted into the house, while the other two quickly checked the stables.

Fletcher barked orders into his phone as if he were commanding troops. Some were ordered out to the ranch, others to the trotter stable, others to various roads to keep an eye out for the horses. He mentioned an address that Ilka didn't recognize. The whole front lawn was suddenly a command center, and no one seemed to worry about Amber, who still lay on the ground over by the wall.

Ilka finally caught Jeff's eye when she jogged over to her half sister. She was about to say something, but he turned away quickly, obviously ignoring her. She reached into her bag for her phone, and while orders flew through the air around her, she called 911 and asked for an ambulance. She still had the slip of paper with Fletcher's address Artie had given her. She also gave them Amber's name and explained there had been an accident.

"She's unconscious," she said, when asked about the injury.

"Who the hell are you?" someone shouted from above her head.

She looked up at Fletcher but waved him off as she repeated the address clearly.

The old man was still standing over her when she hung up. She laid a hand on Amber's shoulder, though she didn't know if the girl was aware that someone was with her. "I'm Paul Jensen's daughter from Denmark. She needs to go to the hospital."

He studied her for a moment, then he slowly nodded and returned to his men.

Amber didn't react when Ilka spoke her name. She shut the surrounding voices out and concentrated on speaking calmly to her half sister. Her head was bleeding, and she lay in an alarmingly twisted position. Out of the corner of her eye, Ilka noticed Mary Ann and Leslie by the front door, the mother sitting erect in her wheelchair, the daughter standing behind her in a beige cardigan with her soft, wavy hair, both looking as if yesterday's events had never happened. They stared down at Ilka and Amber.

The ambulance's siren cut through the air and drowned out the men's loud voices. Ilka stood up when Fletcher approached her again. He sounded much less harsh now as he asked her to follow Amber to the hospital. "I can't leave here until we find the horses. Stay with her until I come."

"But I hardly know her," she said. "Don't you think she'd rather see one of you when she wakes up?"

She glanced over at Mary Ann and Leslie.

"You have the same father, you'll find something to talk about." He stepped aside to make room for the two ambulance medics. He shouted a few more orders to his men before turning back to Ilka. "Follow the ambulance, make sure she has everything she needs. When you get to the hospital, you'll be responsible for getting her admitted and giving them her insurance information."

The young man—a butler?—who had brought him his clothes now came outside carrying a folder.

"Don't leave her until I get there," Fletcher repeated. He handed her an envelope from the folder and told her it contained all the information the hospital would need.

"I'm not a doctor, you know," she mumbled, irritated over being handed all the responsibility. Why not her sister, or one of the men?

But Fletcher was already on his way to the stable. Just before the ambulance arrived, she'd noticed a few stableboys in flannel shirts head out after the loose horses, and now they were returning with four of them.

"What happened to her?" Ilka shouted. He turned around, his face showing no emotion.

"She was trampled."

Again, he turned to his men and herded them over to a stable behind the other buildings. Mary Ann and Leslie were back inside the house, and suddenly everything was quiet.

The ambulance drove off, and at the end of the driveway its siren began blaring. Ilka was trembling all over, her hands clenched so tightly that her nails sliced into her palms. She tried to shrug off her shock like Fletcher had, but it didn't work. All she could do was run to her car and try to keep up with the ambulance, because no one had told her where the hospital was.

The last time Amber had spoken to Ilka, she'd asked her half sister to stay away. *No doubt she'll be thrilled to see who's here when she wakes up,* Ilka thought as she gazed down at her in the bed.

She'd waited four hours while Amber's chest and hip were examined, followed by a scan of her head and neck. Amber had suffered a serious concussion, her hip was dislocated, and ribs on both sides were bruised, but nothing was broken. Several times hospital personnel told Ilka it was a miracle she was alive. Because of the concussion she would have to lie perfectly still in darkness. She'd been given a neck brace, and a strange contraption had been attached to her hip. It looked like a metal frame with a big vise attached; a nurse explained it was for maneuvering the hipbone back into its socket.

"As long as she's so weak, we don't want to risk any movement that could cause another dislocation."

Ilka couldn't imagine Amber doing more than barely moving in her condition. She wasn't even sure her half sister was conscious, though the nurse claimed they'd spoken to her. She'd been given an IV morphine drip, which was helping her body relax so it could heal, the nurse explained.

Ilka held her hand and sat with eyes closed, trying to imagine what it would have been like to grow up with her. They could have played together, argued. This was one of the things for which she would never forgive her father. She'd always wanted a brother or sister. Not that she was wild about the sisters it turned out she did have, but at least she'd have experienced being closer to someone than just friends.

Earlier a young male nurse in a light-blue uniform had checked on Amber. He'd offered Ilka a cup of coffee and sandwich, but at the time she hadn't felt like eating or drinking. Now, though, she was getting hungry. And she had a headache throbbing in her left temple. It was already past eight, and she had no idea when Fletcher would show up. How long did he expect her to stay?

"How many horses did they get?"

Her half sister's sudden whisper startled Ilka, and she jerked and mashed Amber's hand against the bed rail. "Sorry."

"Did they get any from the south stable?"

Maybe it was the medicine, Ilka thought. Or else Amber had more important things on her mind than reacting to a near-stranger sitting there, holding her hand.

"I don't know what the south stable is. But they've rounded up several of the horses."

Amber lay flat on the bed, looking up at her through two narrow slits. "Which ones?"

"I don't know. I saw four, three dark and one light."

Ilka laid a hand on Amber's shoulder when she tried to sit up. "You need to stay down, you've been seriously injured.

Your grandfather is coming as soon as they find the stolen horses. He knows more than I do about what happened."

Her half sister's shoulder stiffened against her hand. "How many did they get?" she asked again.

Ilka spoke quietly to calm her down. "Like I said, I don't know. They drove off with them before I got there."

"Did one of the ones they brought back have a white star on his forehead, and a white sock on his right leg?"

Amber's eyes were closed again, and suddenly it felt awkward holding her hand; carefully she laid it on the blanket as she tried to remember. "I didn't notice. There was so much going on, it happened so fast."

Several moments later she sensed her half sister looking up at her.

"When I told you to stay away and leave us alone, it was for your own sake." Amber closed her eyes again. "I was trying to keep you out of all this. Trying to protect you."

She paused again. Finally Ilka asked her why someone would steal the horses. "Did it have to do with what happened the other day to your mother and Leslie?"

Amber didn't answer. Ilka thought about going out and calling Fletcher to tell him his granddaughter was conscious now. And to see if he was on his way. But it was actually nice sitting there alone with her. Despite the long silences, she enjoyed the sense of peace they shared.

Amber was looking at her again. "Do you know who Maggie is?" Ilka asked. She told her about the letter delivered to the funeral home.

"No." Now she turned her head to look directly at Ilka. "What happened today has nothing to do with you. They're after my grandfather, not you. We're the ones who have to worry."

71

"It has nothing to do with our father, then?"

"No, not really."

Ilka could sense her thinking about how much to tell. Probably wondering whether the story affected Ilka; whether it was something she should let her in on.

"But he was involved? Our father, I mean. And who are *they*?"

Amber closed her eyes. "You don't know them. It's about Grandpa's stable. It's him they're after. His territory."

"I was there when your mother's house was emptied, I was parked out on the street. And this afternoon I saw them leave with the horses. It's hard to feel I'm not involved." She paused a second before leaning farther over the bed. "Maybe you don't realize how lucky you are. You could've been killed. And all that shooting at your mother's house. Whether we like it or not, we're family, and whatever happens to you, in a way it happens to me too."

"It'll be over with soon."

Lying in the hospital bed with her dark hair gathered in a hairband, she didn't look as gawky as the first time Ilka had met her. Her features were pleasant and a bit girlish, even though her cheeks were round and she had a hint of a double chin. Ilka's heart went out to her as she listened.

"Someone's trying to blackmail Grandpa. But he won't play along, and that can cause a lot of commotion."

"Commotion!" That wasn't exactly how Ilka would have described all she'd seen. Amber sounded aloof and unconcerned. Ilka hoped Fletcher was on his way. She'd almost reached out for her half sister's hand a moment before, but now she drew back, amazed that despite being trampled half to death, Amber made it sound as if blackmail and mafia methods were everyday stuff.

She studied her half sister. She had enough problems of her own, and if her father's own father-in-law truly was being fleeced, it probably wasn't a good time to ask him for a loan.

"Grandpa ran the trotter stable together with Gerald Davidson, but he died last spring. His grandson came back from New York to take things over. And he claims Grandpa owes him money, that he's trying to cheat him, but it's not true. Scott Davidson is just greedy."

"So he's the one who took the horses?"

Amber spoke quietly. "Not personally, but I think his men did. We went to school together. I've known Scott most of his life, even though he was a grade under me. He's always had a temper."

"Was he the one who emptied the house out too?"

Amber laughed almost inaudibly, a puff of air through her teeth. "They showed up and harassed Mom to send a message to Grandpa, that they were coming for him."

She kicked the blanket down a bit. Ilka offered to open the window; she didn't think the room was hot, but beads of sweat covered her half sister's forehead. Amber shook her head, said she was okay. She turned her head again to look directly at Ilka.

"They ran the stable for the last fifteen years, until the track went bankrupt months before New Year's. Just before Gerald Davidson died. I know, because I've worked in Grandpa's stable all my adult life. I'm responsible for the trotting horses, I'm a vet and a trainer too. I moved out to the farm when I finished vet school."

"He must think he has a right to some of what you have, from what he's doing."

Ilka didn't really care what their fight was about, as long as

73

it didn't make life more difficult for her. But it still felt nice being with her half sister.

"Scott Davidson claims we cheated him out of a lot of money. He started making all these accusations while they were settling his grandfather's estate. But we don't owe him a penny, and Grandpa doesn't let people push him around. So now it looks like Scott's going to fight dirty."

She stared off into space and chewed on her fingernail a moment. "I'm not sure Scott knows what he's getting himself into," she murmured.

She sounded a bit scared herself at the thought. Then she asked Ilka how things were going with the funeral home.

Ilka studied her hands and chose her words carefully. "It's not going well, not at all. Our father ran up an enormous debt, and I don't have enough money left to do any more funerals."

She described her meeting with the American Funeral Group, including their ridiculously low offer, then turned away from Amber. "I don't understand why I got dragged into this. He didn't write or call me once after he left Denmark. Not one single time. And yet I'm the one who's left with the entire debt, while your family has so much money that it's causing you different problems—"

Ilka cut herself off, but it did feel good to get this off her chest. Even though this wasn't the best time to do it.

Her half sister's voice was close to a whisper now. "The funeral home was almost holy to Dad. Leslie and I, we've never been in the room where you're staying. At least until that evening I waited for you up there. You probably don't have any idea how jealous we were of you. The time you had with him in Denmark, how you were his first daughter, how he always mentioned you when he talked about his past and his homeland. He said you were named after the horse that won the Derby, the first time he was at the track with his own father. We never met our grandparents on his side, we've never been to Denmark. And our names mean absolutely nothing."

Ilka was sitting straight up, hanging on every single word.

"Another thing. It's a lot because of you that I've devoted my life to horses. I hated them when I was a kid, but I wanted to impress Dad and make him proud. But he never came to Grandpa's stable. Only to the track and out to the Conaways'."

Amber's eyes were closed now, but she looked so torn up that Ilka could barely watch as she spoke.

"You probably can't imagine how hurt we were when he left the funeral home to you. We weren't good enough in his eyes to take over his business. Mom thought he must have kept in touch with you, that he lived a double life."

Ilka couldn't believe her ears. "You tell your mother that's not true. I didn't hear a word from him after he left us, not a single postcard, not one phone call. He didn't even let us know I had two half sisters. And you're more than welcome to take over the funeral home. In fact, you'd be doing me a great service. It's all yours. Also, the few things he brought with him from Denmark. It's all up in the room, take it."

Ilka held her hand out. *Yes, please, take it all. Especially the debt.*

"No," Amber whispered. "What's done is done."

She looked drowsy, as if another shot of morphine had entered her veins. "I have enough to do with the horses, and I hate looking at dead bodies."

Her eyes were fluttering, but Ilka told her she'd driven out to the ranch to ask Fletcher for a loan, to help her get rid of the funeral home. "But then I got caught in the middle of everything." She wasn't sure how much Amber heard, or even if she was still conscious. "So if you know anyone who might be interested in taking over our father's business, please let me know."

She's asleep, Ilka realized as she leaned back in her chair. The male nurse came in and said Raymond Fletcher had just called to say he was on his way.

"I'll stay until he gets here," Ilka said.

The nurse glanced at his watch. "It probably won't be more than fifteen minutes. But then they'll have to unpack the wheelchair and bring it up with them."

Ilka studied her half sister. Her mouth was open a crack, her breathing labored. It was hard to tell: Was it their father's features she recognized in the sleeping face, or her own? She felt like staying and taking care of her, but at the same time she wasn't going to give Mary Ann the satisfaction of throwing her out again.

She lightly stroked Amber's cheek before picking up her bag and quietly walking out.

You both should know that when I come home, I'm bringing a big debt along with me. It's just how it's worked out."

Ilka had gone up to her father's room to call her mother's partner, Jette. The two women had been living together for fourteen years, and Ilka knew that sometimes it was better to talk to Jette, who knew how to put things to her mother. Besides, she was a big coward; her mother had kept warning her that she'd run into trouble if she went over there and cleaned up after her father. No matter how old you got, she thought, nothing was worse than having to admit your mother was right.

Several moments crawled by. "Okay," Jette finally said.

That was exactly what Ilka liked about her. She never judged, and she wasn't prejudiced against her father, which was why she never took for granted that anything he was involved in would turn to shit.

Ilka decided to change the subject. "How did it go with

canceling the last shoots?" When she left for the States, she'd tried to talk another photographer into doing the jobs she had scheduled. She'd helped him when he went on vacation with his family, and when she'd screwed up and booked two jobs on the same day, he'd stepped in for her. But unfortunately, he'd been too busy to take over more than a few shoots.

Ilka had sent her mother out to a school to take student pictures, but that hadn't gone well, to put it mildly. Her mother was far too meticulous and spent way too much time on the photos. The school secretary complained. After that Ilka gave up and asked her mother and Jette to cancel everything else.

"Just fine," Jette said. She explained that most of her customers were understanding when told it was because of a death in the family. "Everything's taken care of, there aren't any shoots scheduled. We also shut down your website and answering service, so nothing more will come in."

"You didn't have to shut down the website!" Ilka hated the thought of being dumped directly into the dreaded welfare system when she got home. "Couldn't you just have written that we were booked up?"

"You can do that when you come home." Jette was discreet enough not to ask exactly how much she owed. Or maybe she was scared to hear, Ilka thought.

"Okay. And thanks for all the help."

She answered patiently when Jette wanted to know how she was doing and what it was like over there.

"There must be a lot of interesting things to see and do," Jette said. "And what about the food, I've heard it's so good."

When Jette retired, she'd begun arranging walking tours around the old city center of Copenhagen. She was fascinated by its history. But food? Maybe it was a new interest, Ilka thought.

"Uh, do you mean the burgers, or..." Suddenly she felt like she hadn't eaten a single decent meal in Racine.

"I read that someone in Wisconsin is the American champion at making cheese. They learned it from European immigrants."

It sounded as if she was just getting warmed up, so Ilka broke in. "I could bring some home."

"There's a cheese museum, you really should stop in and see it."

"Could I borrow twenty thousand from you? And please don't tell Mom. Of course I'll pay you back."

Pause.

"It's just until I get through this last funeral," she explained quickly. "The woman was shot in her home. Artie and I misunderstood each other, he didn't realize we weren't going to arrange any more funerals."

"Shot! So it's true: It's dangerous over there. I read on the Internet that Racine is the tenth most dangerous city in all Wisconsin. I figured they were exaggerating after you told us how peaceful it was. And from all the photos you sent, it looks nice too."

"I haven't been here long, but I haven't seen anything bad happen."

Not until the last two days, at least, she thought. She googled the Racine shootings and skimmed the latest headlines while Jette spoke. "SWAT Unit Called to Racine." "Police Searching for Suspect in Connection with Shooting." And the latest: "Woman Killed and Thrown in Trash." A body had been found close to Sunshine Supermarket. Also, police were looking for witnesses to a robbery at a pizzeria. And late last month a thirty-six-year-old man had been shot to death. But there was nothing about any horses or the showdown at Mary Ann's house. The two episodes were of course minor compared with the headlines. The murder of Margaret Graham was also mentioned, though it was farther down the list now.

"It's good you're coming home soon." Typical Jette. One second gushing about how exciting it was to travel, the next second frightened by the thought of all the dangers lurking out there.

Ilka put on her most convincing voice. "It's peaceful here. It must have happened out in the suburbs. You hardly even see anyone here in town."

"To get back to your question, I can't loan you the money without telling your mother. That's not how she and I do things, you know that."

Ilka thought about giving it one more shot, but then she dropped it. Before hanging up she asked Jette to not tell her mother that she'd asked. And yet ten minutes later Ilka's phone rang. Mom.

She muted the phone; she couldn't bear the thought of being lectured, reminded that she should have listened to her mother. Apparently, the scolding never stopped. She put the phone down and walked downstairs to get things ready for Margaret Graham's husband.

Michael Graham had already arrived. He was leaning forward in a high-backed chair in the reception, crying with his head in his hands. His shoulder blades rose underneath his short-sleeved, light-blue shirt with every sob.

She showed him into the arrangement room. A notebook lay on the table. "Have a seat," she said, then she poured him a cup of coffee and asked if he'd like a glass of water too.

"No thank you, this is fine." He dried his eyes and apologized. "Suddenly everything is just too real. I don't think it's really hit me, what's happened. I was out bowling, I always go bowling the last Monday of the month. I met up with some of the guys, old friends, and we went out to eat before hitting the lanes. Just like we've done the last thirteen years."

He was staring straight ahead. An attaché case lay on his lap, but his hands were draped over it, as if he'd forgotten it was there.

"I'm always home around ten, never any later. Five to ten." He emphasized that, as if it were vital. "She was there in the

81

hallway. The front door lock was broken, and she was just lying there, right inside. One arm stretched out, shot in the forehead."

He straightened up and set the case on the floor. "She was brave. Most people would've probably tried to hide, but she wasn't like that. My wife wasn't afraid to stand up to people, she never was. She always thought people could be talked out of things. I'm sure that's why she walked out to the door when she heard someone trying to break in."

"Was there anything stolen?" Ilka said, to encourage him. Sister Eileen had said it was her father's way of doing things. Let the family get it all out, until they were ready to discuss the details of the funeral. And it looked like Margaret's husband needed to talk about what had happened.

"The police said the killer didn't get past the front door. She stopped him out there." He wrung his hands and looked up at Ilka. "They asked me if I shot her. If I came home early, if I was just pretending to be in shock."

Ilka smiled in sympathy. "I'm sure they have to ask questions like that. Have they arrested anyone?"

He shook his head. "No clues. Nothing to go on. They think professionals did it. But wouldn't they empty the house? If they were so professional, they'd have broken in when nobody was home. The police officer said there's been several robberies in town, he seems pretty sure this was meant to be one."

He began sobbing again, and Ilka waited patiently. She slid the box of tissues over to him and drank some of her coffee.

"If she'd just gone to something, this might not have happened."

Ilka raised her eyebrows. "You mean like self-defense?"

"No, just something, anything to get her out of the house."

That was one way to look at it, of course, Ilka thought. But it could have been so many things. A bus driver could have lost control and run over her.

"It's only the men who bowl." He was quieter now. And he seemed to need to explain why he hadn't been there to protect his wife. "The wives never go along."

After they sat for a while in silence, Ilka decided to move on. "Have you thought about how you'd like to say goodbye to your wife? Do you want a funeral, or just a memorial service?"

"She wanted to be cremated. My wife was a medical secretary, she worked for the clinic here in town for years. She knew exactly what she wanted done when she died. We were married almost thirty-five years, she'd just turned twenty when we met."

"Do you have children?" Should she suggest a memorial service? Or should she just let him go on? No one had ever told her about how to handle the family of a murder victim. Maybe they needed more time to prepare. And a police investigation might also be a factor.

"Ruth was born the year after we were married. She lives in Australia with her husband and kids. Three grandkids, we have. I'd like to hold off on the service until they're here."

"Of course. There's no hurry, take all the time you and your family need."

She saw no reason to mention they had plenty of space in the cold room, now that she'd decided to stop taking on business.

He opened the attaché case and pulled out a thin book. "My wife filled this out several years ago." He handed it to her. "This is how she wants things done. A burial testament, she called it. Like what music she wants, about the urn, the flowers."

He paused a moment. "And she decided what she wants on her gravestone. 'A good and long life.' That's maybe not so good now, though, is it, after what happened."

Ilka nodded and agreed with him. He had a few more suggestions, but she wasn't listening. She'd thumbed through the little book and now was staring at Margaret Graham's signature, written with a black pen at the bottom of the last page. Immediately she recognized the slight loop in the *M*, and if she was in doubt there was also the short dash over the *i*. Precisely as in the letters.

The signature on the burial testament was "Maggie Graham."

She stood up with the book in her hand. "May I borrow this?"

He nodded and stood up too, looking relieved that they were through. "I'd like you to follow her instructions. What she wanted is what I want. There's also something in there about what to serve afterward. My wife wanted to keep it simple, just coffee, but my daughter bakes her mother's favorite cookies. We'll bring them along."

Ilka nodded, and though it was impolite, she asked if he could find his own way out. For a moment she stood watching him while her gangly body seemed to be sinking into her shoes. It couldn't be right. She was tempted to run after him and ask him to come back, then show him the letters, ask if his wife really had written them. But she couldn't do that to him.

After she heard him drive away, she pulled herself together and went out to the reception. She unfolded all five of Maggie's letters and showed them and the burial testament to Sister Eileen. The signatures were identical, there was no doubt, and even the normally stoic sister reacted.

"Did you say anything to the husband?" The nun sounded worried.

Ilka shook her head. "Of course not, but I'll have to contact the police."

Sister Eileen stood up at once and strode off; obviously she disagreed.

"Hello! We *have* to show the police these letters." She waved the five envelopes in the air.

The nun turned. "We don't *have* to do anything. The best thing you could do is stay out of it."

Ilka stared after her in bewilderment. Of course the police had to see the letters! She'd tell them when she'd found the last one and hand it over, together with the others she'd found in the desk drawer in her father's room. From then on it was up to them.

She found her jacket and was about to leave when the front door opened and a broad-chested man wearing dark sunglasses came in. He stood for a moment looking around before walking into the reception. Seconds later he reappeared and walked back out. Before Ilka could do more than wonder what was going on, Raymond Fletcher strode inside, accompanied by the man in sunglasses and what looked like his identical twin. Fletcher wore an elegant pin-striped jacket. There was no sign of the helpless elderly man she'd seen at the ranch the day before.

He looked around as if it were the first time he'd been there. "Could we talk?" He gestured with his hand, inviting her farther inside. Into her own funeral home.

"Of course." She heard the nervous uncertainty in her voice, but he didn't seem to notice. She cleared her throat and straightened up, then asked him to follow her into the arrangement room. Michael Graham's cup was still on the table; she took it away and offered him coffee.

He shook his head and said this would only take a moment.

Settle down, Ilka told herself. "How's Amber?"

They stood facing each other, and he showed no intention of taking a seat. One of his men stood just outside the door.

"She was operated on this morning." Fletcher frowned in worry; now he looked more his age. At least eighty. But with an authority that made it feel as though an army had invaded her funeral home.

She sat down. Let him stand if he wanted, she thought.

"New X-rays showed the injury to her hip is more serious than they first thought," he said. "But it's back in place, and her mother is with her. I want to thank you for what you did. It meant a lot to me that she wasn't in there alone."

Ilka was about to ask why he hadn't told Mary Ann to take care of her own daughter, but she held her tongue when he reached into his inside pocket.

"I understand you have some financial problems." Something in his eyes told Ilka to steady herself, that he might be about to tell her she reminded him of her father. But he simply handed her an envelope. Thick and full of bills.

"This isn't a loan," he said. "It's a gift, to thank you for your help, and for me to help you. You're one of us now. Welcome to Racine and welcome to our family."

Ilka was astonished. He was the first of her father's family to welcome her. But before she could reply, he turned and headed out the front door. She watched from the reception window as he got into the back of a car just outside. As they left the parking lot, an identical black car pulled out right behind them. They turned the corner and disappeared. Normally she would have frowned at such a blatant demonstration of power, but after all that had happened the past few days, the security and bodyguards made perfect sense to her.

When she turned from the window, Sister Eileen was sitting at her desk. Ilka hadn't heard her come in, and it bothered her that the nun could still sneak up on her like that.

"You had a visitor." Sister Eileen showed no sign of how much she'd overheard.

Ilka held out the envelope to her. "Raymond Fletcher was here. He wants to help, and this is a gift, not a loan."

Sister Eileen didn't touch it. "We can't take his money."

"We can, and we will, we have to. We can't afford not to."

"It's not a good idea to let Raymond Fletcher get involved in our problems." The nun spoke sharply and looked Ilka right in the eyes, which she rarely did.

Ilka lowered her hand. "He's helped my father before."

Sister Eileen broke the tense silence. "How much is in there?"

"I haven't looked."

Sister Eileen grabbed the envelope, slit it with a letter opener, and pulled out the bundle of bills. Ilka watched her count them. Twenty thousand, in hundreds.

Ilka felt an enormous sense of relief. A gift, not a loan to be paid back. What luck that she hadn't pressed Jette harder for money. She ignored the nun's frown and told her to pay the most urgent bills. "And set aside enough for Margaret Graham's ceremony. I still don't know when it's going to be held; it might be a while before we're paid. It depends on the daughter who lives in Australia."

Sister Eileen looked disapprovingly at the envelope, but she stuck the money into a small box she pulled out of the cabinet under the desk.

"I wish Fletcher would take over the whole business," Ilka said. She felt much lighter, knowing she wasn't alone anymore. "The house too. His people could sell it, I'm sure they could get more out of it than me. They're tough."

"There's nothing your father would have hated more," Sister Eileen mumbled as she carefully closed the box with the money.

Ilka looked at her a moment but decided not to press her on it, though something in the nun's voice hinted that there was much Ilka didn't understand. Clearly Sister Eileen had a need to emphasize how close she'd been to Ilka's father, and thus knew better.

Why did Sister Eileen keep making that point? Everyone understood she hadn't known her father and had no idea what he would or wouldn't have wanted, so of course the nun knew better!

Ilka rushed past several police cars parked in front of the station. Patrol cars, transports, four-wheel-drives. All of them displaying the Racine Police emblem.

She held Maggie's letters and the burial testament as she approached the front desk and asked to speak to someone working on the Margaret Graham case. The officer behind the desk told her to take a seat in the waiting area, but moments later he called her back and pointed toward a hallway. "This officer will help you."

It was Jack Doonan, a young officer she already knew. "Hi," she called out. She hurried to follow him through a swinging door. When he turned, he looked confused for a moment before recognizing her.

"Oh hi." His chin and cheekbones stood out, the sleeves of his light-blue uniform were rolled up, and his service revolver stuck up out of his belt. They'd last seen each other in connection with the tragic deaths of two young men. Back then his eyes had been red and deep furrows had lined his mouth, but now he looked well rested.

SARA BLAEDEL

"I have something you need to see." She handed him the letters and the thin book.

"What's this about?"

She pointed at the envelopes. "Margaret Graham knew my
father. I don't know what was going on, or what this truth
was that wasn't supposed to come out. But it's obvious she was
blackmailing him."

For a second he looked confused again; then he asked her
to follow him over to a desk against the wall in the large open
work space. Officers in small cubicles were working, and the
atmosphere was relaxed, even though they apparently took on
new homicide cases every day.

Doonan read the few lines of the newest letter.

Ilka grabbed the burial testament out of his hand and
showed him the signature. He glanced back and forth between
the letter and testament before nodding.

"Yeah, looks like we won't need the handwriting experts on
this one." He sat down.

Her phone began vibrating in her pocket as he read the earlier letters. She pulled it out and looked at the display. Her
mother again. She ignored it and looked up.

Stan Thomas, an older officer she'd also met, was walking
toward them. Doonan filled him in on the new information
Ilka had brought. He added that he was sure the letters were
written by Margaret Graham.

"Obviously your father didn't shoot her," Thomas said. "So
what do the letters have to do with the break-in?"

"It can't be a coincidence she was killed," Ilka said. "If
she'd been covering something up, and then used it to
squeeze money out of my father, maybe she was doing the
same with other people. I don't think it was a break-in. They

90

would have taken everything valuable in the house after they killed her."

The two officers chewed on that for a few moments. They seemed to agree with her.

"And if her husband hadn't come to us to arrange the services, no one would have discovered the connection," she added.

Thomas studied her. "What else do you know about Margaret Graham?"

"Nothing. I never met her, I didn't know she existed. And I don't know when the last letter was delivered either." She looked back and forth between the two men. "But I regret not coming to you the second I found it. Maybe it could have saved her."

"Hold on now," Thomas said. "Nobody knows that. If it was your father she was blackmailing, the letter must have been around quite a while. He's been dead about two months now, right?"

Ilka nodded.

"Looks like we'd better take your fingerprints. And I'm going to have to ask you where you were on Monday between five and ten p.m. when Margaret Graham was killed."

It hadn't occurred to Ilka that on top of everything else, she could be accused of killing a woman she didn't even know. She stared straight ahead, trying to remember. It was the evening she'd been with Jeff. But she had no idea what time she got home. And she didn't know Jeff's last name, only that he worked for Fletcher. Anyway, she doubted that Jeff wanted to tell anyone about their rendezvous.

"That afternoon I drove out to visit the Conaway family. They were close friends of my father. They live about an hour from town. Karen Conaway and her younger daughter can confirm I was there. You can also check my GPS, I used it on the way there and back too."

"Well, when did you get back?" Thomas said.

She thought back to the bar. Twilight was falling when she and Jeff were walking to the marina. "Probably around seven."

"And you have an alibi for the rest of the evening?"

Ilka hated to do it, but she nodded and told them about her meeting a guy at the bar beside the old jazz club. The girl working that evening could confirm it. "Then we walked down to his boat."

"So he can give you an alibi?"

She nodded.

"And does this man have a name, so we can confirm that?" Doonan asked. Something sleazy in the way he looked at her made her straighten up.

"His name is Jeff. He works for Raymond Fletcher."

Thomas crossed his arms. "Looks to me like there's spaces in those five hours you weren't with somebody."

"Oh, come on! I didn't kill anybody! Back then I didn't even know who she was, and I don't care what secret she was going to reveal. But you're more than welcome to take my finger-prints, if that makes you happy."

Doonan ignored her outburst. "Are there other letters in the desk drawer?"

"Not with that signature."

"No other letters hinting at what this is all about?" He pointed at the last letter about the blackmail money.

She shook her head.

"But if your father and Margaret Graham knew each other, she must've known he's dead." Thomas was sitting on the edge

HER FATHER'S SECRET

of the desk, his gut hanging over onto his lap. "The whole town knows, it's been in the paper. What if this letter is new? Then it couldn't be him it was meant for."

He scratched his head.

"You mean, it could have been sent to me?" She shook her head. That was crazy; she hadn't even been in town long enough to have something to hide.

"That's not what I'm saying. I'd just like to know the connection between your father and Margaret Graham."

Ilka was beginning to regret coming to the police station. It had never crossed her mind that the letter could have been meant for her. Or for Sister Eileen. Or Artie, for that matter. She thought about Sister Eileen, how strongly she reacted when Ilka said she was going to contact the police. On the other hand, the nun hadn't tried to stop her; she'd just thought it wasn't a good idea. Maybe she was right. And Artie had seemed genuinely surprised when she showed him the newest letter.

She felt Thomas's eyes on her. He turned to Doonan and told him to take a look at the woman's bank account. "If we find anything that might be connected to criminal activity, we'll show these letters to her husband. Maybe he can tell us something that'll make sense of all this."

In her mind Ilka saw Maggie's skinny husband in the short-sleeved blue shirt. She felt sorry for Michael Graham, who in the midst of his grief would probably be questioned. Luckily, she didn't have to be there.

"We'll also need to talk to Mary Ann," Doonan said.

Ilka didn't mention she'd been about to give the letters to the woman. And she saw no reason to bring up the shooting episode at the house. "Do you want this too?" She pointed at

93

the burial testament and asked them to make a copy of everything, so she could take the originals home with her.

The moment she stepped out onto the parking lot in front of the station, Ilka absentmindedly pulled her cigarettes out of her pocket and lit one. She leaned her head back and stared at the sky while blowing out a cloud of smoke, then she inhaled again and eyed the thin trail drifting away in the breeze. If only she could follow along! Away! Back to Argentina to herd cattle, as she'd done the year after beating her cancer. Her uterus had been removed at the age of twenty, but she'd recovered and long ago reconciled herself to being childless. Coincidences and events had affected her adult life far too much, and to put it bluntly she was sick and fucking tired of life not cutting her some slack. If only just once everything would go her way. Peace of mind, that's what she needed. She'd had it once, when she married Flemming, but for a long time after he died she'd been angry, enraged at life and God and whatever the hell crossed her path.

Ilka had never fallen in love after Flemming. She'd tried, but it never came. Instead she'd acquired a taste for men in small doses, with no strings attached. Right now, she wouldn't mind a dose. The sense of being close to someone, their skin, a release that could dampen her nerves.

She crushed the cigarette out on the sidewalk and walked to her father's car. Suddenly she sensed she wasn't alone, and when she whirled around, a dark-skinned man with a cap pulled down over his face emerged from a small clump of trees, like he'd been waiting for her. She couldn't see his eyes, but he headed straight for her with his hands in his pockets.

Quickly she got in the car, started it, and backed out while still struggling with her seat belt. She checked the rearview mirror; the man stood watching her. She couldn't say why, but he frightened her so much that she floored it. Her back tire ran up a curb as she turned and drove off.

She took a deep breath when he was out of sight. Her pulse was racing, and she kept breathing slowly to settle down. The man could have been anyone. It was impossible to say if he'd been keeping an eye on her. And the car that followed her home the other day from the Conaways' could have been her imagination. Ilka shook her head to clear her thoughts; it irritated her that she'd let herself feel weak, fragile. But someone had for sure been on the boat; Jeff had heard the footsteps too. That much she hadn't imagined.

She needed so very, very much to go home. To settle in, be bored, know what was going to happen the next day, the next week. She missed her everyday routine, reading the paper in bed. Telling the kids to line up in a row and smile at the photographer. She missed hearing them laugh and tease and act like smart-asses to each other.

Ilka drove down the main drag past the square, where she turned and headed toward West Racine. Maybe she should have let Artie know she was leaving to talk to the police, but surely Sister Eileen had told him.

She turned onto the residential street and stopped to get a good look at Mary Ann's house. The place looked deserted, so she drove on and parked in front. After staring at the porch a few moments, she walked up and rang the doorbell. No response. She waited, rang a few more times. Finally she worked up the courage to step over to peek in the window. Except for a plastic sack on the floor, the living room looked completely empty. At the next window she peered into a small room next to the living room, also empty. Feeling bold now, she circled the house and rested her forehead against the kitchen window in back. A teapot stood on the kitchen counter, along with some food. A ceiling lamp hung where the table once had been.

Ilka had never been behind the house. The yard was enormous, like a park extending all the way down to a row of tall trees. The lawn was well tended, and large box trees had been trimmed neatly in rounded shapes, while flowers in late-summer colors sprang up from low, stone-lined beds. A bit too formal for Ilka's taste, but the broad tiled walkways broke up some of the perfection. Obviously, they'd been designed to make the area accessible for Mary Ann's wheelchair. Ilka walked over to a glass terrace door and peeked in. The room had a fireplace; otherwise it was also empty. The fireplace was plastered and ornate, but Ilka was only interested in the mantel, where Artie had told her the urn with her father's ashes stood. The urn was gone.

When Ilka pulled into the funeral home parking lot, she realized she'd already made up her mind. Maybe it was while she stared at the empty mantel, or it might have been in the car on the way back. No matter. She couldn't take any more, it was way too much, too many unknown factors that made it impossible for her to navigate the life her father had led. She was in over her head.

After she let herself in and shut off the alarm, she went straight to the front door and turned the sign.

CLOSED.

Sister Eileen and Artie were gone for the day, so to avoid any more misunderstandings she reached behind the desk and pulled out the telephone cord. It was time to get rid of the place.

She'd come to Racine to find answers about her father, maybe to find out why he abandoned them. Or at least to understand why he'd ignored her efforts to keep at least some contact, however sporadic it might be.

She tried to picture him in her mind. There would be no more answers, she realized now. It was time to accept that fact and get rid of him too. Mentally. Get him out of her head. Come to grips with the emptiness he'd left inside her. Live with it. She was old enough to understand you can't always find explanations for what's happened or for the life you've ended up with. That went double for other people's lives. She wasn't one bit wiser, and now she was involved in a homicide, which meant that for the first time in her life she'd had to come up with an alibi.

She turned off all the lights downstairs before going to bed.

At the pub the next day, sitting across from Gregg Turner, she said, "Margaret Graham is the Maggie I asked you about the other day."

She'd slept soundly and had been late getting up. And after one cup of coffee she'd still been determined to stop looking for reasons why her father had washed his hands of her. "Rest in peace," she said out loud from behind his desk, while holding her cup. But damned if she'd let herself be suspected of killing Maggie just because she didn't know what was going on. She could see how that could end. So she decided to uncover as much of the truth as she could. She'd checked the pub several times that morning to see if the ex-undertaker was at his favorite table in back, and finally he'd showed up.

"My father tried to hide something." Ilka leaned in closer to

Turner. "And Margaret Graham knew it, and she was blackmailing him. And of course, my father couldn't have killed her. If the killing has something to do with blackmail, there must be others involved."

Though her father's old friend didn't know what she was talking about, he didn't stop her. The thought crossed her mind that he probably just missed having someone to talk to. But then he set his cup down, scratched his nose, and got straight to the point.

"Paul made a few enemies, but mostly he got along fine with people. I never heard him mention this woman, and honestly, I have a hard time imagining anybody thinking it was worth blackmailing him. He never acted like a big spender. He wasn't a man you'd think a blackmailer would set his sights on, if you know what I mean."

Ilka nodded. "The letter could have been meant for me, like the police said. If she was threatening to reveal something that could hurt me, it must be because my father was mixed up in something Maggie thought I knew about. But what?"

The elderly man held up his palm. He was frowning deeply, but he didn't answer her.

"What's it all about?" she said. "These 'truths' my father kept secret? How in the world am I supposed to know what he was doing?"

The waitress came by and refilled Gregg's cup. He took his time adding two spoonfuls of sugar, and they both stared at the cup as he stirred. Then he pushed his cup a few inches forward and folded his hands on the table. "You can't know, of course not. Your father had a serious run-in with his father-in-law when Frank Conaway was sent to prison."

Ilka looked at him in surprise. She concentrated on blocking out the sportscasters' voices from all the televisions in the restaurant.

"I don't know how much Frank's wife told you about it," he said. "A sad case."

"Nothing. I didn't even know Frank Conaway was in prison." She recalled the young daughter saying her father wouldn't be home for a long time. And she had pressured Karen to set up a meeting with him, without having the slightest idea why he wasn't there.

The ex-undertaker sipped at his coffee. When he set the cup down, Ilka noticed his lips were pressed together. Clearly, he hated talking about this.

"Raymond Fletcher made some serious accusations," he continued, speaking slowly now. "None of us who know Frank Conaway believe he was involved in fraud. But it all happened right after the racetrack went bankrupt—there was a lot of confusion back then. The investors lost a lot of money, and accusations of fraud and insider knowledge were flying around against the men involved in the track. That was before the big loss was finally tallied up. But your father never doubted his friend."

"What did my father do? What happened?" Ilka had trouble picturing her mild-mannered father battling the rich old man, who looked very much like someone you didn't want to mess with.

"Paul didn't believe Fletcher. He claimed Fletcher was the swindler and even hired a famous lawyer in Chicago to clear Frank's name. Until he died, your father was paying the lawyer and fighting to get the charges dropped. Paul had his back to the wall, because Fletcher sent in the cavalry against

Frank. More charges were made, but Paul kept accusing Fletcher of using Frank as a scapegoat to hide his own crimes."

Ilka had no trouble figuring out where the money came from to pay the lawyer. "When was Frank Conaway arrested?"

"A month or two after the track was closed. Around the first of the year."

She nodded thoughtfully. "It all fits. The money came from the funeral home's account; he took out every last dollar he could before he died, starting at the beginning of March."

Turner emptied his cup. She gazed at his furrowed brow as the pieces fell into place.

"It doesn't surprise me," he said. "Close friends could always count on Paul. But why would helping a friend make him a target for blackmail?"

Ilka shook her head. Maggie didn't seem to fit into all this. "How was my father so sure Frank Conaway wasn't guilty? And if he actually went around telling people that Fletcher was the real swindler, isn't that possibly…"

"Slander, yes. The case hasn't come to trial yet, I don't know the details. I don't know why Paul was so sure. All he said was that Fletcher probably paid the police off. Which meant they were covering up for him."

Ilka couldn't believe her ears. Raymond Fletcher was obviously a tough businessman, but he'd come to the funeral home and welcomed her into the family, had given her a large chunk of money to help cover her expenses. If her father really had been saying these things about Fletcher, why was he helping her, meeting her halfway? She wondered if Artie and Sister Eileen knew anything about this.

A roar in the room startled her. She looked up; the TV on the wall showed someone scoring. She was surprised to see the bar half full now. Men mostly, standing around drinking beer, their faces raised to the game. Several women also sat on barstools and followed along. Apparently the game was almost over.

Turner looked up at the TV and read the scores of other games. He slouched a bit. Once again Ilka felt an emptiness settling over her. As if she kept reaching for something beyond her grasp. And it was true: He was dead and couldn't answer the questions he'd left her with.

She stood up.

"If your father pulled money out of his business to help Frank, you can be sure he had a good reason to believe him. Paul Jensen might've been a quiet man, but he wouldn't stand for people being treated that way."

Ilka thought about that as she put on her jacket. After saying goodbye, she went up and paid for the coffee, then elbowed her way out to the street and called Artie. "Come in and get me." She stepped aside to let two men enter the pub. "No, it's not a pickup, this is personal. You're the driver, and I'll be ready in ten minutes."

Ilka hoofed it as fast as she could, all the way back to the funeral home. She looked up when she was reaching for her back-door key and spotted the man leaning against the wall, waiting for her. He stepped toward her.

"That night on the boat, it never happened," he said. "We don't know each other. You don't know my name, and we never talked. Got that?"

Jeff blocked her way. "What the hell's wrong with you, telling the police you were on my boat, and they come marching in, asking me if we were together that evening. What were you thinking?"

Ilka's heart pounded. Not so much because of his aggression, but because she'd been so lost in thought that she hadn't seen him. "If you're so scared of being discovered, maybe you should delete your profile on Tinder." She forced a smile; he wouldn't be the first husband to get caught.

He sneered. "I don't have a profile. And we never had anything to do with each other. I've never seen you before."

Ilka sighed. "So you told the police I wasn't with you that evening?"

Jeff nodded. "I told them I don't know who you are, and if you're smart you'll tell them you made a mistake, you thought I was somebody else."

"Like who?" She was beginning to see where his lying to the police could lead.

"I don't care who the hell you say you fuck, long as you don't tell the police it was me."

"I hope you made sure the girl in the bar doesn't remember working that evening." Her alibi was in danger, which angered her. As she pushed by him, Artie's pickup pulled into the parking lot and caught them in its headlights. Jeff stiffened, then it seemed as if his shoulders broadened when he grabbed her arm.

"What's going on here?" Artie yelled from the pickup. He hustled over to them, but Jeff was already headed to his car around front. Artie had loosened his ponytail, and his long gray hair bounced around his head as he ran.

"It's fine," she said. "He works for Raymond Fletcher, I met him out at the ranch. He just wanted to tell me Amber's doing okay."

Artie stared at her. "He was threatening you, you think I'm an idiot? What's going on?"

She smiled. "He was just mad I wouldn't go out with him." She steered Artie back to the pickup, which was still idling. On the way she told him about her conversation with Gregg Turner.

"Did you know Frank Conaway was the reason my father pulled all the money out of the business last spring?"

Artie shook his head as she punched in her father's friend's address on the GPS. "I knew he was really shook up when they sent Frank to prison, but I don't know how he was involved in everything." He rolled down the window and lit a cigarette. "The papers wrote a lot about the troubles out at the track, but like I said, horses and me, we don't agree. I didn't pay all that much attention.

"But as I understand it, one of the big casinos complained about the track wanting to add some roulette wheels and stuff, other gambling than just playing the horses. Lots of tracks are doing that, trying to pull more people in. They're called racinos. The casino sued the track to stop them, they wouldn't put up with the competition, and the track ended up having to pay eighty-two million dollars, I think it was. Which they couldn't do, so they declared bankruptcy."

"*Hold da op*," Ilka mumbled as she calculated in her head how much that was in Danish kroner.

Artie nodded. "And there were some pretty hefty accusations made against the governor. Corruption, bribery. A lot of people lost their jobs, and there were stories about healthy horses maybe having to be slaughtered after the scandal, but I think they avoided that."

"How was Frank Conaway involved?"

Artie shrugged. "I don't know. Your dad didn't talk much about it, but I could tell it really bothered him. He and Frank went way back."

"He must have really felt terrible, since he risked his whole business." She told him about the envelope Raymond Fletcher had brought her. "We need that money badly. Maybe we should offer him the whole business, everything. You could buy the house from him, if you still want."

"It would solve our problems, for sure," Artie mumbled,

nodding to himself. "I don't think he's interested in running the business, though."

"But really, does that matter? I just want him to buy it, I just want out."

Artie suggested they talk to Sister Eileen before contacting Fletcher.

"I doubt she'll be happy about that plan." She described the nun's reaction when Ilka told her about Fletcher's visit. "She made it clear, the last thing my father would have wanted is Fletcher's help. It's just that right now we can't afford being picky."

"Ow, shit!" Artie threw the cigarette butt out the window and shook his singed fingers. He rolled up the window and started the pickup, and for several moments he drove in silence. "You know what. Don't talk to her about it. You don't need our okay. And I'm sure she'll understand you're doing what you think is best."

He turned on the radio, and the rest of the way he hummed along to several country numbers she didn't know.

When they arrived at the Conaways' house, Karen came to the door in a large sweater that reached her thighs. Her hair was pulled back into a ponytail, and she seemed hesitant as she leaned against the doorframe.

Ilka got out and waited for Artie, then looked up at the woman. "I hope we're not disturbing you? I'm sorry for just showing up like this. I heard about what's happened to Frank, and I just want to ask if there's anything we can do."

Karen stepped forward as Ilka approached. "So you're not here for the money your father loaned us? I promised Paul we'd pay back every cent, as soon as we prove Frank is innocent. Raymond Fletcher is going to pay, and I mean money, for what he's done to us."

Ilka took her hands. "We're not here to ask for anything." She put her arm around the woman's shoulders and walked inside. Artie stood, unsure of what to do, which annoyed Ilka; she waved him in.

Karen looked up at her. "He didn't do it. When you came

107

by the other day, I thought you knew what had happened. I figured that's why you were here. But when you didn't say anything, well, I didn't either."

"Really, it's okay. My father believed in your husband's innocence."

She still didn't know exactly what Frank Conaway had been charged with. Apparently, he had been held for over six months, and Ilka thought there must be some reason the case hadn't been brought to trial yet. But then, she understood nothing about the American judicial system. She did understand why Karen Conaway was sick with worry, though; she was financially strapped and couldn't afford the lawyer.

It was dark outside now, and Ilka assumed the daughter was asleep. At least she wasn't in the kitchen or living room. A bottle of red wine stood on the table, almost empty.

"Would you like some wine?" Karen moved to grab a few glasses from a shelf, but Ilka asked if she could make a pot of coffee instead. Karen nodded and sat down.

Ilka sat across from her after starting the coffee. "What is it your husband's accused of?"

"Charged," Karen said. "The police have charged him. And Frank could be put away for thirty years, for felony fraud. He could be a grandfather by that time, if he's still alive. The prosecutor claims he's taken ten million dollars since the late '90s. But look at how we live! Do we look like people with that kind of money?"

She pointed around the kitchen, at an open cupboard with several pots and pans. A cabinet in the corner with tableware, glasses on a shelf. "We don't even have a dishwasher."

She shook her head and emptied her glass. Ilka guessed she'd been sitting in the kitchen since putting her daughter to bed. Then Ilka remembered there were two daughters, and she asked about the older one. The woman looked down at the table.

"Right now, she's in a treatment center. She stopped eating. She's had a rough time of it. Everyone knows her father is in jail. And everyone talks. It's easier for our younger daughter, she's here all the time."

She twirled her wineglass with three fingers. "It's almost like it's not enough for him to ruin our lives with his false accusations. He's also made sure the case has been in the papers, a lot, so everyone knows what Frank's been charged with."

The coffee had seeped through the filter, and Ilka grabbed a few cups from the cabinet. Artie asked her to bring a wineglass too. He poured a glass for Karen and a bit for himself.

"Frank has worked for Raymond Fletcher since he was seventeen," Karen continued. "He knew your dad from the time he came over, and even after we moved out here and started for ourselves, Frank did work for Fletcher and Davidson Raceteam. He ran the stables during the races, warmed up the horses. Of course, he had help from stableboys, but if you only knew how many family dinners he missed because of a race. How many times he missed a school play or concert, all because of a Wednesday race or a weekend race. A filly race or a mare race or…"

She began crying, and Artie leaned over and put his arm around her. Ilka's fingers tingled from clenching her fists so hard. It was like listening to her mother. The words may not have been exactly the same, but it was the same situation. The same absence.

A bit embarrassed now, Karen gently pulled herself away from Artie. "But we always made it work. And my husband was happy with that life. I don't understand how Fletcher could turn against Frank that way, after all those years. Even if he needed a scapegoat to cover up his own fraud. They've known each other almost all of Frank's life."

She swiped at her tears with the back of her hand and sipped her wine. "Paul used to say that if someone ever made Raymond Fletcher open up and feel even a tiny little emotion, it would kill him." She smiled halfheartedly and collected herself.

"I still don't quite get how they think it was done," she said. She explained that they believed he embezzled the money over a period of years. "Supposedly it was fake bills connected to running the stable. Bills that were signed and paid, but never entered into the books of whoever was being paid."

She paused a moment and looked at them. "Money that was an expense to the company, but never recorded as income anywhere else. And since most it had to do with stable operations, Frank's responsibility, they claim he must've known about it. And because it didn't come out until now, it must be because he's behind it. And that's why the police charged him."

"But what evidence do they have?" Ilka said.

Karen laughed wryly. "Fletcher didn't need evidence. He told them his version, and that was good enough for them. Then later he created the evidence they needed."

"He can't do that!"

"Oh yes he can."

"But the police are involved!" Ilka turned to Artie, but he said nothing. "So you really think Raymond Fletcher can get away with this? There has to be more than just him reporting it to the police."

Artie nodded. "Yeah, money. It takes money and influence to make something like this happen."

"But surely somebody is investigating where the ten million dollars is, since it's obviously not here. Somebody must be tracking the money."

"We first found out about it just after Gerald Davidson died. Fletcher and Davidson owned the stable together, so when his estate was being looked at, the financial reports came out. And it wasn't long after the track went bankrupt, so all the investors' losses were being added up. You could say it was perfect timing for Fletcher. Paul claimed his father-in-law used his partner's death to hide the money he'd been stealing. But nobody knows where it is."

Karen emptied her glass and slumped in her chair. "Your father was sure we could prove all the bills were written recently, even though some of them were dated as far back as 1998. That's when they say the fraud started."

"Could you prove it?"

Karen nodded. "The signature was identical on all the receipts. And they were all written with what looked like the same pen. Of course, it's hard to prove a hundred percent, but isn't it really unlikely they used the same kind of blue pen for eighteen years?"

She looked at them as if she expected an answer. When they didn't react, she said, "But the fact is, it was Frank's signature. At first the lawyer focused on the pen and paper, because it all looked new and identical. They didn't even bother to crumple up the receipts and put some age on them. Like I said, though, it's just hard to prove something like this."

"But…" Ilka was about to argue then thought better of it.

"So the lawyer started in on the dates. His idea was to prove

Frank wasn't in the office on the days the receipts were signed. But we never got that far."

She glanced at Ilka; she'd made it sound as if the lawyer was the worst consequence of Paul's death. "We'll find a way. Fletcher is not going to get away with this."

Her chin rested in her hands. Artie had walked over to the front door to smoke, though it did little good, because the smoke drifted inside.

"The last time I was here, I asked you about a woman named Maggie," Ilka said.

Karen shook her head. "I've tried to remember, but no. The name doesn't ring any bells."

"She was killed. Shot at close range. The killer made it look like a break-in, but I can't stop thinking there might be a connection here, that her last letter maybe had something to do with this case. Since my father was so involved."

"Did she know something about all this?" Karen said.

Ilka scooted over when Artie came back. "I don't know. But in the letter, she demanded money to keep a secret, and I'm wondering if it might be linked to your husband. Because it sounds like someone is trying to hide the truth. What I can't figure out is why my father would want to cover something up."

Karen stared blankly for several moments before straightening up in her chair again. "I've never heard of her, but if she knew something, anything, we have to contact the lawyer. What if she's the one piece of the puzzle we're missing?"

"We can't be certain," Ilka said. She had no idea, in fact, if there actually was a connection, but the possibility was thought provoking.

She stood up to leave. While putting on her jacket, she

promised Karen she would contact the police and talk to them about all this.

"I wouldn't get my hopes up if I were you." Karen followed them to the door. "Not when it comes to the police and Raymond Fletcher. I've got to be careful what I say, I know, but I have this bad feeling he owns the police station, or at least the people leading the investigation. If you get what I mean."

Ilka wasn't sure she did, but she let it go and thanked Karen for the coffee. And she insisted that Karen call if something happened, or if she just needed company.

They barely spoke on the way home. Ilka leaned back against the headrest and closed her eyes, but she was too worked up to nap. Artie had sent her straight into Raymond Fletcher's arms to ask for money, yet he didn't seem surprised to hear how the man treated people. He'd just sat there nodding while listening to Karen's story! Ilka was furious with him; her skin prickled, her arms felt heavy. She felt his eyes on her several times, but she pretended to be asleep. Fortunately, he didn't dare turn on the radio. Maybe he sensed her anger.

He slowed when they reached Racine, and while they drove through downtown she squinted and let the light from the streetlamps fly by like white streaks in the air.

"You want to come home with me, sit for a while on the porch? I could make a campfire."

"No thanks."

He pulled in and parked on the street, and she glanced over at him.

He turned to her. "I'm sorry, I didn't know anything about this. I knew Paul didn't get along with his father-in-law, but Fletcher had helped him before. And in our situation, you have to remember, money is money. Which is exactly what you need right now."

Ilka stared out the front windshield and shook her head. "Just take me home."

Even though it was past ten and Sister Eileen's apartment was dark, Ilka knocked on the door. Artie had called after her when she slammed the pickup door and walked off, but now she heard him leaving. So what if she'd hurt his feelings; what he'd done was not okay, not even close. She had no chance of protecting herself if they didn't bother to warn her.

She hammered on the door again, stepped out on the sidewalk and shouted, knocked once more. She kept calling Sister Eileen's name until the light came on in the hall and the nun peeked out the tiny window in the door.

"It's me," Ilka shouted. As if there was any doubt.

Sister Eileen was wearing a long housecoat. Her narrow glasses were pushed up on her forehead, and she held a book. She said nothing, simply frowned at Ilka while holding on to the doorknob, as if she might slam the door at any second.

"Sorry, but I want that envelope with Raymond Fletcher's money. We're not accepting it." She held her hand out as if she expected Sister Eileen to give it to her right there, but slowly she lowered her arm.

The nun looked tired and pale. Something in her expression made Ilka think it wasn't just because it was her bedtime. The whole situation was obviously exhausting her: all the problems with the funeral home, as well as her mourning Ilka's father. They hadn't spoken much about that. In fact, she hadn't spoken much at all to Sister Eileen, at least not about personal things.

"I used the money to pay bills. As you told me to."

"All of it?"

"There's about two thousand dollars left, but that's for the last funeral."

Ilka hardly noticed when Sister Eileen said good night and closed the door. For several moments she stared into the darkness surrounding the house before walking back.

The night sky looked like it did in Copenhagen, yet it seemed different. Everything did. Also, this feeling of being alone was different from the loneliness she'd felt since Flemming's death.

I'd like to see the documents from the Frank Conaway case," Ilka said when Jack Doonan finally arrived at his desk, a cup of coffee in one hand and a bagel wrapped in a napkin in the other. She'd been waiting at his cubicle by the wall for twenty minutes while the department held their morning briefing.

Last night she'd thought long and hard about going to the police, after the episode with Jeff and losing her alibi. Was it a stupid thing to do? But she knew she hadn't killed anyone; she had nothing to fear, she told herself. She'd tossed and turned, thinking about a million things, and when she did sleep her dreams were a chaos of broken fragments. Now her head felt like an unmade bed, and the sight of the officer eating the bagel, the cream cheese hanging on his lip, nauseated her.

Doonan was visibly annoyed at being bothered so early in the morning. And it was even more obvious he had no idea what she was talking about. He scowled and sat down.

Ilka explained that Conaway had been arrested in March,

and she gave him the name of the lawyer her father had hired. For some reason he let her speak, but when he finished eating he crumpled up the napkin and told her to talk to the crimes against property unit. "I don't know anything about the case, but I'll tell you one thing for sure—they won't give you anything before the trial is over. If the accused is in custody, no one will talk to you. And probably not later either."

"But what if the man's innocent? My father was certain that Frank Conaway is a scapegoat."

Doonan lifted his hand to stop her. "Since we're on your father. I was up until one last night going over Margaret Graham's bank account. And guess what, it turns out that fifteen hundred dollars was deposited in her account every three months, for the past eleven years. Interesting, I thought, so I looked at the bank account the money was transferred from."

Ilka breathed in short, shallow bursts.

"Eleven years, the same amount. Every three months. From an account in the name of the Paul Jensen Funeral Home."

He leaned forward, and for a moment they stared at each other.

Doonan finally broke eye contact. Maybe he was looking for signs of her knowing about this, Ilka thought. He pushed a small stack of papers across the desk.

She hardly knew what to say. "But why for eleven years?"

"That's when Mrs. Graham opened the account. Maybe it's been going on even longer. Her old bank closed that year, so now I'm waiting for a court order to grant me access to your account. I'm assuming I'll be able to see when the transfers from the funeral home began."

He handed her a sheet with the latest deposits and withdrawals. A red circle had been drawn around the amount, and the account number had been underlined. "The last transfer was made in June this year. An automatic transfer."

Ilka laid the sheet aside and absentmindedly began putting her coat on. In a few days the third quarter would be over, but now both Maggie and her father were dead.

"Are you absolutely sure my father died of natural causes?" Ilka had to yell to be heard over the noise from the ventilation.

After returning from the police station, she'd headed straight for Artie's preparation room, where he stood in a lab coat and mask, leaning over Maggie's body, working to cover up the bullet hole in her forehead.

She slammed the door behind her and strode over to him. He was wearing in-ear headphones, and when she ripped them out he ducked his head and whirled around; some of the wax he was using to cover the bullet hole landed on her arms. He retreated a step. "What are you doing?"

Ilka handed him the tiny headphones spouting out surfer music. The Beach Boys. "Are you sure my father died of natural causes?" she repeated. "Did you see him?"

A shadow swept across his face. He looked away and spoke quietly. "He died in his sleep in his room."

Ilka took a moment to settle herself down. "How was he found?"

The ventilation roared as she shivered from the damp cold in the room. Artie studied her a moment before turning and swinging the large vent over Maggie's naked body. He walked over to the sink beside the door, pulled off his mask and lab coat, washed his hands, and opened the door. "Come on."

Ilka followed him to the kitchenette. He poured himself a half cup of coffee and grabbed a Red Bull from the fridge, popped it open, and filled his cup. With his other hand he fished a pack of cigarettes from his Hawaiian shirt pocket and headed for the back door.

His goddamn Hawaiian shirts! It's all he wore. Red, green, yellow, blue. All those palm trees and parrots made her want to throw up. And Red Bull in his coffee! Sick!

He held the door for her and pulled out his lighter, then sat down on the top step. "What's this all about?"

It was cool outside, and some fallen leaves from the big copper beech swirled around in the parking lot. He blew out a cloud of smoke and waited. Finally she sat down and covered her face with her hands a moment.

"I guess this link between Maggie and my father bothers me, and now they're both dead. And it was so cold-blooded, the way she was killed. I want to know what happened to him."

She watched the leaves dance around as she explained about the bank transfers. She couldn't meet his eye. "Do you know anything about it? You might as well tell me, I'm going to find out anyway. Either my father set up the automatic transfer of funds from our account, or else one of you two did. You were both here eleven years ago. What is it you're not telling me?"

Ilka heard him set his cup down. Smoke drifted over to her, and she breathed it in.

"He was in bed," Artie said. "Sister Eileen thought something was wrong—the hearse was still in the garage when she came over that morning. The evening before they'd talked about him leaving early, around six, to beat the morning rush hour. He was supposed to take a body to Iowa. The man's family wanted him home, they were going to arrange the funeral themselves. When Sister Eileen went upstairs and knocked, Paul didn't answer. She said he was lying in bed and had died quietly in his sleep."

Artie folded his hands around his knees.

"I'd like to see the death certificate," Ilka said.

"Mary Ann has it."

"But don't we have a copy?"

He took a deep breath. "What difference does it make? Ilka, listen. He died in his sleep."

"Right now, it's important. To me."

Artie explained that the physical certificate had been delivered to the crematorium. "It's the law. It's used as identification before the body can be cremated. And then they gave it to the family, along with the urn."

"But surely we have a copy?"

He nodded. "Digital. On our computer."

"Did you see him up there in bed?"

Artie studied his hands on his knees; a small fleck of tobacco was stuck in the corner of his mouth, and she was about to lean forward and brush it off when he shook his head.

"No. I was off a few days, fishing up in Canada. The morning Sister Eileen found him, I was gone before sunrise. She tried to get ahold of me several times that day, but I didn't hear her messages until I got back that evening."

Now Ilka understood why he'd acted so aloof. He hadn't been there when her father died, only Sister Eileen.

His eyes were glued to his hands again. It seemed difficult for him to talk about this, and Ilka had to remind herself that unlike her, Sister Eileen and Artie had been close to her father. She waited.

"It was hot the night your father died. His body was already swelling when Sister Eileen found him. He'd probably been dead twelve hours, and there's no AC up there—well, you know that. He didn't really look like himself. Sister Eileen told Mary Ann the swelling would disappear when he was embalmed. She offered to arrange the services, but Mary Ann wanted him cremated immediately and asked to have the urn delivered to her. So Sister Eileen got another undertaker to drive him to the crematorium that same day."

"No service was held?" Ilka was surprised. It seemed odd that no one wanted to say goodbye to an undertaker.

"There was, but not here. Mary Ann wanted it at her home, family and friends only. Nobody with business connections to your father was invited, except for Sister Eileen and me."

After a few moments Ilka stood up and offered to take his empty cup inside. She went into her father's office and shut the door, then she sat down in her father's chair, turned on the aging computer, and waited for it to come to life. Strange, she thought; she'd been thinking so much about her father recently, yet she didn't know what he'd looked like the last several years he was alive. She remembered him only as someone who made her feel safe. All the insecurity he'd left her with had somehow been pushed out by how much she'd missed him while growing up.

She typed his name and waited for his death certificate to show up. August 16. He'd died exactly ten days after her fortieth birthday. But she hadn't been contacted until Artie called her two weeks after that, asking her to come to Racine. The doctor had determined the cause of death to be cardiac arrest. Artie had told her that in the hearse, the day he picked her up at the airport. She'd also been told that her father had died in his sleep, but she hadn't needed to know the decomposition process had already begun because of the heat.

The death certificate had been scanned and saved in the computer two days after his death. She turned on the printer.

Most of the information was hard for her to understand, but it didn't matter; after skimming through the last page, she stopped abruptly. She pulled the paper out of the printer and turned on the desk lamp.

The death certificate had been signed by Margaret Graham.

Ilka shot up from her chair and banged her knee hard against the desk. It hurt like hell, but she humped over to the door, eager to find Sister Eileen and shake an explanation out of her. She was the one who'd found her father in bed, the one who had saved a copy of his death certificate in the computer, and yet she'd said nothing when Ilka showed her the letters together with the burial testament.

She stopped at the doorway, and after thinking a few moments, she tossed down the death certificate and limped over to the cabinet where the funeral home's books were kept in ring binders on the lower shelves. She'd spent considerable time going over the finances for the past five years to get a picture of their financial situation, but now she was looking for a specific expense from this year.

Fifteen hundred dollars had been transferred on March 28, as a decorations expense. She checked the end of June; the same amount had been entered the same way. Then she went back to March 2010, and there it was again.

Expense: decorations.

Nothing about whether it was for flowers, candles, table decorations.

She went through the books from other years; the same entries had been made, of course. Finally, she slumped forward, her palms cupping her forehead. For the past eleven years the money had been transferred to the account Doonan had showed her at the station. And before that, starting in 1998, the same amount had been transferred to a different account. Always as a decorations expense. Glancing through the other expenses, she'd recognized a coffin supplier who had shut her off recently, as well as a crematorium. Then there were the usual expenses. Electricity, water, the chemicals Artie used to prepare the bodies.

She sat up and thought about her father entering the same amount every quarter for eighteen years as an expense, for decorations. Money that had ended up with the woman who had signed his death certificate.

Ilka closed the ring binders and stood up. All she felt now was exhaustion as she opened his most recent calendar. The last meeting he'd scheduled had been at Margaret Graham's address.

"Can I borrow your pickup?" Ilka said, when she ran into Artie in the hallway. Her father's Chevrolet had an empty tank.

At first the look he gave her made her think she'd have to walk to Michael Graham's home, but then she realized he wasn't angry. He was about to say something, but he changed his mind and stepped aside.

She headed out the door. "Take the hearse," he said. By the

time she turned around, he was already in the preparation room. She stared at the closed door. Clearly, she'd hit a very sore spot when she pressured him to explain he'd been fishing in Canada when her father died. After all, Artie had known him since moving to Racine in 1998.

Nineteen ninety-eight.

Ilka burst through the door. "Exactly when in 1998 did you come back to Racine? When did you meet my father? Was it spring, summer, fall?"

Artie was about to pull a mask on, but he stopped. His hair was hidden in a net, and he looked a bit sad and tired. "It was September 1998. My father died just before Christmas, and I inherited his house. And when your father offered me a job, I decided it was time to move back."

When Ilka arrived in Racine, Artie had explained that he and Paul had met at Oh Dennis!, the pub, while he was still taking care of his own father. Artie had lived in Key West since finishing at the California School of the Arts in San Francisco. He'd run a small gallery down there, Artie the Artist. Ilka had made fun of the name, laughed at it. She wasn't laughing now, though. "Were you here earlier that summer, to check up on your father?"

Artie looked fed up. He took a step toward her. "What's going on, what is it you want to know?"

"I want to know what *you* know about the transfers of money made to Maggie. Four times a year for eighteen years, beginning the year you came back to town."

His eyebrows shot up. "Nothing. I don't know anything about that, and I've never transferred money to Margaret Graham either, if that's what you're asking. I have zero access to the funeral home's bank account. That's been Sister Eileen's territory the past few years, after your dad left all the book work to her."

They stared at each other long enough for it to feel awkward in the cold, damp room. Ilka realized they'd been arguing only a few feet from Maggie's dead body.

"I'm sorry," she said. She'd gone too far, and she knew it. He was pale and obviously hurt, but she also felt let down, confused. It didn't matter who knew what. If they had cheated or bribed somebody, well, that was in the past. *Look to the future,* she'd told herself years ago when she'd been widowed. And now she needed to get back to that mantra.

"Really, I'm sorry," she said. "I didn't mean to hurt you. Or accuse you of anything. Listen, I'm not used to people being murdered or put into prison for nearly the rest of their life. The longest sentence back home is sixteen years for first-degree murder. No one sits in prison for thirty years, unless they're insane and a threat to everyone, then it's an open sentence. If Frank Conaway is found guilty, he won't be celebrating Christmas with his younger daughter before her own children are out of high school. And Maggie blackmailed my father, and now she's been shot."

"But that doesn't mean the two things are linked." He put his hands on her shoulders, which cheered her a bit. Even though she was at least half a head taller than Artie.

"If Margaret Graham really was blackmailing your dad, it says more about her than about Paul. And I'll bet the police will investigate. He might not be the only one being blackmailed."

Ilka nodded; she'd had the same thought.

Of course, Artie was right, she should leave all of this to the police. Yet she knew she couldn't let it go.

L ow ranch-style houses lined both sides of the street. Identical houses, laid out as mirror images of each other, with
small front lawns, low fences, and driveways on both sides of
each house. When Ilka turned onto the street, she felt she was
entering some sort of model town, an exhibition carefully displayed and tidied up every day. No clutter, no contrasts. She
kept an eye on house numbers and slowed down at number
forty-two to look it over before driving to the end of the cul-
de-sac and turning around.

She'd taken ten dollars from the coffee can in the kitchen
to gas up her father's car. Arriving in a hearse would be too
much, she'd decided. As she'd told the police, she'd never been
in this part of Racine; it amazed her that there were so many
large residential areas, yet the town seemed nearly deserted.
The same went for the marina, where the boats were packed
like sardines without a boat owner in sight.

Ilka parked four houses down from number forty-two,
and when she got out she looked around. Several times

she'd had the feeling someone was watching her, but she was alone on the street. Except for the woman who glanced up from a flower bed she was weeding. Ilka nodded politely when she passed by, but the woman was already back to her work.

When she reached the steps to Michael Graham's front door, she noticed traces of the police investigation. They'd stuck several small pieces of tape on the windowsill and around the lock on the door, which gave her a certain sense of relief; her alibi may have been ruined, but apparently there were fingerprints. Though surely Stan Thomas didn't really believe she'd shot Maggie. Why should she? Presumably he was simply looking into every possibility.

The house had no doorbell or knocker, so she rapped firmly and stepped back so Graham could see her through the spy hole. A moment later he unlocked the door and opened it, but before he could speak, Ilka apologized for not calling in advance.

"I'd like to talk to you," she said. "Not about the funeral though. It's something private. Is this a bad time for you?"

But Graham had already stepped aside for Ilka to come in. He didn't seem all that surprised to see her either.

"Are you here to talk about my affair with your father's wife?" He added that he could understand if the gossip had flared up again, seeing what had happened. "It ended a long time ago, and I haven't spoken to Mary Ann for years."

He showed her into the living room. She noticed the rugs, in contrast with the hallway's bare wood floor. Ilka stood for a moment and imagined Graham coming home from bowling to find his wife just inside the door.

After she sat down on the plush leather sofa, he took a seat in a chair across from her. "I hope the rumors aren't about me shooting my wife, so I could run off with my ex-mistress."

He smiled sadly. His attempt at lightening things up made her realize the police hadn't talked to him yet about the letters.

"I haven't heard of anyone accusing you of that."

His expression changed; he was probably wondering now why she'd stopped by.

"Your wife signed my father's death certificate." She handed him a copy.

He thumbed through to the last page, then he handed it back. He looked relieved. "There's nothing strange about that. She worked for Dr. Vincent after quitting the hospital, he was Paul and Mary Ann's doctor, so he must have been called in when they found your father. She told me once it's normal here for doctors to sign the death certificate of their patients, long as there's a witness. Coroners only must sign when a sudden death looks suspicious, but usually that happens at the hospital or the morgue. My wife worked in the reception. She made sure all the papers got sent out, and she signed as a witness too."

Ilka stared at the stamp mark proving the death certificate had been certified by the Racine Health Care Clinic. It was signed by Dr. Vincent and witnessed by Margaret Graham. His signature was simply a few tall strokes, while hers was legible.

No matter what, Maggie had definitely known that Paul was dead. Now the letter made even less sense to Ilka.

The living room window was open a crack, and cool air seeped into the room. Graham watched a scooter zip by outside, then he turned to her. "I was so much in love with your dad's wife. I never meant to cheat, it never crossed my mind, not really. Back then, I thought of myself as a faithful husband with a solid marriage; definitely not a bad one. Not fantastic, but okay. I've thought about what happened a million times. It doesn't make sense, it just happened, I fell head over heels in love. Couldn't stop myself. Couldn't walk away."

He threw up his hands, as if gesturing helped. "I tried telling myself it was an obsession, like that made it okay, but no. I wasn't crazy or anything. It wasn't like some virus and I could be cured. I was one hundred percent in love with another man's wife, and I wasn't strong enough to walk away. She fell in love with me too. The same way. We had an affair, but Maggie found out and told your dad. I figured that's why you showed up here today, to get some answers, an explanation. I can tell you this, I was going to leave my wife to live with Mary Ann. She would have left your dad too, even though we'd have had to move out of town while the kids were still in school."

He sat straight in his chair and looked her right in the eye as he spoke. A sad man, yet composed. He paused for a moment, seemingly to give her an opportunity to ask questions, or even to come down on him hard, but she said nothing.

"We met at a wedding reception. Both of us were friends of the couple. Mary Ann came by herself, but Maggie was there too. Funny, she's the one who introduced me to Mary Ann. Which she also blamed herself for, plenty of times over the years."

Graham fiddled with his shirtsleeve and smiled wistfully as he shook his head. To show that he'd put it all behind him, Ilka thought. But something in his eyes told her that though it happened long ago, and Mary Ann was just a part of his past now, she wasn't the least bit forgotten. Bringing back all these memories livened up his face.

"There was something magical and light about Mary Ann back then. It hit me like a ton of bricks. She claimed we drank the wedding couple's love wine by mistake, out there on the lawn, looking out over the lake. She gave me her phone number, and right then and there I should've thrown it away, but I called her that night. And the next day we got together. She'd made a picnic basket, and we sat down there by the lake. She knew so much about things, she was so sunny, happy. And she had a great voice."

Ilka could hardly believe her ears. Mary Ann, magical and sunny? And she couldn't at all picture her father's wife singing. On the other hand, she'd never have imagined her shooting at people either.

"I loved my wife, but I was ready to give everything up for Mary Ann. Then they had the accident. All those years ago, in May, a horrible day. And I haven't seen her since. She wouldn't see me, she returned all my letters. I did all I could to get to her, but she made it real clear. It was over between us."

He leaned forward and rested his forearms on his thighs, folded his hands over his knees. He spoke with compassion, as if Mary Ann could hear him. "Life hasn't been easy for her. It wasn't easy being married to your dad. He was very busy, and she felt all alone with their first daughter. I think she was lonely. Then they had Amber, and they fell into a routine."

"Did my father never do things with his family?" Ilka said. She was alert now to something opening inside her, something she recognized.

"Of course he did, sure, it wasn't like that," he said. "He took care of them, provided for them. Mary Ann's dad gave the house to them for a wedding present, but it looked to me like Paul took care of the rest. It was more that he didn't pay her all that much attention. That's what she was missing."

He shrugged and raised his eyebrows, as if he was a bit embarrassed at being the one who gave her father's wife what she'd needed.

"I could be wrong about that last part, though. I tried to fool myself into thinking I wasn't taking anything away from him." He smiled shyly. "Don't misunderstand me. Mary Ann cared about your dad, and she loved her two daughters, but when you fall in love it's hard not to be blind. And that's what we were. Blinded by each other."

He looked down at the floor. Ilka nodded, even though that had never happened to her. Flemming was the only man she'd really fallen in love with, but it hadn't happened as it did with Maggie's husband and Mary Ann. It was a love that slowly grew and gave her a sense of security without blinding her. She'd just known they were going to stay together.

"So anyway, the day Maggie came home and caught us, there was no turning back. Mary Ann and I agreed the time had come, even though we hadn't chosen it. And we hated all the secrecy, we wanted to get it out in the open. We just hadn't done it yet. I asked Maggie not to tell Paul, but she was crazy mad and hurt, she said she already knew what was going on, and she'd told him. But your dad hadn't said anything about it to Mary Ann."

He glanced at the open window again. It was quiet outside, no traffic, not even a bird singing. "Before we got caught, Mary Ann talked to a lawyer about what would happen with the house in case of a divorce. But then they had the accident. And like I said, I never saw her again."

He spoke in earnest when he turned to her. "Mary Ann was the love of my life. But I've never felt so empty before, now that Maggie's gone. We've been together two-thirds of my life. She was my wife, seems like forever. Maybe I never really knew how much she meant to me. I can't tell you how many times I regretted not running away with Mary Ann, back when we had the chance, but now I regret even more not seeing how much I loved my wife. Maggie forgave me, and we had a lot of good years together, even though we almost broke up a few times. I sort of bottled myself up right after what happened with Mary Ann, couldn't let go of it."

Ilka felt she should stand up and leave. Thank him for talking to her, for telling her this love story her father was indirectly involved in. Tell him he was welcome to call if he had questions about the funeral. Yes, she should get out of there, right now. But she couldn't.

Graham was leaning over with his head in his hands, though he wasn't crying. It seemed that he too was trying to absorb everything he'd said. As if it had been buried inside him all these years, and now it had clawed its way out. He looked exhausted. It moved Ilka to see how burdened with grief he was at discovering how much he'd loved Maggie. And yet she leaned forward and said what she should have waited to say until after the funeral.

"Did you know that since the summer of 1998, my father deposited fifteen hundred dollars in your wife's account, every three months? Over one hundred thousand dollars in all. And it looks to me like she was blackmailing him. But maybe you have an explanation."

She didn't mean to sound belligerent; she tried to smooth it over by telling him that because of a few letters, the police had gone through his wife's bank account and had discovered the transfers from the funeral home account.

He sat with his mouth open, but he waited until she had finished to speak. "I don't...I don't know anything about that, it's...But that can't be right. That much money, I would've known about it."

True, she thought. It *was* a lot of money, something that would have affected their financial situation.

He walked over to a low bureau behind the dining room table and brought back a dark-green ring binder. His finger trailed down the latest entries in their bank account, occasionally stopping, then he turned the page and kept checking. Page after page. Finally, he straightened up and nodded, though now he was pale and shaking. He closed the ring binder.

"I don't understand. If it started eighteen years ago, that was about when Maggie found out about Mary Ann and me, but if she was blackmailing someone, wouldn't it be...one of the guilty parties?"

He sank back in his chair, completely lost. As if he were trying to grab on to something that wasn't there. "She never said a word about this. Why would she ask him for money? What was in those letters that made the police look into this?"

Ilka hesitated a moment before picking up her bag and finding Maggie's letters. She handed them to him.

As he slowly read the letters, he looked at least as shocked as just before, when he'd learned about the blackmail. "What did she mean, *finally*? She makes it sound like your dad deserved the credit for Mary Ann and me breaking it off."

He shook his head. "The accident did it. Two people were killed, that was tragic, and she was paralyzed. They all could've died. I don't understand how my wife could be so heartless, to see the accident as a good thing for her because it saved our marriage."

He stared at the letters lying on the table between them.

Ilka had thought the same thing. Artie had told her how much the accident had affected her father. She couldn't imagine his reaction when Maggie's letters came, making it sound as if he'd done her a favor.

Graham sat up and made a great effort to pull himself together. "I have no idea why she would blackmail Paul. We didn't lack for anything, she didn't need the extra money." He seemed to feel he owed Ilka an explanation on behalf of his dead wife.

"Maybe we'll never find out." Ilka saw no reason to mention how much his wife must have felt betrayed and rejected by his affair. "But the police will probably want to talk to you about this. They might ask if she was blackmailing someone else, who'd then have a motive to kill her."

"I always felt my wife was well liked and respected," Graham mumbled. "She got along with people. I can't imagine anyone wanting to kill her."

She let him think about it.

"Are you saying it was a...a hit? You think she did something so bad that they came here to kill her?"

Ilka had no answer for that. She asked him if he could think of anything that connected Maggie with her father. "Did they stay in touch after you and Mary Ann broke it off?"

"Not that I know of, but if he's the one who gave her this money, then they must have."

"Forget about the letters for a moment. Could your wife have been doing some sort of work for my father, that he paid her for? Decorations for the funeral home?"

"Decorations!" He looked confused for a moment, then gestured for her to look around. "Does it look like we have a lot of decorations here? Maggie didn't like knickknacks, why in the world would she make decorations for the funeral home?"

"I'm just trying to find a logical explanation for why my father gave her so much money. And one reason could be that she did something for him."

"I didn't hear her mention Paul Jensen one single time after what happened. I didn't even know they knew each other. Just what are you thinking about?"

"I'm not thinking of anything, really. Maybe your wife knew something about my father that made him willing to pay her off, even though he didn't have much money. Did he do something wrong? What did she have on him?"

"Well, the money was put in her account, that's for sure," he said, as if stating the obvious somehow helped make sense of it. "We had a joint account, but we kept separate accounts too. I kept my nose out of my wife's money. I did get a letter from the bank two days after she died, and it surprised me how much money she had, I can tell you that. But she didn't spend a lot, and we paid our regular expenses through the joint account. Besides, she earned a decent wage working for Dr. Vincent, so I didn't think a thing about it. I guess I'd better give all these papers of hers to the police."

Graham ran his hand down his face and took a deep breath. "It's just so strange. It's a side of her I never saw. I can't imagine what she knew about your dad, but the way it goes back to when everything happened with Mary Ann and me, now that makes me wonder. And the letters, it's nothing she ever talked about. It's just really confusing. She couldn't talk about her work at the clinic, but as far as her private life goes, I can't think of anything involving your dad."

His shoulders slumped, and Ilka waited until he looked over

at her again. "Maybe I didn't know her as well as I thought I did," he said, his voice small now. "I wish I had some answers for you. I don't know what to say."

"I understand, it's okay. My problem is, I can't stop thinking he might have been killed too." She thought about her father's urn and the bare mantel at Mary Ann's house. She needed to find out where it was.

"Could it really be true somebody came here to kill my wife?" Graham asked again, as if the idea was just now beginning to soak in. "They must have been keeping an eye on her. So they'd know she was alone when I went bowling. I need to talk to the police again. This changes everything."

Ilka stood up, and she wanted to grab hold of him, now that his world had been shaken for the second time in a very few days, but before she could make a move he held his hand out.

"Thank you. I don't know what my wife was involved in, but thanks for coming here and being honest with me. I can't excuse anything she's done, but I'm sorry if it caused problems for you and your dad."

On the way to the car, his last words hung in Ilka's mind. Problems! Everything that happened seemed to cause problems that blasted her from every direction. But right now, one overshadowed all the others: her father's ashes. Where were they?

Ilka had just started the car when her phone rang.

"Now don't hang up!" her mother yelled. "We need to talk. You're avoiding me, and I can understand if you feel ashamed. You can't call Jette and ask for money and expect her not to tell me you called. What were you thinking? She's not like your father, always going behind my back."

"Don't start in on that again," Ilka said. She'd had enough of everything being about her father's mistakes. Michael Graham had said it very well, she thought. He'd let himself and his emotions get stuck in the past, and he ended up overlooking what he'd had.

"But I mean what I say."

"I know. And I'm sorry, it was a stupid thing to do. Of course she had to tell you. I was under a lot of pressure—I *am* under a lot of pressure. I'm in debt, and I don't know how I'm going to get out of it. And unfortunately, you were right, I got pulled into this and I lost my head."

Immediately Ilka regretted what she'd said.

"Oh no, honey!"

Would a person really still call their forty-year-old daughter honey? Ilka thought.

"Do you have enough money for the ticket home? I'll buy it for you."

"It's not that simple," Ilka said. "I can't just come home. I think Dad was murdered."

"What? What do you mean?"

"I'm not convinced he died in his sleep. And in fact, I think he was doing what he could to be a decent human being." She explained how the funeral home's debt came from him helping a friend. "He didn't gamble it all away."

She sensed her mother holding herself back.

"It's like these skeletons keep falling out of the closet. He was involved in a traffic accident many years ago; two people were killed, and his wife became an invalid. So the situation isn't that simple. His life wasn't exactly a bed of roses. And his wife had an affair once."

Ilka stopped; it was getting too complicated.

"We'll fly over to you. I'll find out how soon we can leave."

"No! Don't. I'm coming home. It's all going to be okay, it's just that it's taking longer than I'd thought."

She couldn't even begin to explain that she was going out to look for her father's ashes.

"But I'm worried about you being over there alone. Honestly, it sounds to me like your imagination is running away with you."

"Mom, I have to go."

"If Paul got himself mixed up in something, the police will have to take care of it. It's not your problem."

"Dad's youngest daughter was seriously injured," Ilka said.

"I'm on the way to the hospital to see her now, I have to hurry."

"So they've accepted you after all, have they." Her mother's voice sounded brighter now. "That's so nice for you, having a connection with your half sisters. Do you remember the time you came home from school, when you told your classmates you had a little sister? And when they wanted to see her, you told them she lived in a foreign country. We had no way of knowing back then, of course, but in a way it was right."

Ilka remembered. She'd felt at the time it was right. She wanted a brother or sister so much, and one day she told the two girls she sat beside in class that she was a big sister now. A few days later one of them gave Ilka a few of her little sister's onesies. Ilka took them, though her two friends might have been suspicious. At any rate they didn't talk any more about it.

"It's not that I've gotten to know them that well," Ilka said. "It's only Amber, the younger one, that I've really talked to. She's the one in the hospital. Which means she can't really turn me away, can she."

"You'll figure it out." Her mother suggested she invite the two half sisters to Denmark, so they could see where their father came from. The thought seemed absurd to Ilka now, but she said nothing. She did promise to call and keep in touch, though, so they wouldn't be so worried.

I'm family," Ilka said as she leaned over the hospital recep-tion counter. She showed her driver's license, pointed to her last name, and explained that Amber Jensen was her sister. It turned out she'd been moved, first to surgery for an operation, then to a rehab ward.

"You'll have to come back tomorrow," a nurse said, after Ilka had finally found the right hallway and asked where she could find 10222C. "She's already had visitors today, she needs to rest."

"I'll make it a very short visit."

"Sorry."

"I just need to give her some clean panties and a picture of her boyfriend, and then I'll leave. She called and asked me to bring them."

The nurse was unsympathetic. "She's not allowed to wear her own panties. We provide clothing here."

Ilka smiled at the nurse, a younger woman. "You know how it is, you feel healthier when you wear your own panties. And right now, Amber needs to feel she's getting better."

The nurse seemed to be thinking it over.

"And it would help her rehab if she had a picture of her boyfriend. It's something for her to look forward to, motivation. You know how that is."

Finally, the nurse relented and followed Ilka down the hallway. "Could I see his photo?" she asked, adding that she wouldn't tell anyone about the panties.

Ilka stopped and fished around in her bag, relieved the nurse didn't want to see the underwear. She had a photo of Flemming in her billfold, inside a clear plastic pocket, from when they'd just met. He looked good in his turtleneck sweater, with his dark hair swept back. She showed it to the nurse. Her Flemming, forced into the role of Amber's boyfriend.

The nurse backed off a step. "That's her boyfriend?" She made it sound as if she'd rather stay in the hospital than hurry home to him.

Ilka nodded. "He left his wife and small children to be with her. He's incredibly rich, so even though he's a lot older, you can't blame her for going for it."

The nurse nodded knowingly. Ilka stuck her billfold back in her bag. The nurse's reaction had hurt, but it was true: He could have been Amber's father. Very young father, but anyway.

"Don't stay too long. She didn't feel well after physical therapy today, so we gave her pain meds. She might be asleep."

"I'll make it quick." The nurse showed her into what looked like a large hotel room, with a small sofa group by the window and a balcony door that was open a crack. A long, sheer curtain swayed. "Wow."

The nurse smiled. "Wow is right. You can see why your

family moved her to a private room. Unfortunately, not all of us have that option."

Ilka closed the door when the nurse left. It didn't surprise her that Raymond Fletcher took good care of his granddaughter. As well he should. He was the reason Amber lay there with a damaged hip and a serious concussion. Ilka walked over to the bed.

On the way to the hospital she'd worried that Mary Ann or Leslie would be there. Or even worse, Fletcher himself. She would have hurried away before anyone noticed her. But Amber was alone and awake. She sat up and stuffed the pillow behind her when her half sister walked in. Ilka helped her.

"How are you? Are you in pain?"

Amber nodded. She looked drowsy, but at least she was strong enough to sit all the way up. She reached for a glass of water and drank. "I'm glad you came, I was going to call you. You need to go out and check the horses."

That sounded like an order. Ilka saw a bit of Amber's grandfather behind her pale, tired face. "I can't stand lying here without knowing they're okay, even though everyone says they are."

"But if the horses came back like they say, then they're okay."

Amber looked annoyed. "We can't trust them. Right now, they'll say anything to keep me from getting worked up."

She reached out to Ilka and looked her straight in the eye. "We're talking about horses worth millions of dollars. They're my ticket out of Racine and my retirement too. I can't just lie here not knowing if I've lost everything. I have a bad feeling about it, that's all."

"But I don't see how I can be much help. I don't know what to look for; I don't know which horses are yours."

"I'll explain everything to you."

"But what about the men working in the stable, can't we call them?"

Amber let go of her hand. "I tried to call Tom, the stable foreman. He takes care of all the practical stuff, I take care of the horses. But he's not answering. The horses must be looked after twenty-four hours a day. Somebody's there; they have to be, and I need to know what's going on. If all the horses are back. Please, will you please go out there?"

The look on Amber's face was too much for Ilka. She promised to drive out to the ranch the minute she left the hospital.

"The others don't need to know you're doing this for me. Drive around back and use the door that leads out to the pasture."

"Okay. But tell me, how are you feeling?"

"Forget about me, the horses are the important thing right now."

Ilka had that figured out already. She pulled a chair over to the bed. "Actually, I came by to ask you what's happened to our father's ashes. They're not in the house, I drove out and checked. The place is empty."

At first Amber looked confused, but then she slid down a bit against the pillows. "The urn was on the mantel above the fireplace. Did they take it too?" Her voice sounded small.

Ilka nodded. Amber stared straight ahead. "Then he must have it."

"Who?"

"Scott Davidson."

"If he has it, I'll get it back," Ilka said.

"You can't, don't go out there!"

"Tell me about him. I've heard he's a part owner of your stable."

"Only the racetrack stable," Amber said. "He helps run it, but he doesn't own any part of our private stable or the horses we breed. He's got nothing to do with the ranch."

"What's he like?"

"Strange. Scott's always been a loner, even when he was a little kid. After the accident he lived with his grandfather, and he shut himself off from the world even more. He was about ten when it happened, I think. After I finished college I heard he was accepted at some fancy university, and I haven't seen him since."

"The accident?" Ilka straightened up.

Amber looked at her. "It was his parents whom Dad hit in the head-on collision."

A bell rang in the hallway, and Ilka jumped. There was a draft in the room from the open balcony door, and suddenly she felt cold. She rolled her sleeves down. "Our father killed his parents?" She barely recognized her own voice.

"He didn't *kill* them. It was an accident, he lost control of the car. It was on a curve, and nobody knows really what happened. But you can't say he killed them."

"But that's how you'd think if you're only ten years old," Ilka said.

"I don't know how other people think," Amber snapped. "After the accident, Grandpa became partners with Scott's grandfather, Gerald Davidson. Probably to make sure everybody moved on after what happened. Davidson got a good deal. At the time he had two horses that were promising, but neither of them had qualified for any major race. He made a lot of money out of the partnership. Scott should thank Grandpa for the fortune he inherited, instead of fighting him. It's a fight he's going to lose."

Ilka thought for a moment. "Why was the urn there at your mother's?"

Amber had slid all the way down now, as if all this talk had exhausted her. "What do you mean?"

"Why were our father's ashes on the mantel? Why wasn't the urn buried?"

Ilka realized that sounded like a criticism, but before she could soften her words Amber shook her head and said her mother wanted it that way.

"But did she love him?"

Amber looked as if she didn't understand the question. She shrugged. "I don't know if she actually loved him. It's been a long time since Mom felt strongly about anything. When I was a kid, she loved her garden. She always smelled a special way when she was out there snipping flowers and planting things in the beds. And she was happy when she came back in the house. Now that doesn't happen much anymore, but that's just who she is. She doesn't go around clapping her hands and jumping for joy."

Ilka walked over and closed the balcony door, then she glanced out in the hallway, but the nurse didn't seem to be keeping an eye on the clock. She decided now was as good a time as any.

"I heard our father fought with your grandfather when Frank Conaway was arrested. And he tried to get the police to drop the charges. I can't help it, I keep thinking he might have been killed."

Amber raised up on her elbows and pulled herself back against the pillows. Ilka saw what was coming, and she hurriedly added, "I'm not saying your grandfather had him killed."

"I've never heard that before," Amber said. She sounded as if she took what Ilka said seriously. "I knew Dad wasn't getting along with Grandpa, but they never really did get along."

Ilka said she'd visited Maggie's husband. She described the warmth in his voice when talking about Mary Ann, how magical she was, how beautifully she sang. Then she told Amber about Maggie and the letters.

Amber frowned and looked sharply at her half sister. "I don't know anything about this." She paused a moment. "Is it the letters, is that why you want the urn? To see if you can find something that would show he'd been killed?"

Ilka shrugged. Mostly she just wanted to get it back, but of course she could have the ashes examined. Though she doubted anything would come of it.

"Don't go to see Scott Davidson," Amber repeated. "If he has the urn, he won't give it to you, and it could turn out bad for you. Even dangerous. You saw what he's capable of when he came out and stole the horses. He attacked us, it got violent. But things might even be worse now, after Grandpa sent his men out to get the horses. Stay away from him."

"Are you saying they might have killed somebody to get the horses back?" Ilka couldn't believe her ears.

Amber shrugged in a way that told Ilka it was very possible. "I'm just trying to make you understand, this is serious. Grandpa won't let anybody push him around. And he'll push back hard if he has to."

That Ilka could believe, even though it shook her to hear

Amber make it sound like a necessary move. Something to be expected if you went up against Raymond Fletcher.

She stood up. "So what is it exactly you want me to look for in the stable? Do you want me to lead them out of the stalls, to see if they've been injured? I'm not so sure I could do that."

Amber shook her head. "You don't need to. At this moment, I just need to know if my horses are there. I'm worried about Tom not answering me."

She grabbed a sheet of paper, her rehab schedule, and turned it over and drew an outline of the stable, with stalls on both sides. In each space representing a stall, she jotted down the color and markings of the horse that belonged there, without even having to pause to remember.

She handed the drawing to Ilka. "Go down to the south stable. Right now, the other buildings don't matter. It's these five horses I'm interested in. If you have time, and nobody sees you, try to find Tom and ask him why the hell he doesn't answer. He knows I've been calling and sending him a bunch of messages. He can't just ignore me this way. I'm afraid something's happened and he doesn't dare tell me."

She wrote down his number at the bottom of the sheet. "If you don't find him, call him. Maybe he'll answer if it's you."

"I'll find him." Ilka was on her way out when she remembered about the car. "I need to borrow some money to drive out there for you, I'm low on gas. And I'm broke."

"Didn't Grandpa come see you?" So. Amber had sent him to her.

"Yes, but I had to use the money to pay bills."

Amber had already grabbed her billfold from the drawer of her night table. She took out all the bills and handed them to Ilka. Four hundred seventy dollars. "Tell me when you need more. I'll have them help me out to the ATM in the main hall."

When Ilka reached the parking lot, the thought hit her: She should have warned Amber that someone might ask about her panties.

It took less than twenty minutes for her to drive from the hospital to Fletcher's ranch. On the way she tanked up and bought a sandwich with some of the money Amber had given her, without feeling the slightest bit guilty. She still had four hundred dollars rolled up in her pocket, a nice little security blanket.

Ilka knew the road from the first time she'd been here, and she slowed down at the series of curves where she'd met the truck carrying the horses. The big pastures were on her right. Amber had told her to go past the ranch house entrance to the next curve; the driveway there ended behind the stables.

Tall trees on both sides of the road cast shadows onto the car when she turned in. According to Amber, the southern stable stood next to the pasture. Two cars were parked there, but Ilka drove by them and stopped beside a truck with the Fletcher and Davidson Race team logo on the door. She took the path around the building and immediately spotted Amber's stable. Expanses of grass stretched out beyond it.

There was no one around, but she hurried around the corner of the stable and stopped at the sight of a small tractor parked at the next stable, where someone was mucking out the stalls. Quickly she opened the double Dutch door, and when she ducked inside she was surrounded by the familiar pleasant odor of horses. And silence. No sound of jaws munching on hay, muzzles sweeping the floor for food, tails flicking at flies. No sounds at all.

Ilka walked farther in. Was the stable really empty? The stalls were. She would have guessed the horses had been turned out to pasture, but Amber had explained they were never all outside at the same time. Too many injuries occurred when they ran around together, and these trotting horses were much too valuable to risk that.

She entered a stall and noted that it had been swept out. There was food in the trough, and the water bowl was clean but empty. She checked the stall on the other side; it looked the same. She closed her eyes and leaned against the stall bars, thinking of how to break the news to her half sister, how to explain it. The horses could have been moved to another stable. They could be under special surveillance. At worst they might be stabled at a vet clinic, in which case no one could blame Fletcher for not wanting to add to his granddaughter's worries. She decided to try to find Tom.

Suddenly someone grabbed her shoulder and brutally jerked her around. Pain shot down her arm, and it took her a moment to recognize Jeff's bitter face. She nearly stumbled in her struggle to keep up as he pulled her over to the stall door.

"What the hell are you doing here?" he snarled in her ear. "Who sent you?"

She wrenched her arm free, shoved him back, and yelled, "What's wrong with you?" She rubbed her shoulder. "Amber asked me to come and check on her horses. She's my half sister, and maybe you've forgotten because you're so busy running around beating people up, but she's in the hospital!" She was so mad that she almost slugged him.

"Where are they?" she said, pointing to the empty stalls.

"What are you doing here? This is a private stable, you've got no right sneaking in."

"Who the hell do you think you are?" she shouted. "I just told you what I'm doing, and I have every right to be here, but I'll gladly leave when you show me where Amber's horses are."

He took a step back and studied her. "Who sent you?" he asked again.

Ilka couldn't believe her ears; hadn't she already explained? "What is this, what's the problem?"

He stared coldly at her. "You were at your father's house when it was emptied out. You were here minutes after they stole the horses. You expect me to believe all that's a coincidence, you didn't know what was going on?"

Before she could answer, he slammed his forearm across her breasts, pressed her against the wall, and roared, "Are you in cahoots with Scott Davidson? Did he send you here? We're watching you, we've seen that car following you. And you heard yourself, someone was up on the deck of my boat."

It was more a reflex than anything, a reaction to the pain in her chest and her struggle to breathe, when she kneed him in the groin. For once she felt fortunate to be tall, because she'd obviously hit the perfect spot. He lay on his side, doubled over, and she threw herself on him and pressed her knee against his throat. She'd never hit anyone in her life, never been in a fight, but it all happened so fast that she didn't have time to think. "What the hell do you mean, you're watching me? Are you following me too?"

She pulled away and stood up.

Slowly he got to his feet. "A black car with Wisconsin plates is on your tail, all the time. Ever since they came here and attacked Fletcher. And I want to know what you're up to." He explained they'd been tracking the car, which they'd discovered had been rented with a false ID.

"I'm not up to anything." She'd stop yelling, though she was still mad. "I've just been at the hospital, visiting Amber. You should know that if you're watching me."

"Yeah, we know. And we know they were there too, parked just behind you."

Ilka grabbed onto the stall door, short of breath again. She hadn't noticed any car, but then, she hadn't been watching either. Hadn't thought about it. Again, she felt vulnerable; she noticed her hands trembling. "I don't know who it is. I've spotted a black car following me several times, but I was never sure it was the same one."

Finally, Jeff seemed relatively calm. "You went out to Frank Conaway's wife. Keep away from that family."

"Stop telling me what to do! I have every right to visit my father's friends."

"The black car was out there too. What's your connection to Scott Davidson?"

"I don't know anything about Scott Davidson."

He stepped close to her again, so close that she felt his breath on her face. "Was it one of his people on the boat that night?"

Ilka's heart hammered away, and she felt short of breath, but she stared him down. "You mean that night that never happened? How could you tell the police I lied about that?"

They stared at each other a moment, then he tucked his shirt into his pants and brushed the dust off his clothes.

"I don't know Scott Davidson," Ilka repeated. "I don't know what he looks like or who he is."

"And you don't know who's following you?"

Ilka shook her head. "I told you, a few times it felt like someone was watching me. Like when I walked out of the police station. I didn't spot the car, though, just a man walking toward me. Was that one of you?"

Jeff snorted. "Believe me, you'll never see us when we're trailing you."

"Shouldn't you be concentrating on finding Amber's horses?"

"Shouldn't you be concentrating on your funeral home? I hear the American Funeral Group made sure no crematorium in the state will do business with you. And they've sicced the undertaker association on you, too."

"What for?"

"Because you don't have the training to run a funeral home, it's the law. They say you don't have a certificate or the skills or experience to live up to the association's high standards." He seemed to be enjoying every word he spat out at her.

"Artie Sorvino does. And all our paperwork is in order."

"But you've been driving the hearse. You've even been inside the morgue."

Ilka spoke quietly. "How do you know that?"

"Because we know everything about you."

"Is it the American Funeral Group following me?" She'd had enough. "What have I ever done to you people? I'm just trying to sell my father's business, so I can go home and get back to my life."

"Then you'd better get going, the sooner the better."

"But what have I done wrong?"

His eyes showed a hint of sympathy. "You've started something you shouldn't have."

"Is this about Frank Conaway and Fletcher's false accusations against him? Or is it this Scott Davidson I don't even know?"

He grabbed her shoulder again and shoved her toward the stall door.

"Has something happened to the horses?" she said.

Jeff glanced quickly around before leaning in close to her. "Go back to your car and go home. No more questions, got it?"

"If you're not going to tell me anything, let me talk to the foreman, Tom, and then I'll leave. The horses are Amber's life, she needs to know what happened to them."

He led her over to the old Chevrolet.

She twisted free of his grip and unlocked the car. "Are the horses back yet?"

"We haven't managed to find them yet," he finally admitted. "But don't tell your sister. We'll get them back."

So Amber was right after all, Ilka thought. She wanted to ask about Tom, but Jeff opened the door and shoved her inside. "No more questions. Do a deal with the American Funeral Group and go home."

Minutes later, after Ilka had driven through the series of curves, she pulled over and gazed out over the pastures. What should she tell Amber? She had no idea, but she had to tell her something. She closed her eyes, leaned her head back against the headrest, and breathed out. Then she pulled out her phone and sent a text: *Just left the ranch. All horses are okay. Love Ilka.*

She shut her phone off so Amber couldn't call back and ask for details.

Ilka was almost back to the funeral home before she suspected the metallic blue SUV was following her. She'd noticed it after turning off the county road onto the highway. And now it was the only car that had stayed behind her for several miles. Downtown she almost ran a red light from watching it too closely in her rearview mirror.

She turned just before Oh Dennis! and began weaving through the streets to show them she knew they were there. Soon it became obvious they didn't care whether she knew or not, though the driver never got close enough for her to see anything other than his cap pulled down over his head. Pathetic, she thought, as she pulled into the funeral home parking lot.

The SUV slowed down but didn't stop, and soon it was out of sight. Even though Jeff claimed two people were having her followed, Raymond Fletcher and someone else, this car was the only one she'd managed to smoke out. She stood for a moment. The parking lot was deserted except for her car, Artie's pickup, and a station wagon probably owned by the parent of a student in the school across the street. Her arm still hurt from Jeff's rough treatment, but at least her heartbeat was back to normal. At least she could breathe.

She ran into Artie when she walked in through the rear door. Maggie's body was finished now, and he'd cleaned the prep room. And Michael Graham had called; his daughter's plane had landed that evening, and she wanted to stop by the next morning to view her mother.

"They asked if they could hold a small memorial here for the immediate family, when they get the urn."

Ilka nodded and asked when.

"Monday," he said.

"We can't, we won't be ready by then. I just found out none of the crematoriums will take our business." She walked by him.

He followed her into the office. "Hey, what's wrong?"

She sat down. "We're going for a little drive."

"But you just got here."

Ilka nodded. She decided she'd better bring him up to date, since he'd be smuggling her out of the funeral home. She told him about her run-in with Jeff.

"That bit about the crematoriums is true enough," Artie said. A friend who worked for one on the outskirts of town had called earlier that day; his boss had told him they'd blacklisted the Paul Jensen Funeral Home. And his friend had heard from someone else that every crematorium in Wisconsin had been told to do the same. The message was clear: If the crematoriums didn't toe the line, the American Funeral Group would take their business elsewhere.

"Those assholes," Ilka said. "They're acting like some sort of undertaker mafia."

"We'll handle it."

Ilka understood. Now was the time they needed Dorothy out at the former crematorium.

"After the daughter and her family leave tomorrow morning, we'll drive Maggie out to Dorothy," Artie said. "Then I'll pick her ashes up the day after tomorrow, and we can tell them it's okay to hold the ceremony the day after. They won't need catering, they just asked for some music while they say their goodbyes."

Artie made it sound so simple, which was exactly what she needed to hear. But then he frowned deeply and tilted his head while eyeing her skeptically. "You really think someone's following you? Sounds a little fishy to me."

"I know, but yes, I really think so." She told him about the black cars, the metallic blue SUV, and all the times she'd sensed someone watching her.

"A light-blue four-wheel-drive, now that's original! What do they think you're up to?"

"I don't know. But it must be something to do with my father's battle with Fletcher. It's like they know exactly what I've been doing, and I don't like that."

She felt the worst might be that they'd watched her every pathetic, embarrassing attempt to get rid of the funeral home. Also, it aggravated her that Raymond Fletcher was trying to run her out of town while pretending to be on her side.

"But why?" Artie still looked puzzled.

"I really don't know." The quarrel was the only explanation she could come up with. There had to be a lot at stake for Fletcher, since he was accusing Frank in the fraud case.

"I need to go out to Hollow Ranch. It's just outside of town, and you have to drive. I don't want anyone to see me or know where we're going."

"What for?" he said, setting aside her asking to be smuggled out of the funeral home.

"To visit Scott Davidson. But you don't need to go in with me. All I want is my father's urn."

"Weren't you just told to stay away from him?"

Ilka tipped her chair back. "Don't you start telling me what to do." She sounded braver than she felt. Everything was beginning to get to her again—Maggie, the funeral home chain, Frank Conaway, Scott Davidson. She was caught in the middle of all this tangled-up, confusing mess, and she couldn't escape without somehow getting rid of the funeral home.

"Like I said, all I want is my father's ashes."

"Okay."

"Right now I don't know what to do about the business. Maybe we should talk to the IRS and the bank and hand it all over to them, so the house doesn't get auctioned off. Then you can take it over if you want."

She was well aware it made no sense for Artie to start up a business reconstructing bodies if no one was going to hire him.

"You mean, just throw in the towel." He smiled, thinking she was just kidding.

She nodded.

"C'mon, don't make everything out to be worse than it is," he said.

"I think Sister Eileen has lost faith in me too. I think she's avoiding me. I hardly ever talk to her; every time I see her she's busy. Has she said anything to you?"

Artie looked out the window and shook his head. "Don't worry about Sister Eileen. She's sort of closed up sometimes."

That might be, Ilka thought. But what about all the times Sister Eileen had knocked on her door upstairs and offered her tea and cookies? Ilka was sure the nun had been concerned. Not anymore, though. She wasn't really there, at least when it came to the teamwork Ilka had tried to build among the three of them.

"She's keeping me at a distance."

"Forget about her. You really think we need to smuggle you out of here? And what, you'll hide on the floorboards all the way there?"

"Yes." She asked him to back his pickup beside the hearse in the garage, so she could crawl inside.

He fished his lighter out of his pocket. "You're sure no one's keeping an eye on me too?"

She shook her head. "No, but we'll take the chance. I need to go out to Davidson's, and the only thing I know for sure is that someone's following me."

Artie seemed to accept that. She went upstairs for a sweater while he got the pickup.

Her father's room looked like a battlefield. She was still busy sorting his papers, dividing everything up into two piles: keep and toss out. She'd emptied the desk drawers, leaving only the boxes along the wall. At first, she'd planned to throw most of it out, but now she was thinking about giving it all to Karen Conaway. It might be useful for her husband's defense.

Outside Artie started his pickup, and moments later she heard the garage door open and the pickup backing in. She grabbed her sweater and hurried downstairs.

167

They drove through a wooded area, and Ilka was about to google Hollow Ranch to bring up a map, when Artie pointed ahead. "That might be it; I see guards at the driveway."

Ilka still lay curled up on the floor on the passenger side. It felt like she'd never get her long legs straightened out again. First, they had stopped by Artie's, where he threw some fish he'd caught that morning into the freezer. She'd insisted on staying inside, even though her legs were starting to cramp. His house was the last one on a dead-end road, no one could drive there without being seen, and it wasn't visible from the highway; Artie thought she was being paranoid. He'd asked her if she was going to play this game everywhere they went, but she'd ignored him.

She looked up at him. "What do you mean, guards?"

"Guards with guns. One on each side of the gate."

Ilka crawled up onto the seat. Her legs stung when her blood began circulating again.

HOLLOW RANCH was elegantly written on a large sign beside a

169

shiny cast-iron gate, and as Artie had said, two uniformed men stood with guns in their holsters.

"What's going on?" Ilka was scared for a moment, thinking the men were police sealing off the area—had the feud between Fletcher and the young Davidson escalated into another shootout? Then she noticed the printing on their uniform jackets: SECURITY GUARD. "Is that legal?"

Artie pulled over. "Is what legal?"

"Carrying weapons out in the open like that, when they aren't police."

His look told her to stop comparing everything with Denmark. She dropped it.

"Drive on up," she said.

The two broad-shouldered men were already staring at them, their hands on their weapons, alert and ready to act.

"What should we tell them?" Artie said.

"Let me take care of it, just drive."

He inched forward and signaled to turn, even though there wasn't a car in sight for miles. Both guards stepped forward, and Ilka rolled down the window and leaned out.

"We'd like to speak to Scott Davidson."

The guard on her side simply shook his head, not even bothering to ask if they had an appointment.

"I'm Ilka Nichols Jensen. Please tell him I'm here." She guessed they might react to hearing her name if Davidson had ordered his men to keep an eye on her.

"He's not home," the guard said.

Ilka gazed down the length of the fence, which extended beyond her sight. "I'm here to pick up my father's ashes."

Artie didn't say anything, but he grabbed her when she opened the door to get out. She broke his grip and walked over to the guards, then pointed at their walkie-talkies and offered to deliver the message herself. She repeated her name and added that she came from the Paul Jensen Funeral Home. "I came for the urn with my father's ashes."

The walkie-talkies came to life, and the gate began to open.

"*Out of the way!*" both guards yelled, signaling to Artie to move his pickup. They pushed Ilka to the side, and two black four-wheel-drive vehicles appeared, barreling down the highway. They looked like the ones she'd seen earlier. She tried to wrestle out of the guard's grip, and when the car slowed down to turn in, she waved her arms. Before the guard could react, she ran after them through the gate, yelling at them to stop. He caught her several feet down the driveway, but she kept yelling, even though the cars sped toward the house. The safety on a gun clicked behind her, and she doubled over when the guard twisted her arm and shoved her back toward the road. Her hair hung in front of her face as she stumbled along. Artie came running, and when she heard one of the cars backing up from behind, she tried to straighten up, but the guard held her down. Pain shot up her arm as she flashed on what her mother had told her: It's America, it's not like back home in tiny Denmark, it's dangerous, and you're naïve if you think nothing will happen to you, because anything can happen over there.

Artie was saying something, but her ears were ringing. She didn't dare raise her head until a man behind her spoke up. The guard loosened his grip, and Ilka winced as she slowly straightened up and turned.

Scott Davidson was in his late twenties. Stocky, with an angular face. Not nearly as intimidating as she'd imagined, knowing what he was capable of. He asked what he could do for her.

"I'm Ilka Jensen, and I—"

Suddenly she was startled to see who was getting out of the backseat of the nearest car. Karen Conaway had been crying, and the man at her side smiled hesitantly as he held his hand out and introduced himself as Frank Conaway. He also said hello to Artie, but he turned back to her abruptly and said he'd been good friends with her father.

Ilka nodded, though she was staring at Karen, trying to read her expression. What was going on, were they scared? What had Davidson done? The guards retreated, and the cast-iron gate closed behind them, cutting her and Artie off from his pickup.

A few moments later Ilka understood that Karen was crying from relief and joy; she kept repeating that it was finally over.

"What's over?" Ilka asked quietly.

"Scott has offered to help us, and he posted Frank's bail."

Davidson turned to her. "You're Jensen's daughter, I've been told. And I understand you three already know each other."

He asked Ilka and Artie to go along with them to the house. Ilka crawled in the backseat of the car with the Conaways. She was sore and still shocked by how the guard had handled her, and she felt guilty about not asking Artie what he wanted to do, but she had to find out what the hell was going on. To her relief, Artie got into the lead car with Davidson. She shut the door and they took off.

"So what's going on?"

Frank Conaway's curly hair hung over his ears; he was thin and short, half a head shorter than Ilka. They took stock of each other, though not impolitely. More out of curiosity. Gregg Turner had said her father almost thought of Frank as his son, but it wasn't jealousy she was feeling. Rather a strange, unfamiliar sense of connection with him, without really knowing why.

"After you came out the other evening, Scott contacted me and offered to help," Karen said. "Of course I knew him, he's Davidson's grandson, but I couldn't figure out what he was up to. Or what was in it for him. Like I told Paul, I can't pay anything back before we're awarded damages, for Frank being falsely accused. And that could take a while. But Scott seemed really up front; he said he wasn't doing this to help me or my husband. He wants Raymond Fletcher's scalp."

Karen fumbled with her scarf. Her hair was brushed back, and she held her husband's hand while she talked. "Scott's sure that Frank didn't embezzle any money. If he had, it would have been discovered a long time ago. He's sure that Fletcher transferred money over the years to Scott's grandfather, 'cause it turns out that Gerald Davidson had a separate account, with just under ten million in it when he died. The same amount the company was missing."

Frank took over. "Scott says his grandfather's books show it's ten percent of the total winnings from the races. In other words, every time Fletcher and Davidson Raceteam won a race, ten percent of the money was taken out of their joint account and deposited in Gerald Davidson's account. Scott doesn't know anything about this deal the two partners must have made, but after Gerald died the payments stopped. And Scott won't stand for that. To him, the deal is still on, as long as they jointly own the stable. Fletcher used me as a scapegoat to cover up the deal. And that's what your dad found out about."

"But do they still own the stable together?" Ilka said.

Frank nodded. "At least on paper. They share the expenses and winnings, and they hire employees to run Fletcher and Davidson Raceteam. The stable is one of the biggest winners in North America in harness racing; these horses are too valuable to ax a deal just because of a change in ownership. And if they don't have to actually see each other, the partnership works."

"So Scott Davidson took the horses in Fletcher's private stable because he thinks his partner owes him, that he's not being paid the percentage of winnings." Ilka wasn't completely sure she understood.

"Right. He's not going to let the old man screw him around."

They had passed through a patch of woods and were now in front of an elegant white building that in no way resembled Fletcher's ranch. Also, she saw no stables on the property. Davidson and Artie stepped out of the car in front, and a little dog ran up to them and barked. It looked more like the peaceful home of a wealthy man than the gangster headquarters Ilka had been expecting after Amber's warning.

"Gerald Davidson bought this place several years after going into partnership with Fletcher," Frank said after they were all out of the car. "He used to live down the road a way, on a smaller place."

They walked up to the front steps, and Davidson invited them in, but Artie held back. Ilka whispered to him that he didn't need to go along, that she'd be out as soon as she had the urn.

He nodded and pulled a pack of cigarettes out of his pocket. She glanced back just before the door closed behind her; Artie was already sitting on the step, with a wispy thread of smoke trailing away in the wind. The dog was curled up beside him.

D avidson showed them into a spacious hall with a broad stairway leading up to the second floor.

Ilka stopped just inside the door. "Could I talk to you a moment?"

He turned while the others went on. "Aren't you coming in?"

She shook her head. "I don't want to interfere. It's very generous of you to help them. My father and Frank were good friends, and he tried to help too, but he couldn't keep Frank out of jail. I'm sure it's an enormous relief to his family that he's home until the trial starts."

"There won't be a trial," Davidson said. "Frank didn't steal from anyone. Fletcher's the one who should be in jail, and he will be."

There was nothing threatening or aggressive in the way he spoke, just as nothing about him indicated he'd once been a shy, quiet boy. He seemed down-to-earth, an ordinary guy whose eyes may have narrowed when he said Fletcher's name, but otherwise he came off as straightforward and harmless.

175

"My father's urn was on the mantel in Mary Ann's house. I'd like to have it. I wasn't here when he died, and it would mean a lot to me to be able to say goodbye to him."

He gazed at her for a moment, as if he was trying to understand what made her think he had the urn, but then he nodded. "I'll see what I can do." He turned and headed for the stairway.

Ilka felt relieved, and she also turned to leave, but Frank came over and stopped her. "I'm really sorry I wasn't around to welcome you when you came to Racine."

She was about to smile, but his look told her he had something private and confidential to say. Something she wasn't sure she could handle.

"Paul was my best friend," he said. "And I always hoped someday I'd get to meet you. There's so many things I want to tell you, so much you should know about him."

His curly, much-too-long hair hung in his eyes, and he swept it aside. He seemed unsure of himself, as if he was trying to sort out what he had to say.

"First of all, your dad hated himself for leaving you and your mother. That doesn't help you now, I know, but he thought about you a lot. One time he said he had plenty of regrets, things he wished he'd done different. But not being able to shake off what he'd inherited, that was something he never forgave himself for. That's why he left, to escape from the man he was becoming. Did you know that?"

He spoke quietly. "He was afraid of ending up like his own dad. Gambling was like some demon inside him. He couldn't stop it. He was afraid of totally losing control."

Ilka stood frozen as a chasm opened inside her.

"He wanted to protect you and your mother. Get control of

himself before he came back to you." Conaway hesitated, then asked her if she knew why her father became an undertaker.

"To take over my grandfather's funeral home when the time came, is what I always assumed."

Frank shook his head. "Your dad wanted to be an engineer or physicist. Instead he left school when he was sixteen and started working for your grandpa."

She'd never heard this before. "So what happened? Why did he do that, leave school?"

"To take care of his mother. And his little sister. He thought if he stuck around, he could protect the family when his dad got violent. Did you know Paul supported his family by the time he was eighteen?"

Ilka was shocked to hear he'd grown up in an abusive home. "I didn't know my father even had a little sister, I had no idea…" All she'd known about was the two cousins her mother had kept in touch with, even after her father left.

Frank glanced at the window and nodded thoughtfully, then turned back to her. "I remember one time your dad and I were in the pub, we'd had a good day at the track and we were celebrating with Irish coffee. A few too many of them. That's when he started telling me about his childhood home."

He gave up on swiping his hair off his face. In a way it was easier for Ilka to not see his eyes while he spoke.

"His sister was twelve when she died. Their dad was out of his head one night, and when he saw she was scared of him, he got really violent."

Frank paused for a moment before adding that Ilka's grand-father might not have known what he was doing when he took his anger out on his family. "Paul said his dad let the demon inside him take over. Sometimes he was a loving father, well liked and respected, also at the racetrack. But occasionally he couldn't get a handle on himself, and it was scary."

Ilka looked away.

"His sister crawled up in a window to hide. Your dad and his mom were in the room when she fell. And no one ever talked about it afterward, ever again. That must have been almost the worst. His folks called it *the accident* but wouldn't talk about it. Your dad stayed with his grandpa and grandma several weeks after she died, but nothing changed when he came back. And he started working again at the funeral home."

Ilka barely remembered her grandmother, and she'd never seen her grandfather; he died several years before she was born. "What do you mean, my father wanted to escape from the man he was becoming?" Two things he'd said kept turning in her mind: *losing control*, and *couldn't get a handle on himself*.

"He…" Frank looked at her. "What is it?"

Ilka shook her head and stared at the floor. It wasn't just a weakness she'd inherited from her father; it went all the way back to her grandfather. She was certain the same demon lived deep inside her. Maybe she was better at holding it down, but it unnerved her to learn the family had been battling it for generations. And that a little girl had died because of it.

After several moments she said, "But why did he think leaving us would help?" Out of the corner of her eye she noticed Davidson on the stairs with a few ring binders under his arm.

"Your dad recognized what was happening to him. He saw a pattern, but he couldn't control it. That demon kept growing inside, and he started in on your mom. He told me he was scared he'd hurt you. So he left to protect you from the man he was turning into."

His voice was weakening, and he cleared his throat before

going on. "The first time we talked about it, I had the feeling he was planning on both of you coming over here. He never hid the fact he had a family. And he bought you a pony too. But then later he told me all this about being scared of himself and what happened to him when he…yeah, started losing control."

Ilka stepped over and leaned against the door for support, unable to speak.

Frank stayed put. "I saw your dad like that. How he was when he lost control. Several times, actually. First time was one afternoon at the track, we didn't know each other so well back then, but usually he was a lot of fun to hang around with. He was going to buy me lunch before the race."

For a second his lips trembled at the memory. "We had good seats, and there were two horses in particular your dad was keeping an eye on. The first race went okay, and we walked over to the stable between races to hear what they were saying. Your dad was there to set up a few meetings, he was helping start up the new stable. *Trotter Magazine* had written about how he'd been brought over all the way from Denmark, so people knew who he was, they wanted to meet him. They bought us beer, drinks, the best whiskey, and I wasn't even twenty-one, under the drinking age, so I had to stay sober and drive home."

Ilka squirmed, but she didn't interrupt him.

"Then the last race, he changed all of a sudden. I noticed it when he didn't answer after I said something to him. I was just a kid, I didn't want to be impolite, didn't dare say anything either. But I couldn't help hearing how much he was betting on horses he didn't know anything about. He'd just moved here, he'd never seen them run before, knew nothing about their training, their stable. But still I figured he knew what he was doing. Even though he was acting crazier all the time. He even started talking to himself."

He glanced at Ilka to see how she was taking this, but she nodded for him to go on.

"He was scaring me. I didn't understand what was happening. It was like he was in his own world, out of contact. On the way home, I realized he'd lost every cent he had. I was really shocked—I remember that. And embarrassed too; I didn't know how to handle the situation. So we didn't say a word all the way home, and the next day we didn't talk about it. A year or so went by before he opened up about that day and told me why he left you and your mom."

Ilka caught herself clenching her fists in front of her mouth while trying to hold back tears. She lowered her hands and shook her head in apology. "I never knew. Thank you for telling me."

They looked at each other a moment, then she explained she'd come to pick up her father's ashes. "I think Davidson has the urn, and I asked if I could have it back."

She told him about the episode at Mary Ann's house. "I'd like to hold a small memorial ceremony for him. Would you like to come? You didn't have a chance to say goodbye to him either."

Frank nodded. "I'd like that, very much. Your dad meant a lot to us, and when Karen said you'd stopped by the house, I felt terrible that you and Paul didn't have even a little time together."

"Why didn't he ever answer my letters? I've gone through his room, and I found a stack of letters he wrote me. Why didn't he send them?"

He looked surprised. "I didn't know you two wrote each other. He never mentioned it."

"We didn't write each other. Well, we both wrote letters, but I sent mine and he didn't send his. They were bundled up in his room."

"I don't think it was so easy for him. He used to say that sometimes you just have to stop looking back. I think he meant you can't always control what happens, sometimes you just have to play out your hand."

Ilka let that sink in for a moment, then she nodded and said her father might have been right. "I'll let you know when I have his urn."

Artie was still sitting on the step when she came out. He'd just lit another cigarette, and without a word Ilka snatched it out of his hand and inhaled deeply. The smoke burned her lungs before she breathed out. After a few more drags she walked over to the lead car and asked the driver to take them back to the gate.

Ilka went up to bed right after they got home. She'd had the presence of mind to hide on the floor of Artie's pickup before they reached the funeral home. Not that she cared right then if anyone knew she'd been smuggled out, but something told her that later on she might need to shake Fletcher's man tailing her.

Shadows flickered behind the curtains in the darkness that night as she lay thinking about what Frank Conaway had told her. She could barely breathe from the horrific thought that she carried her father's demon around inside her. But by morning she'd cooked it down to a single fact: Her father had left his family to save them from the man he was becoming.

She was all too aware of the reason he had fled. Not that she'd seen the demon's face clearly, but she'd met it. She knew how it was to not be able to stop, that sense of being overwhelmed by an irresistible temptation, an intoxicating feeling of free fall.

What scared her was not knowing how to find a way back to herself without leaving behind way too many casualties. It had already cost her dearly. Ilka had let people down, broken off friendships, cheated people she cared about. And turned her back on those who had tried to help. She knew exactly what Frank Conaway was talking about.

But then she'd met Flemming.

One afternoon at the racetrack, when she was sitting alone in the stands, he came over and put his arm around her. The race was over, the horses had left the track long ago, the spectators had filed out, and the stands had been swept. But Ilka couldn't go home. She was twenty-five and had already burned all her bridges.

During the night, while lying curled up in bed, images had flashed by in her mind like a slideshow. Glimpses, short episodes from the past twenty years of her life. Some were overexposed, others so dark that they barely registered. Generally, though, she'd viewed much of what she'd gone through. After high school, the world had been hers for the taking. Her grades were good enough for her to choose any career she wanted, and she chose law, but after her first semester the pains started in her abdomen.

The tumor turned out to be malignant, and the doctors at Rigshospitalet wanted to remove her womb and both ovaries. The sooner the better. Her clearest memories of that time were of the female doctor who came to her bed, took her hand, and explained that Ilka might regret not letting them remove some of her eggs before the operation, that she should give it serious thought. The eggs could be frozen and used later if she changed her mind and decided to have children.

"You're not thinking straight now," the doctor said. "And you're so young."

Ilka insisted she knew what she was doing. She turned

down the offer. She didn't want children, she didn't want responsibility for a human being she might deceive. The doctor persisted, telling her over and over it would be too late after the operation, but Ilka stood her ground. And she'd never regretted her decision. After the doctors gave her the green light, she hoisted her backpack and set out to see the world. She was gone for almost eighteen months.

She'd been home a year when Flemming showed up that day at the track. He sat with his arm around her shoulder for a long time without saying a word. He was fifteen years her senior, though she didn't find that out until later. And though he was a total stranger, she followed when he stood up and said it was time to go home.

Flemming convinced her to seek help. He also set up a meeting with her bank, and together they wrote down a list of people she owed money. Her mother stood at the top of the list, which included girlfriends from school and Torkild, who owned the local grocery where she worked behind the counter three days a week.

Later Flemming told her he'd noticed her several times when he was at the track to take photos (besides being a school photographer, he did freelance work). He knew she came alone, and he claimed it was her vulnerability and desperation that had attracted him. Many weekends Ilka had simply wanted to soak in the atmosphere and the sound of the horses' hooves thundering toward the finish line. And when the last race was over, she went home at peace with herself. Other times she was barely aware of placing a bet until she noticed the ticket in her hand.

Each Monday, Tuesday, and Wednesday she made plans for the coming weekend. She tried to keep Sundays booked so she wouldn't have time to go to the track. But when the weekend rolled around, she would find herself out there anyway. Her friends gave up on her; they'd gotten tired of her canceling plans to get together, of loaning her money she never paid back.

Flemming saved her. Though it did take time. They'd been living together over a year when his youngest son from his first marriage was to be confirmed. Ilka had been invited, and Flemming was looking forward to the rest of his family meeting her. For a long time, he saved up for the confirmation party, including the food and his son's confirmation gift. He kept the money in a hand-carved wooden box in his desk drawer. She only meant to borrow it; she was still working at the grocery, and she would of course put it back when she got paid. The thing was, harness racing season had just begun. It was a month before the confirmation.

She won in the first race, but it went downhill after that. Several in the group she was with that day had known her father, and everyone, including Ilka, was buying rounds of beer and schnapps. The drinking was part of the scene, especially early in the season when it was hard to stay warm if you stood outside to watch the races.

That morning, on his way to lunch with his mother, Flemming had inexplicably sensed something was wrong. He'd gone straight home after lunch and discovered his wooden box was empty, so he drove out to the track. At first she didn't recognize him when he grabbed her. She threw a fit when he asked her to leave with him, but soon after she broke down. And since that day Ilka hadn't touched a drop of alcohol or been at a track. She hadn't even been near a horse or stable, at least until she'd driven out to Fletcher's ranch.

Ilka went along to the bank when Flemming borrowed the money for the confirmation. Back when they'd moved in together, she had told him about her father and how she missed him, but it was only after her breakdown at the track that she told him the whole story. After the confirmation party, she quit her job at the grocery and began working with him. Flemming was her soul mate, her best friend. And her world fell apart the day he collapsed on the kitchen floor.

Ilka understood exactly what her father had run away from. He'd allowed that inner demon to grow, until at last it was too big to handle. He realized what it could do, he'd seen that with his own eyes. And he'd left before it happened, because he loved her and her mother.

She cried all night and into the morning, when Artie came up and sat on the edge of the bed. Finally she stopped shaking when he lay down beside her and held her. They lay without moving or speaking a word, until eventually Ilka slowly turned to him. No hands stirred, though; no lips searched each other out. His eyes were filled with sorrow, and that was enough, he didn't have to comfort her, she thought. But now he knew her secret, that there was a darkness inside her that must never be allowed to come out.

They heard Sister Eileen arrive downstairs and walk around, shut a door. Ilka was familiar now with the nun's routine: turn on the coffee machine, go out to pick up the paper, wait for the mail. But today wouldn't be business as usual. Margaret Graham's daughter was coming to view her mother before the cremation, and that was it for the day.

Ilka pulled herself up onto her elbows and whispered *thank you* to Artie. She swept the gray hair from his face and for a moment her hand rested against his rough chin. "Thanks," she repeated. Then she sat up, folded her arms around her knees, and rested her head back against the wall.

Artie got up. "Stay here and rest."

She shook her head. "Please," she said, her voice hoarse now, "would you call Dorothy and ask if she could cremate Maggie for us? She's the only place we can go."

Artie nodded and said he'd go down and call her while Ilka took a shower.

After her shower, she changed the bed and opened the window wide. Artie had coffee and bread from the bakery waiting for her when she came downstairs. Her eyes were swollen, and her head hurt from too little sleep and too many tears.

She hugged him long enough to feel the warmth of his body before sitting down and buttering a roll. "I just don't know what to do with all this." She threw her hand up in resignation. "I don't even know what to do with myself."

She smiled sadly, feeling like she had to explain, but it was too soon for her to put it into words; she needed more time to think it over. And the first person who deserved to hear from her was her mother. As soon as she settled down, she needed to call and tell her what Frank Conaway had said. And explain to her how helpless she felt at the idea that she couldn't stop something inside her from taking control.

"I couldn't get ahold of Dorothy," Artie said. "But you can just drive out there. Graham's daughter has already been here and gone, and the hearse is loaded up and ready."

"Are you coming along?"

He shook his head. "I think you ought to go out there alone. Dorothy was close to Paul; it would be good for both of you to have a talk."

Ilka almost said she couldn't. She wasn't sure she could stand more heart-to-heart talk.

This time Ilka was sure no one was following her. The road was deserted, and she flew over the hilly landscape, fields stretching out on both sides like shallow waves. She slowed down when she spotted the tall crematorium chimney and turned onto the gravel driveway. The old hearse protested at every pothole until she finally had mercy on it—and Maggie in back—by slowing to a crawl on the final stretch. Dorothy Cane was definitely not spending her under-the-table income from them on driveway repair, Ilka thought, as she pulled up in front.

Officially the crematorium was not in use. It stood behind Dorothy's red-brick house, and the chimney seemed enormous to Ilka when she got out and noticed the wispy smoke snaking up into the blue sky.

Dorothy was a potter and artist. She'd bought the place to use the enormous furnace for her work, and as far as Ilka knew she made a living at it. But no more than that. She'd helped Ilka's father with several cremations when a deceased's family couldn't afford it. Artie had mentioned many times how Paul insisted that every dead body be treated with dignity, including those without the money to cover expenses.

Ilka wasn't sure what she thought about the furnace being used for cremations even though the crematorium had been closed down when Dorothy moved in. But right now, she felt fortunate to be able to get Maggie cremated without having to drive out of state. And Dorothy could use the money to keep the furnace going, Artie had explained the first time they'd been there.

Wisconsin law stated that if Dorothy had a valid license, and the cremation was performed by a certified undertaker, it was all legal. Artie would be coming out to pick up Maggie's ashes to help satisfy the latter requirement. Maybe it wasn't strictly legal, but at least it came close.

Ilka was still staring at the smoke when Dorothy walked up to her. The middle-aged woman was wearing dark-blue coveralls, with a scarf around her longish gray hair. She wasn't smiling, but she did hold out her hand and say hello. It wasn't often that six-foot Ilka met another woman her height, but Dorothy might even have been half an inch taller. They eyed each other a moment before Dorothy said that Artie had called and told her Ilka was on her way.

"Should I back up to the door?" Ilka was hoping for help in wrestling the coffin inside. She wasn't experienced enough to manage it alone. "I have four hundred dollars for you," she added as they lifted the coffin onto the small wheeled cart Dorothy brought out.

It took some work to balance the coffin on the cart, then they pushed it to the room at the end of the tiled hallway. On Ilka's first visit, two open coffins had been lying around, as if two people inside had simply stood up and walked off, but the coffins were gone now. The room was warm and clean; over by the wall stood a lathe and a table with two beautiful floor vases waiting to be finished. A radio was playing, and the air smelled of clay.

"You don't need to pay," Dorothy said. "This one's on the house, a gift to Paul."

She parked the coffin to the side and locked the cart's wheels as she explained they would have to wait for the oven to warm up to around eighteen hundred degrees, which might take some time. "Come on inside, let's have a cup of coffee."

"Artie probably told you I'm broke." Ilka's sense of dignity flew out the window. She searched in panic for some excuse to wait out in the hearse, anything to not have to keep the conversation going.

Dorothy nodded. "It's okay. I want to help."

The warmth in her voice puzzled Ilka. She seemed completely different from when they'd met, when she'd demanded to be paid even before unloading the coffin. Ilka followed her over to the house, politely taking off her shoes in the entryway.

The living room was comfortable, and Dorothy's knitting lay on the coffee table beside an empty cup. The yarn reminded Ilka of her mother, who after retiring had started an online business selling yarn and teaching knitting classes over the Internet. She'd even written a small book with knitting patterns and instructions that she sold on her site. Her mother was practically the epitome of Danish *hygge*; several popular bloggers had also recommended her knitting classes.

Ilka was about to comment on the knitting to break the ice,

but when she turned to the kitchen she noticed the photo on the shelf. Of her own father, smiling and holding hands with Dorothy.

Dorothy came in and saw what Ilka was looking at. She pointed at the sofa and told her to have a seat, then sat in an armchair facing her. The tall woman's coveralls tightened across her thighs when she tucked her feet under her. "Your dad and I had a relationship."

For a moment she gazed at her hands folded on her lap, and when she looked up, the tenderness in her eyes reached across the coffee table to warm Ilka.

Ilka fidgeted a bit, but she didn't respond.

"I can understand if you think that's sleazy and wrong, but we were happy. Paul and Mary Ann had an open marriage, you know."

Ilka could hardly believe her ears.

"They agreed on that from the start. I don't know if you're aware of this, but they were forced to get married."

It took a moment for Ilka to realize she was sitting with her mouth agape. Slowly she shook her head and pulled her legs underneath her as she settled into the corner of the sofa.

Dorothy looked as if she didn't know where to begin. She went out to the kitchen for the coffee, and while she was gone Ilka looked back at the framed photo beside a vase filled with flowers.

Dorothy carried the coffeepot into the living room. "I miss him. Every single day. We only saw each other a few times a month, but we talked on the phone almost daily. Just to say hi, how are you doing."

She placed two cups on the table and went back for the milk. Ilka took the opportunity to compose herself.

"What do you mean, forced to get married?" she said after Dorothy sat back down. Forced marriages were something she associated with the Muslim world.

"They screwed up. Both of them did, but separately. They had no choice, or at least your dad didn't. Mary Ann might have been able to get out of it, but she didn't dare. She toed the line and did what she was told."

Ilka looked questioningly at her.

Dorothy poured milk in both their cups. "She got pregnant with a guy who wasn't good enough for her. At least according to Raymond Fletcher."

"So my father was good enough?"

Dorothy shook her head. "Not in the long run, no. But back then he was a better option than the boyfriend. Paul was a stranger from Scandinavia, and the papers wrote about how he'd been headhunted to take harness racing here in Wisconsin to the top. He was the state's great hope. And people who represent hope are always an attractive asset." Dorothy handed her one of the cups.

"But then he screwed up," Ilka said.

"Did he ever. But no one found out about it. Fletcher covered for him. He replaced the money Paul gambled away."

Ilka thought of what Karen had said about her father losing all the money he'd won just before leaving Denmark. The money he was going to put into Fletcher's new stable. The money behind the job offer he'd been given.

"Paul lost every cent. But the worst was that the investors would have lost all faith in him if it came out. That was the scandal Fletcher saved him from. So they held on to the investors, but Paul would never be able to pay that much money back. Not even a tenth of it. Fletcher forgave the debt when he married Mary Ann. It was the only way out of the mess he got himself into."

"Was it because he was afraid of going to prison?" Ilka thought about the insanely long sentences in the US compared with Denmark. "I mean, if what he did ever came out?"

Dorothy shrugged as she gazed at the steam rising from her cup. "I don't think so. No, he wasn't scared of that."

Ilka waited, but Dorothy didn't go on. "So where did he meet Mary Ann?"

"At the stable. But Mary Ann wasn't interested at all in your dad, she was in love with her boyfriend. Paul told me he'd only seen her a few times before the day he was hauled into Fletcher's office. They'd hardly even talked before Fletcher gave him the ultimatum."

"But if my father wasn't afraid of prison, why did he agree to the marriage?"

Dorothy bit her lip and thought for a moment, then took a deep breath. "He was afraid for you and your mother. If he didn't accept Fletcher's offer and marry his daughter, they would have gone after you two. They would have taken everything from you."

Ilka shook her head. "That's absurd. We didn't own anything."

Dorothy nodded. "Fletcher showed your dad photos of you on the way to school, playing with your friends. And they followed you when you visited your grandparents. They knew everything about you, and it terrified Paul. He knew Fletcher was serious when he said he'd go after your mom and have you taken away from her, unless he played along. Fletcher would do practically anything to save his stable and his reputation, it was all he cared about. Even if it meant deciding his own daughter's future."

Ilka covered herself with a blanket.

"Your dad didn't have a choice, not really. He accepted the deal, and that included cutting off all contact with you and your mother and his former life in Denmark. Fletcher told Paul that if he ever got back in touch with you, and Fletcher found out, he'd come after you. And they reminded him of it over the years."

Finally, everything began falling into place for Ilka. "Fletcher used me to threaten my father. Also, to make sure he wouldn't leave his new family here."

Ilka was slumped in the corner of the sofa now, cold and miserable. She wiped her tears off with the back of her hand.

"Fletcher had photos taken of you now and then to show Paul. There was nothing your dad could do."

"So he got married," Ilka mumbled. "But what about the baby?"

"They were married before she was born."

"Leslie."

Dorothy nodded. "Leslie isn't your dad's biological daughter, obviously." She set her cup down on the coffee table. "He could hardly talk about it, he was so unhappy. He never forgave himself for putting you and your mother in danger."

"But it wasn't his fault that Mary Ann let her father push her around and decide for her."

"It was the only way she could keep the baby," Dorothy said. "Fletcher told her he'd have it removed either surgically or by adoption, if she chose to give birth."

Ilka drew her knees up to her chin. "But he couldn't force her to do that! Why did she let him?"

"She had no choice either, when it came down to it."

"Everybody has a choice."

Dorothy shook her head. "Mary Ann didn't, if she wanted to see her child grow up."

"She could have run away with her boyfriend."

"Fletcher would've found her and dragged her back. Paul asked her about it back then, and Mary Ann said she wouldn't live the rest of her life running from her father. So she gave up and did what she thought best for herself and the child."

"Then what about Amber?" Ilka said, her voice low now. "She's not my father's child either?"

"Yes, she is." It had been part of the deal, Dorothy explained. "The idea was that they were supposed to be a family, with more than one child. But Paul never regretted that, he loved Amber, adored her. He never had quite the same feelings toward Leslie, but they made it work as a family. And I have a great deal of respect for that."

"Respect! What's there to respect?"

Dorothy shrugged. "I can understand you blaming him, but he blamed himself even more. He had to come to terms with the situation he'd put himself in."

"What about Leslie's biological father? Did they threaten him to keep him away from Leslie?"

"They never told him Mary Ann was pregnant. He didn't know he had a daughter."

Ilka buried her face in her hands and began rocking while waiting for her rage and pain to ease off. Finally she looked up and said, "Did anyone ever tell Leslie she's not my father's biological daughter?"

Dorothy shook her head slowly.

Silence.

"It was so many years ago. Leslie and Amber are adults now," Ilka said. "Why didn't he and Mary Ann get a divorce?"

"After the accident your dad didn't feel it was right to leave her, when she was confined to a wheelchair."

Ilka nodded. That he was driving the car probably played a part in his decision too. He did have *some* sense of responsibility.

Dorothy cleared her throat. "I think over the years they also relied on each other. They were each other's fate, so to speak. They built something up together. Not a marriage in the traditional sense of the word, if there even is much left of the traditional nowadays, when two people choose to live together. I've never been married, I really shouldn't be talking. But they were there for each other, they were loyal to each other. They had an alliance, you might say."

While Dorothy was talking, Ilka slowly realized that the rage roiling inside her was actually sorrow. And it literally took her breath away.

Dorothy nodded; she seemed to understand what Ilka was going through. "I know. It's almost too much to bear."

She was right, Ilka thought. It was really and truly almost too much to bear. Also, because the story she'd been carrying around inside her for her entire life turned out to be false.

She barely managed to drag herself off the sofa and carry her cup into the kitchen. Dorothy followed, and apparently, she saw Ilka was struggling, because she offered to do the cremation herself. Artie could come by the next morning and pick up the ashes.

Back in the car, Ilka realized that Dorothy might be the only person who had loved her father after he left Denmark.

"What in heaven's name is going on?" Sister Eileen said from the doorway of the reception the next morning.

Ilka jumped; she hadn't heard her come in.

"There's a coffin outside under the carport. And what about those tables you've set out in the parking lot?"

Ilka wiped the sweat off her forehead. She was standing on a ladder, unscrewing the big gold-framed mirror on the wall above Sister Eileen's desk. "We're having a clearance. The tables are for a yard sale. We need to be ready before school's out and the parents come for their kids."

"Have you lost your mind?"

"Everything in here of value, we have to sell."

Sister Eileen leaned against the doorframe. "So you're selling a used coffin in a flea market in our parking lot," she stated, without emotion. "You might at least have waited to empty out the entire house until Margaret Graham's memorial service tomorrow."

Ilka could understand if Sister Eileen resented not being

consulted. "I have to pay back Raymond Fletcher. I don't want anything to do with the man. You were right, it was a mistake to take his money. And all I can sell is what's inside here."

Ilka had racked her brain for a way out, and this was the only solution she could come up with. She had no one to ask for help, no place to go to borrow money. It was all on her. She'd even considered going to the hospital and begging Amber for a loan, but no. She was finished with that family.

Dorothy's story had torn her apart. Not only because of her father's monumental screwup, which forced him to put his life in the hands of a man who treated others as pawns in his own cynical game, including his daughter. While Ilka was pushing the furniture together, she'd realized what hurt most was learning that her anger with her father all those years came from a story that wasn't true. Her story. Everything she'd imagined, all her life, had been wrong.

"But the coffin," Sister Eileen said. "People will be offended by it out there. Think about the school across the street. It will hurt our image."

Ilka hopped off the ladder and shouted, "We don't need an image! The business is closed. This is now a former funeral home."

Sister Eileen straightened up. "We still have a memorial service tomorrow at ten, and honestly, it would be nice if you could show a little bit of respect for Maggie's family." She turned and walked off.

Ilka trotted after her and stopped her in the foyer. "I'm sorry, I didn't mean to yell."

She asked Sister Eileen to come into the arrangement room, where nothing had been moved yet. She pointed at the sofa and plopped down in the easy chair facing it. Sister Eileen sat stiffly, her hands folded in her lap, as Ilka told her the story about Raymond Fletcher, about why her father had been forced to break off all contact with the daughter he'd abandoned. About how the old patriarch had taken her father from her. "You can see why I have to return Fletcher's money. And I hope you'll help me."

The nun nodded when Ilka asked if they still had the last two thousand dollars Fletcher had given her.

"That means I need eighteen thousand dollars, plus whatever this last ceremony costs. I have to get ahold of that money."

She glanced around at the worn furniture. Everything in the house was old, and even if she managed to sell it all, it wouldn't be enough. They'd have to sell the vehicles, she thought. She'd ask Artie to take care of that.

The nun looked as if she was the one who had lost everything. Her hands were still in her lap as she nodded almost imperceptibly. Ilka waited for her to speak; she looked fragile, vulnerable.

Artie had offered to contact a thrift store in West Racine. He'd also made a list of businesses that bought estates. Not that Ilka had any great expectations for how much they would pay. "Artie's bringing a trailer after he picks up the urn at Dorothy's. He'll haul some of the bigger pieces away."

From out of the blue Sister Eileen said, "That's why your father included you in his will. He wanted to make sure you came and found out why he had to stay away from you."

Ilka stared at her. She'd been thinking exactly the same thing: that he'd wanted her to know why he had abandoned his family. That was why he'd kept the old letters. He wanted to make sure Ilka knew he'd never forgotten her, and that all his life he had done his best to protect her. But it was a surprise to hear that Sister Eileen knew about it.

"We'd better get busy if you want everything out there before school is over," the nun said. She offered to take out the cremation jewelry in the glass cases. "It's worth something. The boxes are in my desk. We also have several toys in the cupboard. Your father brought them out whenever there were children."

She pointed to the tall cupboard in the corner where they also kept various papers and order forms. "If we make sure the toys are in front, they'll get the children's attention when they come out of school. The parents will follow." It felt as if she'd suddenly taken charge. They stood up and returned to the reception, where Ilka glanced through the window and saw the director of the American Funeral Group walking up to the front door. When he came in, the scent of his aftershave was so heavy that Ilka drew back.

"I'm here to give you a final offer," he said. He looked every bit as arrogant as at their last meeting.

She stared at him, irritated at the timing of all this. As if he was aware that she'd hit bottom. He held out a check, and she stared at him in disbelief when she saw the amount: thirty thousand dollars, ten thousand less than his first offer.

"No thanks." She walked angrily past him and opened the door.

"This is my last offer," he warned, still holding the check out. "You keep the house and its contents, but you have to shut down the business and give us your clients."

"Over my dead body."

"We take your clients, but also your debt. Sign the contract, and this check is yours. You can go home to Denmark."

"One hundred thousand," she said. "The same conditions and a hundred thousand, and it's a deal. You take over the clients and the debt, we keep the house and contents."

Even his smile was arrogant. "You're making the mistake of your life." He folded the check demonstratively and stuck it back in his inside pocket. "There's nothing here worth what you're demanding, and you know it."

That may be, she thought. But the very fact that he'd showed up was proof he wanted the business. It was definitely worth something.

His smile disappeared. "I won't take your refusal as a dec-laration of war. I'm assuming you're naïve, that your lack of experience in the business is why you're acting against your best interests. But I will remind you, we've been accommodat-ing and willing to help with your difficult situation."

She didn't answer, and after a moment he added, "If you'd been the least bit responsive, if you'd bothered to learn about the business, you'd have known that our first offer was excep-tionally generous. And now I'm even offering to relieve you of your debt. You're making a grave mistake."

Ilka stood holding the door open for him. Seeing there was nothing left for him to say, he walked out.

The door closed slowly as she watched him leave.

"That was dumb," Sister Eileen said.

Artie walked in with Maggie's ashes in a dark-brown urn. He laid it on the desk and said he couldn't open the garage door. "The remote's not working."

"Maybe we need new batteries," Ilka said.

Sister Eileen walked over and looked at the ceiling light while she flipped the switch. Nothing. She tried to turn the lamp on, but it didn't work either.

The next five minutes she and Ilka walked around trying every outlet while Artie checked the fuse box. The fuses were fine. Sister Eileen brought out a file from her desk and read for a moment, then looked up sadly and said that she'd forgotten to pay the electric bill.

"They've shut us off."

Artie seemed to suddenly remember something. "Who was that guy that just left?"

Ilka told him about the offer. "The man has no shame." She felt the energy draining from her.

"You should have taken the offer," Sister Eileen said again. For once there was nothing disapproving or superior in her voice. Only worry. She looked at Ilka. The nun was right, she should have said yes. And yet.

She shook her head. "I won't be treated this way. I don't want their money when it's so obvious they're taking advantage of my situation. And if it's Raymond Fletcher who told them about my financial situation, then I won't have anything to do with them."

"This might not be the right time to think about your pride. They'll take over your debt and leave you the house. In any case it would solve a lot of problems."

Ilka sank down in a chair and nodded. It would solve many problems, and she could put it all behind her. She wavered; of course she should have accepted, she should have snatched the check out of his hand, taken the money and run. As fast as she could.

"He'll be back," Artie said. "He's just playing the big shot. We'll be worth just as much to him tomorrow as we are today. He'll come back if you change your mind."

Ilka smiled at him.

Sister Eileen checked her watch. "We'd best get to work if we're going to be ready by the end of school." She stood up from behind her desk and turned to the mirror Ilka had tried to unscrew from the wall. She asked Artie to get it down, then opened the showcases in the foyer and carefully removed all the jewelry displayed on the mounds of velour. Then she moved on to the cabinets and emptied them. Ilka stood and watched in a daze. Finally, when Artie brought the mirror out, she got going.

"There's more velour in back," Sister Eileen said. She suggested they carry out the tables used for memorial service buffets. "We can use the velour for a tablecloth. The larger things we can put on the ground beside the tables."

Cupboards, tables, her father's entire office—everything was to be carried out. Lamps, mirrors, paintings. Porcelain from the kitchen. Stacks of plates, coffee cups, saucers, cake forks. Vases and candleholders. The two sofas in the memorial room by the dais for coffins. Also, several floor lamps. They had 150 identical chairs in the memorial room, but they decided to take only 10 of them out and tell people there were more inside.

"We have boxes of tissues," Sister Eileen called out from the kitchenette, where the top shelves were used to store supplies. "And three boxes of small chocolates. I'm sure we can sell them."

"Remember, Michael Graham and his family are coming tomorrow," Ilka said. She suggested they concentrate on the back part of the memorial room, the section used only for large services.

The piles were growing, and Ilka began carrying them outside. Meanwhile Artie wrestled to open the garage door manually. Sister Eileen spread the velour out over the white folding tables and arranged them in a wide horseshoe open to the street and the school across from them. Then she began setting out the vases and candleholders. Artie ducked into the garage to look for anything that could be sold.

If Ilka accepted the offer from the American Funeral Group, there would be enough money to pay back Fletcher. The rest she would give to Artie and Sister Eileen; then she could pack up and go home. But she was in the grip of a melancholy that puzzled her. After all, she had the explanation she'd come for. More than that, she thought: The answers she'd gotten were already filling the emptiness she'd endured for so long. She felt closer to her father. And yet she hadn't completely come to terms with everything. The fact was, she simply wasn't ready to sell at any price.

Sister Eileen interrupted her thoughts. "We also have eight boxes of square candles, should we set them out too?"

Ilka nodded and went over to help Artie carry a buffet from her father's office. As she was about to go back inside, a woman approached and asked if everything was for sale.

That was easy, Ilka thought. She smiled and nodded at the woman, who was mainly interested in the vases, but when Artie came out with one of the armchairs from the arrangement room, she fell in love with it. When she found out there were two of them, she bought them on the spot. She'd recently moved to Racine, her son had just started in the school across the street, and she needed furniture. Could she go inside and look around to see if they had more she could use?

Artie opened his mouth to say yes, but Ilka broke in and asked what specifically she needed. It was better that the woman believe it all came from a private home, not the funeral home.

"An armoire, and a dining table and chairs."

Ilka handed Artie her phone and asked him to go up to her father's room and take a picture of the old armoire. It wasn't large, but it was a beautiful teak piece with shelves on one side and room to hang clothes on the other.

When Artie came back down and showed her the photo, the woman bought it. And the table in the middle of the foyer, used for the large flower vase. Along with six chairs from the memorial room, they could be used in her dining room. Moments after she paid, the next customer showed up, and before Ilka knew it all the vases were gone. Only two candleholders were left. Several large paintings and the glass cabinet were also sold. They hadn't even brought out the jewelry, nor the toys. Basic necessities for a home went like hotcakes, she thought. She folded the bundle of bills and went inside for more.

She spotted the car when she came back out to the parking lot. Davidson's black four-wheel-drive wheeled into a parking space as far from the yard sale as possible. Sister Eileen was dickering with someone on the price of her father's desk, and Ilka thought she heard the nun swear when the customer walked away.

Davidson approached her carrying an urn. He looked stern as he nodded at the tables. "What's going on here?"

"We're selling out." Before she could stop herself, she'd explained that she was trying to get out of her debt to Raymond Fletcher.

Davidson eyed the table with the unopened boxes containing twenty individual boxes of tissues that Sister Eileen had just set out. "How much do you owe him?"

Ilka regretted having mentioned the debt. "Twenty thousand

dollars." She added that they'd already brought in $380, even though they'd barely gotten started.

"I'll buy the rest," he said. "Tell them to shut it down."

Ilka looked at him in confusion. "But most of it's inside, we haven't even carried it out yet."

He already had his checkbook out. She stared at his pen as he signed the check for twenty thousand dollars. She hadn't even known that people over here still used checks, it had been so long since she'd seen one in Denmark. She hesitated before accepting the check when he handed it to her. Why was he doing this?

"Let's go inside, I'll show you what you've bought."

Davidson waved her suggestion away. "I'm not taking any of it, you keep it. Unless you really want to get rid of it. I can send a few of my men over to haul it away."

Ilka shook her head and looked at the tables as she told him she'd rather keep it all. The funeral home would have to be emptied at some point, but it didn't have to be right then. The rush of customers from the school had ended, the last few cars had driven away, but Sister Eileen stood attentively behind the porcelain and glasses, waiting for new customers. Ilka walked over and laid a hand on her shoulder. "You can start packing it up. I'll get Artie to come help. It's all over, it's all been sold."

Sister Eileen glanced over at Davidson, then she nodded and started gathering up the glasses.

I need your help," Davidson said.

Ilka had been expecting that. She hadn't believed he would hand out so much money without wanting something in return. "Why don't we go inside?"

Still holding the urn, he followed her to the back entrance. Ilka glanced at him as she held the door. She hadn't noticed before, but he looked sad, solemn.

He stopped and looked over at the hearse in the garage. In principle it was his, though it seemed he'd already forgotten the yard sale and the check he'd just written. Artie was cleaning up. There weren't any coffins inside, and the blankets used for covering the dead were stacked in a pile. Corpse blankets; at least they got out of trying to sell them, she thought.

Most of what had been in the office had been sold, and the desk was still out in the parking lot, but she pulled over two chairs and told him to have a seat.

He went straight to the point. "I know this sounds a little bit morbid, but could you help me get something that would determine your father's DNA?"

They both stared at the urn. "The ashes won't help," he said, answering her unspoken question.

Ilka fidgeted in the chair. It must be important to him, given the size of the check he'd just made out. And that worried her.

They sat for a few moments in silence, but then she nodded and said she would look around. "There's a comb up in his room, and a pair of glasses. Would that help?"

He laid the urn down in the windowsill, and she wondered if she should offer him something to drink.

"Did you know your dad wasn't Leslie's biological father? Fletcher claims my dad was the guilty party, and he says he can prove it." He laced his fingers together, as if he needed something to hold on to. "His lawyer contacted me this morning. They're making a claim on the money I inherited from my grandfather. They say it should be divided equally between me and Leslie."

His face was white with anger as he continued. Ilka tried to absorb all this. "That's half of everything my grandfather owned. His properties, his half of the stable, the companies he built up in his lifetime. Fletcher wants her to have as much of it as I do. Because he was her grandfather too."

"But don't you already have the inheritance?" Ilka was confused; she'd thought that was part of the reason behind the dispute between the two partners.

He nodded and explained that he'd received an advance on his inheritance. Plus, he'd been given control of the assets that needed to be managed. "But it's a long, drawn-out process, and the estate isn't completely settled yet. The will can still be contested, and that's what Fletcher's doing."

Ilka tried to sort all this out in her head, but it wasn't easy;

the scope of the tragedy was too much for her. Apparently, the man killed in the car accident was the man Mary Ann loved and had been denied.

"I know my father wasn't Leslie's biological father, I just found that out. But I didn't know your father was her father. Mary Ann was pregnant when she and my father were forced into marriage."

"Forced? What do you mean?"

Ilka couldn't meet his eyes. A bird flew by the open window, and she heard the droning of the buoy in Lake Michigan, reminding everyone of the danger out there.

Finally, she straightened up and looked at him again. "Back when Mary Ann got pregnant, Fletcher didn't think your father was good enough for his daughter. He forced her to break it off, and your father never found out about the pregnancy. Fletcher was the one who decided *my* father would claim he was *Leslie's* father. It's a long story."

She shook her head, hoping he understood that she didn't think of her father as being better than his.

"So Dad never found out that Leslie was his daughter, that's what you're saying?"

"I haven't spoken to Mary Ann about that, but I don't think he did."

"But your father knew the baby wasn't his?"

Ilka nodded. "That was part of the deal. It was supposed to look like he was Leslie's father."

"So. Dad wasn't good enough for Raymond Fletcher. He worked in his stable, but he wasn't good enough for his daughter. And now the old bastard wants to get his hands on part of the inheritance." A tight-lipped Davidson shook his head and stared at the floor.

"Mary Ann was very much in love with your father," Ilka said. As if that was any comfort. "She kept her pregnancy a secret because otherwise Fletcher would have made her get an abortion or give the baby up for adoption."

Ilka couldn't see him well enough to know how he took that, and she stopped guessing his thoughts. First her father had accepted the child as his own, then he'd caused the accident that orphaned Davidson.

Suddenly he stood up. "This isn't about money." His eyes were clear and steely, and he looked determined. Ilka winced, but he didn't seem to be blaming her. "I have plenty. But I'm not going to let him get away with this. They don't need the money either, he's out to humiliate me. It's because I'm trying to prove that Frank Conaway is innocent of the charges against him. Raymond Fletcher is going down. He doesn't realize who he's up against." A vein bulged at his temple.

Ilka spoke softly. "Be careful." She understood him, and she wanted to help if she could. She felt miserable about the situation her father had been in, yet something hard and unyielding was building up inside her: a hate of a man she hardly knew. Raymond Fletcher.

"Why do you need my father's DNA?" She would search for any possible trace of her father if it could help.

"Before my lawyers get started, we need to know if Fletcher is telling the truth. I've had an oral sample taken, and we intend to contact Leslie for a sample from her. And then we have to eliminate your dad as her biological father."

"Leslie still thinks he is," Ilka said.

"I'm aware of that, but that's going to change."

She nodded. And really, it was fair enough that she knew the truth. Ilka asked him to wait while she went up for the comb in her father's desk drawer. Back downstairs she found an envelope, carefully laid the comb inside, and handed it to him. "I hope there's something on it you can use. And thank you for bringing me the urn. It means a lot to me."

He stood up and told her that the lawyer working on Frank Conaway's case could already prove that Conaway hadn't been in the stable office four of the days he'd supposedly signed a receipt.

"We're going to get him off. And I'm going to see to it that Fletcher goes to prison for fraud. But I still don't know why he deposited ten percent of the race income in a special account for my grandfather."

Out in the parking lot, Davidson said he realized his grandfather's reputation might be damaged if it turned out that he and Fletcher had somehow been cheating.

"But if my grandfather's name has to be ruined, at least Fletcher will go down with him."

He opened his car door, and Ilka remembered something. "What about the horses? Where are they?"

He frowned at her, as if suddenly recalling her connection to the Fletchers.

"Amber's worried," she said. "It was her horses you took, not his. I really think you need to return them."

Ilka explained that she'd visited her half sister at the hospital, and that Amber had asked her to drive out to the ranch to make sure her horses were okay.

"I know they're hers," he said. "That's why we took them. I'm sure she'll pressure Fletcher to deal with us, if it becomes necessary. If the horses had been his, he'd just have written them off."

Unbelievable! Ilka thought, and she almost yelled at him, but instead she stepped back and watched in disbelief as he stepped into the car and slammed the door. She stared while he drove away. Kept staring even after he'd vanished.

Ilka walked into a cold blast of air when she came down the stairs the next morning. A door slammed out back, and she folded her father's robe around herself and headed for the kitchenette. Her father's office window stood open, and the curtain had been sucked out and was fluttering in the breeze. A cable drum lay on top of the desk, which was back in place now. Someone had pulled a red cable through the window; it lay slack on the asphalt around the corner.

Naturally Ilka was curious. On her way to the back door, she passed the memorial room and noticed the chairs gathered around the dais and the candles in the two floor candelabras. Sister Eileen and Artie must have been up early, she thought, preparing for the memorial service. No trace remained of the yard sale; everything was in its place, except of course what they had sold before Davidson arrived.

She called out for Artie and tried the door to the preparation room, but it was locked. She slipped into a pair of his rubber boots by the door and walked out to find him. At

Sister Eileen's front door, she froze at the sight of Artie strad-dling the low fence to the neighbors. A cigarette hung from his mouth as he concentrated on plugging the red extension cord into an outlet on what looked like a shed. The neighbor's shed.

She couldn't believe it. "Are you stealing electricity?"

Artie started at the sound of her voice, and instinctively she ducked. He glanced quickly at the neighbor's house, let go of the extension cord, and swung his leg back over the fence. He kicked some leaves over the cord to hide it.

Suddenly she was very aware of what she was wearing. She nudged the cord close to the building with the tip of Artie's rubber boots, hoping that would hide it better.

"They asked for music, and we need to make coffee after the memorial," Artie said. "We need electricity. I'll pull it when they're gone."

Ilka didn't know what to say. He was right, they had no choice, even though Sister Eileen had promised to get ahold of the electric company and make sure the bill was paid.

Back inside the house, Artie plugged in another extension cord to reach the kitchen. "We have a little less than an hour, so one of us needs to get the tables set."

Ilka was still wearing her robe.

"Looks like Sister Eileen's got everything ready in the memorial room," he continued. "All we lack is the table for coffee."

It was Sister Eileen's job to set out the cups and plates, fill the bowls with chocolates, and generally make sure everything was ready when people arrived for a service.

"Where is she?" Ilka asked.

Artie said she'd been there when he showed up. She'd

helped him put everything back into place, but then she'd left. "Some guy came by and asked directions to the harbor, and when I was getting our city map in the reception I saw her walking across the street. She disappeared somewhere down by the school."

Ilka frowned. "Where was she going?"

Artie shrugged. "She didn't say, but we're out of milk. She's probably doing some shopping."

Ilka couldn't remember any stores in the residential area behind the school. But as long as Sister Eileen was back before the memorial service started, it didn't matter. She asked Artie about the flowers; she'd already grudgingly accepted him picking them up from the common grave. Before he could answer, though, she heard herself say that she'd handle it.

Artie went into the cold room for the urn containing Maggie's ashes. Without electricity the room had warmed up. Ilka had gotten used to the odor of cold and chemicals, but now the smell seeping into the hallway was rank and nauseating. It didn't seem to have affected Artie, though, as he walked out carrying the urn. He set it down on the dais, and when Ilka came over to smooth out the tablecloth, she noticed that the urn stank. On her way to the kitchen to get a wet rag, she decided instead to run upstairs for her deodorant and a quick change of clothes. Back downstairs, she wiped down the urn and sprayed all the deodorant on it. After a moment she leaned over and sniffed; it worked. The smell was gone.

Michael Graham would be there in less than forty-five minutes, with no sign yet of flowers or Sister Eileen to greet him. Even though she breathed deeply into her stomach, she felt the pressure inside her chest. This memorial service would be it, she reminded herself.

"Where the hell is she?" she hissed, unable to hold it in. The plan was that Maggie's husband would show up before the rest of the family, and he would take care of the music. Ilka noticed Artie staring at her as she walked around talking to herself. She broke off her monologue, and he offered to take care of the flowers if she thought she should stay there.

She shook her head and fished the car keys out of her pocket. "I'll be right back." She reminded him that the daughter was bringing home-baked cookies to serve with the coffee. "We'll need some bowls."

By now Ilka knew the way there; she didn't need the GPS. Other than a few big semis up ahead of her, the traffic was very light. It took her less than ten minutes. She'd brought along a pair of garden shears she'd found in the neighbor's shed; she hadn't even checked to see if anyone was around when she jumped the fence. Soon it would all be over, then she would resurrect the morality she'd temporarily buried inside her when she took over the business.

A young guy with a dog was walking her way when she parked at the curb. She slumped down in her seat and looked away to hide her face. When she peeked up, he was obviously more interested in his phone than her, and after he passed by, she grabbed the shears, jumped out, and trotted up the sidewalk and around the house. For a moment she stood admiring the bed of golden flowers; they hadn't been weeded lately, but the blossoms were magnificent. Quickly she snipped off all the asters and dahlias and carried them back to the car. It pleased her to know someone would get some enjoyment out of them, now that Mary Ann wasn't around anymore.

Without a single glance at the neighbor, she opened the trunk and dropped the flowers in, making sure she didn't mash them when she shut the lid.

She left West Racine fifteen minutes before Graham was to arrive.

Back at the funeral home, she had to find something to put the flowers in, now that they'd sold all the vases. Artie had a few tall glass jars in the preparation room, but they seemed a bit too plain. When she went into the memorial room to see how many they needed, Sister Eileen was standing there with three large ceramic vases. It took Ilka a moment to see they were urns without lids.

The nun was setting out boxes of tissues on chairs, and she also had stacked coffee cups and cake plates on a table against the wall. Ilka waited in the doorway and gave her a chance to say something about where she'd been, but the nun simply said hello and pointed at the urns. "I've already put water in them."

Ilka fetched the trunkful of flowers, carefully carried them inside, and laid them on the wheeled cart with the urns. Several of the blossoms were already hanging, but sorting them out would take too much time. At once she began arranging them, and was about to start on the last urn when Artie walked in.

"What about the music?" she asked. She plucked out a few flowers that were simply too sad-looking.

"We don't have any more extension cords that can reach the stereo, so I brought my little CD player in from the prep room. It's enough, long as there are only a few people here."

Ilka realized she wasn't listening, not really. She heard what he said, she understood the absurdity of the situation, but it didn't sink in. It was as if she'd resigned herself to it all. Right now, the only thing that mattered was giving the Grahams their money's worth. After that it was over. She gazed at the dead woman's urn, thought about the one containing her father's ashes that Davidson had given her. She'd taken the deep-blue urn up to her father's room and put it out of her mind before going to bed. Something inside her had shut off, or else she was subconsciously pushing everything away, not allowing herself to think things over.

"Sorry, but before we stopped yesterday I sold all the small chocolates to a mother holding a birthday party for her child," Sister Eileen said. "Did we promise them anything for the coffee besides what they're bringing?"

Ilka shook her head, but then she thought she'd better check. Artie had lit the candles on both sides of the dais and tested his small CD player, and now it was ready for when Graham arrived with the music. The family had made a playlist on an iPhone; it was simply a matter of plugging it in. At least some things were turning out okay, she thought.

She walked out into the hallway and almost ran into Stan Thomas. It surprised her to see him, and yet maybe it wasn't so unusual for the police to show up at a service for a homi-

222

cide victim. She remembered the extension cord running over to the neighbors' house; hopefully he'd come in through the front door.

Sister Eileen nodded politely at him when she walked by with an urn of flowers.

Ilka noted how the deep-red dahlias brightened up the memorial room, then she asked, "Is there anything new in the case?"

The policeman crossed his arms and shook his head. "No witnesses, nobody saw a thing. All we have to go on is the caliber of the bullet fired, and that it matches a number of automatic weapons on the market. I'm inclined to agree with you, it doesn't look like a break-in that went all wrong. It looks like a professional job. But other than the situation between the deceased and your father, we haven't dug up any motives that could explain a hit on her."

He studied Ilka for a moment then looked her right in the eyes. She refused to look away, and finally he broke it off. "Obviously your father didn't do it. But we're keeping our eyes and ears open. And we do have one person we're looking at."

The front door opened, and Michael Graham stepped in wearing a dark-blue suit with a narrow, lighter tie. He seemed to be okay.

Ilka greeted him and showed him into the memorial room, where she tried to make him feel at home. She pointed at the small CD player, thinking that if he was going to complain about it, this was the time to do so. Before anyone else arrived. But he simply nodded and smiled at the sight of the flowers.

"My wife loved dahlias." He thanked her for the elaborate

decorations, then began placing small folded sheets of paper on the chairs. Texts of the songs they would be singing.

He guessed about twenty people would be showing up, including his daughter and three grandkids. And siblings, cousins, and a few close friends. Though he wasn't sure. He apologized and said he'd sort of lost track. Ilka assured him there would be plenty of coffee, and of course they were bringing along the cookies. She hadn't had time to check the agreement, but he didn't seem to expect anything more.

She hurried upstairs; she'd hoped to have enough time for a shower, but now she simply changed clothes. Pulled on her father's coat, buttoned the white shirt all the way up, tightened the belt, hoisted up the pants. Her father had been tall, and he hadn't gotten any shorter with age, she'd noticed. She brushed her hair and made it back downstairs just as the car doors began slamming.

A short time later Ilka left the memorial room. Music played softly behind the closed doors. The coffeepots in front of her were full, the bowls overflowed with cookies, and one of Maggie's friends had set two bottles of sherry on the table and asked if they had any small glasses. Somehow Sister Eileen had come up with fourteen nearly identical cut liqueur glasses with flower designs. Ilka had never seen them before; they'd definitely not been set out for the yard sale. Yet there they were, next to the coffee cups. She closed her eyes and listened to the soft, soothing music accompanying the farewell ceremony. Someone was speaking, but the words flowed together from inside the closed room, and she let herself float away for a moment without thinking of what had happened before Maggie Graham's death.

Her eyes were still closed when the back door leading to the parking lot opened and someone cleared his throat. Ilka turned and looked at the stocky, bearded man. She walked over to show him into the memorial service, but then she noticed his old jeans and thick sweater. "Can I help you?"

He looked her over. "I'm looking for a guy by the name of Javi Rodriguez."

Ilka hesitated. "Is he attending the memorial service?"

He walked all the way into the hallway before shaking his head and explaining that the man was a friend of the owner of the funeral home.

"I'm afraid I can't help you," Ilka said, trying to sound polite, even though she felt extremely uncomfortable when the man began forcing her back to the door of her father's office. "The owner died almost two months ago."

The music and voices from the service had stopped, and she heard Artie and Sister Eileen speaking in the reception. The man would have gone right on into the foyer, but she planted herself in front of him. "We're closed. This is a private memorial service, and I'm going to have to ask you to leave."

The man pulled a photo out of his pocket and handed it to her. It looked like an enlarged passport photo. A black-haired man in his forties, she guessed, staring sharply straight into the camera. His mouth seemed to be pulled up on the right side. He was a total stranger to her.

She shook her head and handed the photo back to him, but he asked her to keep it. His eyes blurred for a second, then he straightened up and looked over her shoulder; when she turned there was no one there. She stepped toward the door, but he didn't take the hint, so she raised her voice and told him to leave. Artie walked in and glanced at the man and nodded before asking what was going on.

Something in the man's expression changed, and finally he retreated a step. "My friend there is missing." He nodded at the photo in Ilka's hand. "His phone was last registered here, at this address, and no one has seen him since."

Ilka asked Artie if the name Javi Rodriguez rang any bells. He thought for a moment before shaking his head. He went in to ask Sister Eileen, but when he returned he shook his head again. "Sorry, I don't think we can help you."

They followed him to the door. He stopped and said, "Who owns this place?"

Ilka's hand was on the doorknob, and she was about to close the door. "I do, I recently took over the business."

"And when did the former owner die?"

"August."

"I don't believe I caught your name," Artie said. He was behind her now, backing her up.

The man kept staring at Ilka without answering. She thought about Stan Thomas. "There's a policeman here. If you're searching for this man, he's the one you should talk to." She asked Artie to get him.

The man shook his head, then stared at Artie a few moments before whirling around and walking off without a word. They stood in the doorway and watched him leave.

She closed and locked the door.

"What did *he* want?" Artie said.

"He just wanted to know if we knew the guy in the photo, that was it."

Artie glanced at the grainy photo before walking into the office and standing by the window.

She followed him. "Have you heard the name before?"

He shook his head. "But the guy who was just here is the same guy who came by this morning, wanting to know the way to the harbor."

After they'd finished cleaning up, Ilka felt the service had gone better than she'd dared hope. Apparently, nobody noticed they didn't have electricity; they even complimented her on the candles in the bathrooms. And the neighbor hadn't barged in to ask what the hell they thought they were doing.

All in all, she felt it would have been a total success, if not for Stan Thomas hanging around afterward. He'd been more than a little interested in Michael Graham and her conversations with him. He also wanted to know if she was certain the relationship between Graham and Mary Ann was over, but he seemed to accept Ilka's explanation that the affair had ended shortly after the car accident. Nothing Thomas said set off any alarm bells with Ilka, though she had the feeling he was holding something back. Not that she had a right to know everything, but after all, her father had been the one being blackmailed, and they should be keeping her informed. At the same time, it was a relief to know the police were no longer interested in her. She'd love to find out why the sudden interest in Maggie's husband, though.

Ilka followed Thomas out the door and asked if he happened to know a Javi Rodriguez. "A guy came by asking about him." She showed him the photo.

Thomas shook his head. "I don't recall the name." He nodded curtly and headed for his car, his mind on other matters.

Ilka thought about Michael Graham. The red-eyed widower had been clinging to his oldest grandchild when they came out from the service, struggling to not break down.

Back inside the funeral home, she noticed Sister Eileen standing in the kitchenette with a stack of dirty plates and cups in her hands. Ilka was still holding the photo. She asked the nun exactly what the man had said that morning.

Some of Sister Eileen's head covering fell into the sink when she shook her head. Without a word or a single glance at the photo, she lowered everything she was holding into the sink, elbowed past Ilka, and vanished.

Ilka was staring after her when Artie walked in. "He's a long way from home," he said. "Texas plates. Quite a little trip he's taking."

Artie had already rolled the heavy-duty extension cord up on the drum. She went in the office and closed the window.

"Was the guy looking for Rodriguez this morning too?" Ilka said.

Artie shook his head. "No, he only asked where the harbor was."

Ilka went upstairs to take off her father's suit. She noticed that Amber had called; she needed to go see her half sister, but she had no idea what to tell her. She'd already written that everything was okay. Lying in a text was one thing, though; she couldn't sit there and lie to her face. And no way could she explain that Scott Davidson had specifically gone after her horses. That he was using her to pressure Fletcher.

She picked her jeans up off the floor. Amber would know that her grandfather wouldn't hesitate one second to sacrifice her horses, if it got to that point. Davidson might think Amber was the old man's soft spot, but the truth was, he had no soft spots. That much Ilka understood.

She'd asked Artie to cash Davidson's check at the bank, and now she had an envelope with a bundle of bills like the one Fletcher had given her. She needed to take it out to him before deciding what to do about Amber.

Instead of sneaking around the back way, this time Ilka drove straight up to the house and parked next to the front steps. With the envelope in hand, she walked up to the door, but it opened before she rang the doorbell. In front of her stood the young man who had brought out a clean shirt for Fletcher the first time she'd been there.

Ilka wasn't surprised they were aware of her; she'd noticed the surveillance camera when she'd turned into the driveway. And she'd braced herself for Fletcher's security people. If she ran into Jeff, she'd ignore him.

But the young man politely invited her inside. He wore a suit, which made Ilka think he was a butler or something similar. He wasn't a bodybuilder type either, unlike the others she'd seen on her first visit. He led her down the hallway without asking why she was there. A door was open, and sunlight cut a sharply defined pattern on the wood floor inside the room.

"He's expecting you." He ushered her in.

Fletcher sat behind his desk, and they stared at each other as Ilka walked over and laid the envelope in front of him without saying a word.

"Is this the smart thing to do?" His voice sounded weaker than when he'd come to the funeral home.

Ilka held his eye as she nodded. "Tell me what happened back then."

She sat down in the high-backed chair and pulled it closer to the desk; she didn't intend to leave before getting some answers.

Stone-faced now, he picked up the envelope and stuck it in the right-hand drawer of his desk, then leaned forward and laced his fingers. Ilka guessed he was trying to figure out why she'd come.

"Why him? Why did you pick my father for the job?"

Fletcher raised his eyebrows.

"The racetrack, back in Denmark. How did you find out about him? How could you know he'd just won a small fortune? Did you have spies? Were they the same ones you sent after me, when you needed my father to toe the line?"

She took a deep breath.

He still didn't answer her.

"He'd just won the largest payout of the year at the Charlottenlund Racetrack. If I didn't know better, I'd think you went after him because of the money. Over one hundred fifty thousand dollars. In 1983 that would've been enough to pay off our house in Brønshøj and his funeral home's debt, with quite a bit left over for him and my mother. If you hadn't made that offer. Why him?"

Fletcher's eyes twitched, as if he were thinking back to that time. Or trying to. Maybe he didn't really remember anymore?

Finally, he spoke. "We believed in him. I sent a few of my men to Europe, to get an idea of the standard over there and find the man I felt we needed. They happened to be in Denmark during that race your father cashed in on, and it caught our attention. We needed a man with a sharp eye for winning horses. Someone who didn't just play it safe and go with the favorites. A man who could see something nobody else could. After that race, my men asked around and found someone who knew him well. He said Paul had been around racetracks all his life. We became convinced he was the man for the job. So, we made him an offer, and he took it. Later on, your father turned out to be a complete dud, but of course I didn't know that back then."

Ilka thought she heard anger behind every word he spoke. Or was it disappointment? A frustration that had grown with the years and affected him personally.

"If you investigated him, you must've known he had no experience running a stable. It was his hobby, his passion, but he wasn't a professional."

"He took our offer, didn't blink an eye."

Ilka clenched her fists and tried to hold herself back. "You showed up at a difficult time in my father's life. You offered him his dream for a new start, to get away from his problems. His inner demons, even. Who fooled you into thinking he was the right man to bring over here?"

"Like I said, we needed a smart horse man, and we found someone who knew your father and recommended him."

"You needed an undertaker from Copenhagen?"

Someone walked by out in the hall, and she lowered her voice. She was sweating. Dorothy had mentioned photos from her confirmation in Denmark, from her time in school and beyond. From Flemming's funeral. Suddenly the pieces began falling into place. She remembered the old photos she'd found in her father's office.

Fletcher was squinting now, and a vein stood out on his forehead.

It came to her. "Freddy! It must have been Freddy!"

Fletcher didn't react, but he didn't need to. She knew.

Her father's two cousins had been close to him, according to her mother. They'd been at her confirmation, and one of them had also attended Flemming's funeral. Freddy in particular had stopped by their house often, so it seemed natural that he kept in contact after her father abandoned them. And not long after his disappearance, Freddy moved into a large house in a Copenhagen suburb.

"You asshole! How did you get him to do it? Did you pay him to convince my father to come over here? And what about the photos? Maybe you told him, what, that they were for my father, so he could see how his daughter was doing?"

Ilka was standing now, leaning over the desk as she yelled in his face. She clenched the edge of the desk to keep herself from strangling him.

"And what about the photos from my husband's funeral? How did you explain that to Freddy?"

Fletcher was suddenly wide awake. He shrugged, as if he couldn't care less. "I didn't need to explain anything. The check I sent was enough."

Ilka let her hands fall to her sides. Everything she'd meant to say about Amber's horses, about wanting the funeral home chain to leave her alone, about the explanations he owed Frank Conaway and Scott Davidson—none of it mattered now. She was speechless.

On the way to the door, she realized she'd never actually hated anyone before. Not even her father. But she was absolutely certain she hated Raymond Fletcher and the cynicism and inhumanity he stood for. She hated him for taking her father from her, which meant nothing to him. And for keeping her father over here when he obviously despised him. She hated Fletcher for his power and influence. And money.

She turned at the door. "I'm going to tell Amber she won't be getting her horses back. And to call you to find out why."

She closed the door behind her and stopped to catch her breath.

She had no idea how long she'd been standing there when she was startled by the sound of something being smashed behind a door farther down the hallway. The butler was nowhere in sight. On her way to the room she heard screechy female voices and more porcelain breaking, shards rattling when they hit the floor. She was sure it was Leslie yelling, but only when she reached the door did she recognize Mary Ann's voice, sharp but calm in comparison with Leslie's.

"That's no excuse!" Leslie shouted. Something heavy rammed the wall beside the door. "I had a right to know he wasn't my father, I had a right to get to know my real father!"

Ilka couldn't hear Mary Ann's answer, only the murmur of her voice. She glanced around to make sure she was alone, then she leaned against the wall and listened. Mary Ann was closer to the door now, maybe only a step away. Ilka put her ear to the wall.

"You're right, I should have told you. We were going to tell you, but after the accident it didn't seem to matter."

"How can you say that? I have the right to know the truth about my father. Even though Paul killed him."

Ilka had the feeling Mary Ann was crying.

"I was twelve when the accident happened, and I've spent all my adult life taking care of you," Leslie yelled. "How can you treat me this way? Did you think I'd never find out?"

Mary Ann's voice was resolute. "It's not as simple as you think. Paul didn't kill anyone. And if I could have, I would've told you everything. But I couldn't. You can't imagine how many times I wished Frank Conaway had never called me."

The women stopped talking. Ilka was shocked by what she heard, and she backed away. What did Mary Ann mean, that her father hadn't killed anyone? And what did Frank Conaway have to do with the accident? She hurried out and closed the front door behind her as quietly as she could; she didn't want anyone to know she'd been eavesdropping.

The second she pulled out of the long driveway, she parked on the side of the road. How she'd gotten in her car and driven that far, she had no idea. She rolled down the window and breathed in the fresh air.

No one had told her exactly what happened at the accident eighteen years ago. Only that her father had been reckless. Her hands shook as she rummaged through the glove compartment for something to smoke. She plucked out a broken cigarette from under a map. Suddenly she realized she was crying.

For a moment she closed her eyes and let the smoke surround her. It was a cowardly thing to do, but right now she couldn't help it. She grabbed her phone.

The horses aren't back. Talk to your grandfather about it. He's the only one who can get them back again.

She pushed SEND, leaned her head back against the headrest, and finished her cigarette.

After driving for half an hour, she pulled into a filling station for gas. Neither Sister Eileen nor Artie had been around when she'd returned from Fletcher's ranch to get the Conaways' address and give Frank a call. She'd wanted to make sure he was home before driving all the way out there.

She bought a cola and emptied out her coin purse on the counter. Graham would be paying them for Maggie's funeral soon. They also had the money from the flea market. They could get by for a while.

She saw the message from Amber when she got back into the car. *Call me.* Ilka left it as unread and opened her cola.

She'd been aware of the car since leaving Racine. Even though it kept a good distance behind her, she was positive it was following her. Now, though, after she pulled out of the station, it seemed to be gone. She kept an eye on the rearview mirror, but she more or less had the road to herself. If they really had been following her, they'd turned around, she thought as she pulled into the Conaways' driveway.

Their dog ran out and barked at her when she pulled up to the house. Frank Conaway came out of the stable. Ilka hadn't told him why she was coming, and he checked her expression to see if the news she had for him was good or bad.

"Let's go inside," he said. He explained that Karen had taken their daughter over to her parents' house. "We're trying to get back to normal around here."

He showed her into the kitchen and offered her one of the sandwiches Karen had made before leaving.

Ilka politely declined and said that a cup of coffee would be more than enough.

She came right to the point. "You were with my father at the track the day of the accident. Could you please tell me what happened that day?"

Conaway had been taking food out of the refrigerator, but he stopped and slowly turned to her. He laid the sandwiches down, pulled out a chair, and sat down facing her. "That's right, I was with your dad that day. I was the one who called Mary Ann."

He laid his hands on the table and looked down, as if he were inspecting his fingernails. His long curly hair had been cut, and he'd tucked his checkered shirt in his pants and tightened his belt to the last hole. He still looked a bit worn out from his time in jail, but not exhausted like he'd been out at Davidson's, just after his release. Now he sat up straight and began by telling her that already that morning, when he picked Paul up, his friend had been grouchy.

"I knew he didn't always get along with Mary Ann's family. Fletcher was mad as hell at him, and her mother didn't think he was good enough for the family. Anyway, we made it to the racetrack. I had five horses racing, one of them in the first race for mares. I went in to check the horses, and Paul went on up into the stands to study the program. When Fletcher was in the stable, your dad stayed away. And after they fired Paul, Fletcher bad-mouthed him every chance he got. So of course your dad avoided him."

"When did you see him again?"

"Just before lunch. And later early in the afternoon, before the last two races."

He hunched forward and looked down at the table. "First time I went up to him, I asked if he wanted to eat lunch together, but he was already part of the group sitting at the table. Russians or something, somewhere from Eastern Europe anyway. It was their accent, it sounded like they chopped their words out with an ax."

He wiped off his forehead. "I don't know where they were from, I just noticed they spoke weird, and we didn't know any of them."

"Was he drinking with them?" Ilka felt a strange chill creeping up on her again.

Conaway looked puzzled and shook his head. "They were too involved with the races, working each other up, but Paul was the one who knew the most about the horses. So I figured he was just enjoying the attention, having an audience. I told him I'd be back when I finished with the last horses, and I left."

Ilka closed her eyes. She knew exactly how it felt, up in the stands, together with people as wild about racing as she was. The tension just before a race started, opinions on the various horses flying around. The scorn for the losers hanging in the air. Time flew by, and it was like being in a room with no door.

"Gregg Turner came over to the stable to get me," Conaway said. "He insisted, told me I had to drop everything and go with him. I was busy bringing out a sulky, the jockey was standing there waiting for me, but Gregg dragged me away. And even before we got to their table, I saw how bad it was."

He looked away and bit one of his knuckles while Ilka waited, dreading what she was about to hear.

"The Russians were playing in another league money-wise, and your dad was swept up in it. And we couldn't get to him, he wouldn't listen to us, he got mad when we elbowed our way over to him."

He looked down at his fist. "He wasn't himself, not at all."

Conaway looked at her as if he wanted to make her understand, but she already did.

"He'd lost all his money and written two checks that wouldn't clear. When we finally got to him, he was about to sign an IOU, with his house to back it up. Gregg managed to grab it and tear it up before he signed it, while I tried to drag Paul out of there."

He pointed at his skinny body. "Fat chance of that happening. Your dad was a big man."

Ilka nodded. Conaway was at least four inches shorter than she was, and he'd stand little chance against someone six-three.

"I offered to drive him home, but he wouldn't listen. Gregg wanted to run back to the stable and get Fletcher, but I talked him out of that. I called Mary Ann from the office and filled her in, and I asked her to come out and talk some sense into him."

For a moment he hid his face in his hands; then he looked up at her. His expression said it all. "I went back to at least stop him from gambling until Mary Ann got there, but he told me to go to hell. And then I got mad. It wasn't the first time I'd had to step in, and usually I managed to get him out, but not this time. He blew up, he acted like a real bastard."

He threw up his hands. "I mean, I wasn't his mother or anything, but I knew how it was going to end. He'd regret it all and blame himself. And me too, probably, for not stopping him. It was those Russians, getting him all worked up. Laughing at him, daring him, and he kept betting more on every race. It was pure entertainment for them, but Paul was blind to it. Then his phone rang, and he was told there'd been an accident."

He paused a moment. "A mile from the track."

Ilka raised her hands to her mouth and spoke in a near-whisper. "So he wasn't even in the car when it happened?"

Conaway looked away and rested his forehead in the palms of his hands. He shook his head.

Ilka's ears began ringing in the silence. She stared to prod him on.

He wet his lips, as if he could barely speak. "We got there before the ambulances and emergency people. Mary Ann had been thrown from the car, she was lying in the field several yards from the accident. Fletcher arrived just after. I don't know who called him."

The inside of her mouth throbbed where she'd accidentally bitten herself, and though her jaw was nearly locked, she said, "Who reported the accident?"

Slowly he shook his head. "I don't know. Nobody else was around when we got there."

"Fletcher forced my father to take the blame. What, did he make him get in behind the wheel?"

"He ordered me back to the stable when he showed up. I wasn't there when the police arrived. Fletcher's security guard drove me. I don't know what happened, but I saw the other car, way down in the opposite ditch. I heard later on it was Davidson; that he and his wife were killed instantly. But the boy survived, he'd been in the backseat, and he crawled out the back window, it was all smashed up. They had to cut the Davidsons out."

He cleared his throat and said that he and Paul only spoke about it one time afterward. "Your dad blamed himself. I wanted him to tell the police the truth, but he refused. He kept saying it was his fault she'd been driving out there. To pick him up. If he hadn't lost control at the track, the accident would never have happened. I think he felt that what he'd done was worse than if he'd been behind the wheel."

"But Fletcher knew the truth."

Conaway nodded.

"And you knew," she said. "And Mary Ann. What about the boy, did he know, did he see anything?"

Conaway took a deep breath. "Right after the accident, Fletcher formed a partnership with the boy's grandfather, Gerald Davidson. They owned the racing team together. It was an enormous opportunity for the old man; his horses weren't in the same league as Fletcher's. A lot of us wondered about that back then. But Fletcher never explained. It was a hell of a deal for Davidson."

"So maybe, if the boy had seen something, Raymond Fletcher made sure he wouldn't talk, by making Davidson his partner."

"Or if he said something, his grandpa probably convinced him he was wrong. And it wouldn't be all that hard to question what a ten-year-old boy remembered."

They sat in silence again for several moments, until Ilka leaned forward. "Was my father punished?"

"They took away his license for a few months. If he'd fought it, he could've gotten off scot-free: There was no alcohol in his blood, no proof he'd been driving too fast, no sign he'd done anything wrong. The case was closed, the deaths were accidental. A tragedy that orphaned a ten-year-old boy."

Ilka's phone rang in her coat pocket, and she took it. "You have to drive out to Artie," Sister Eileen said. "I think something's wrong."

"I can't." Ilka explained she was at the Conaways'.

"You have to. I just called him, but I couldn't understand what he said. Something's happened."

"The keys to the hearse are in the desk, take them. I'm at least an hour away from his place."

"I can't," Sister Eileen said, then she lowered her voice. "I think he's hurt, I think he's been injured."

Ilka drove way too fast, even though the sun riding the horizon blinded her.

She'd run out to the car and thrown her bag on the front seat, leaving Conaway sitting at the kitchen table. She'd called Artie several times, but all she got was his answering service. And when she tried to get ahold of Sister Eileen to find out more, no one answered at the funeral home. Her chest tightened, and she pushed the old Chevy even more.

Finally, Sister Eileen picked up. "Where are you?"

Ilka checked her GPS. She was close to Kenosha, the nearest town to Racine. "What happened when you called him?"

She slowed down when the red warning light began flashing. Low on gas. She swore at herself for being too rushed to fill up on the way out.

"At first he didn't answer though I called several times. And when he finally did I couldn't understand him, it was more noise than anything. Then the connection broke off."

Ilka could barely recognize her voice. "Have you called the police?" she yelled.

"No, I, I called you," the nun stammered.

Ilka sped through town and on out to the lake, her hands stinging from gripping the wheel as she took the sharp curves. "What did he say?"

"He tried to speak," she wailed, "but I couldn't understand him. How far away are you now?"

At last, Ilka turned in the driveway to Artie's house and spotted the rear end of his black pickup. She told Sister Eileen she was there now, and with the phone to her ear she jumped out of the car and headed for the terrace overlooking Lake Michigan.

Artie lay motionless just inside the gate. A black cotton sack like the ones used in executions in American movies had been pulled over his head, and a pool of blood had spread out on the walkway. He lay in a fetal position, his hands covering his face, as if he'd been protecting himself before losing consciousness.

Ilka screamed his name, then she tossed her phone aside and threw herself on the ground to loosen the cord tied around his neck.

"Artie!" She stuck one hand under his head and pulled off the black cloth, crying quietly as his long brown hair, matted with blood, came into sight. Immediately she wrestled off her jacket with her free hand, rolled it up, and slid it under his head, then she turned him slightly; his face was a bloody mess, but to her enormous relief his skin was warm. Blood still oozed from the cuts and scrapes on the back of his head. At least he was alive! But he lay twisted in an awkward position, and he didn't respond to her voice. Ilka sniffed to clear her nose, which was clogged from crying, then grabbed the phone beside the walkway and stared at him while she pressed RECALL. Now she was the one who spoke quietly when Sister Eileen answered.

"Call for an ambulance."

She couldn't remember the address. She knew her way there but had no idea what the street or road was called.

"What happened?" Sister Eileen sounded calmer now that Ilka was there.

"Someone tried to execute him." She explained about the black cloth sack. "But he's alive."

"Are they still in the house?"

"Call the damn ambulance!" she yelled. "He's unconscious, we have to get him to a hospital, *now*. And call the police."

"Is anyone in the house?" Sister Eileen repeated.

Ilka noticed that the glass door leading into the living room was shattered; shards of glass littered the floor inside. Over the phone she heard Sister Eileen talking to 911, briefly explaining about the assault and that the victim was unconscious and presumably bleeding to death. She gave them Artie's name and address. Ilka hadn't known Sister Eileen had a cell phone.

Artie's pant leg was torn, and a shoe lay under the picnic table a few feet away. Sister Eileen's voice was unclear now, but Ilka heard her speak about calling Artie earlier that evening and not being able to understand what he said. That she'd been worried and called her boss to drive out there. She must be talking to the police now, Ilka thought.

She hung up and pocketed the phone, then she sat down and quietly told Artie that help was on the way. That she would stay with him, and to hold on. She held his hand, stroked it. Should she move him? No, not a good idea. She thought about covering him with a blanket, but she didn't dare go inside the house. In the silence she studied Artie's damaged face, and suddenly his body jerked from a mild spasm, his swollen eye-lids fluttering for a moment. He didn't react, though, when she spoke his name again.

She swiped at her tears and noticed that her arms and hands were covered with snot and Artie's blood. She wiped most of it off on her pants, then took his hands and carefully began stroking them again. The glass had cut the back of his hands. She thought about Raymond Fletcher and his men, who had been keeping an eye on her since she'd come to Racine. How much did they know about what she'd just found out? She'd been so certain no one followed her out to the Conaways', but maybe she'd been wrong?

Ilka shuddered, and her hands were shaking when she leaned over to stroke Artie's hair. She glanced over at the table on the terrace, past the walkway to the front door, then over to the broken sliding glass door.

Finally, she heard them coming, the sirens cutting through the evening air, and she ran up to the road and waved both arms when the ambulance appeared around the curve. A police car with blinking lights followed, and she stepped aside and gestured where they could come in and park beside her car. Then she ran back to Artie. More sirens neared the house, and she whispered to Artie, told him again to hang on.

At once their footsteps and voices transformed the stillness into a crime scene, and she was told to move away. Even though it wasn't completely dark yet, a floodlight was set up, and soon it illuminated the entire terrace. The paramedics were already attaching a drip to Artie's hand, and orders flew around as efficient hands applied a compression bandage to the back of his head and tried to stabilize him before lifting him onto the stretcher.

Ilka looked away. The stretcher's undercarriage reminded her all too much of the pickups she and Artie had made together.

They began rolling Artie to the ambulance, then they decided to carry the stretcher instead. He lay on his side, still unconscious, with a gray blanket covering him. Ilka had been focused completely on him, but as she stood up to follow, she noticed that the whole area was sealed off with barrier tape.

An officer came over and asked her name. He also wanted to know why she was there. She answered mechanically while staring at the open ambulance doors. Shadows moved behind the matte glass high on the side of the ambulance. They were busy inside. Saving Artie's life.

She gave him her date of birth, her address, and her Danish phone number. She explained her relationship to the victim. They already knew that Sister Eileen O'Connor had reported the assault. Ilka explained that the nun worked for the funeral home, and she'd been trying to contact Artie, and that's why she'd called Ilka. The officer wanted to know why they hadn't called the police immediately, but she couldn't answer that. Just as she couldn't explain why she hadn't immediately called for an ambulance when she found Artie, but she did explain about the black sack pulled over his head. And she apologized for loosening the cord without being careful of ruining fingerprints. She hadn't been thinking of anything like that, she'd been focused on freeing him and making sure he survived.

"Was anyone around when you arrived?"

"I don't think so," she said. "But I didn't go inside. I haven't been inside since I came."

The officer eyed the broken glass door but didn't say anything.

She asked if they needed her to stay, or could she go along to the hospital? The officer checked to make sure he had her number written down correctly before letting her go. He added that they might need to talk to her again, depending on Artie Sorvino's condition.

Ilka bit her lip. Depending on whether Artie regained consciousness, is what he meant. If not, they would need someone who could tell them more. The only problem was, she didn't know what more to say. She mentioned that Artie's father was dead and that he had no other family. He was single, a bachelor. He was alone. But he had Sister Eileen and Ilka. She wrote their names down as next of kin on the form he handed her.

Back at the funeral home, Ilka pulled off her bloodied clothes and washed her hands and face.

Sister Eileen was very quiet as they drove to the hospital. She held her hands folded in her lap and stared straight ahead after Ilka said that Artie still hadn't regained consciousness when the ambulance drove away. Nor did she react when Ilka confronted her about not first calling the police.

"He was lying on that walkway for an hour and a half! Did you understand anything he said?"

It was a wonder he could even answer his phone, Ilka thought. Usually he kept it in his pocket. He must have managed to jimmy it out. But of course he couldn't speak clearly, with his battered face and that black cloth over his head.

"You didn't think you should call for help immediately?"

"I called you," Sister Eileen said.

Her face was white as snow, and Ilka realized she was frightened out of her wits. Ilka tried to reassure her, saying that Artie would be fine, that he was in good hands. But Sister Eileen began shaking when they drove in the hospital parking lot. She sat with bowed head when Ilka got out, not moving until Ilka opened the passenger door to help her.

The nun was a small, frail woman, though usually it wasn't so obvious. Or at least Ilka never thought about it anymore when they were at the funeral home. In front of the hospital, however, she seemed to vanish inside the gray habit that hung below her knees.

Ilka spotted Information, a glassed-in booth in the middle of the foyer. She explained that they were there to see Artie Sorvino, who had just been brought in. Ilka jotted down where they were to go, but when she turned around she stopped. Over by the automatic doors, staring out at the parking lot, stood Jeff and another of Fletcher's men.

Immediately she grabbed Sister Eileen's arm and guided her to the hallway that led to the emergency room. When she realized she was nearly dragging Sister Eileen along, she apologized and let go. She stopped a harried-looking man in a white coat to ask directions, and he pointed ahead and told them to walk to the end of the hallway and around the corner.

Family members sat around in small sofa groups. Some were stone-faced, others were reading magazines in their laps with small children sleeping beside them. It wasn't crowded, but the mood was gloomy from the fear and worry in the room.

The woman behind the counter asked for Artie's birth date, and Ilka was startled when without hesitation Sister

Eileen said, "April twenty-nine, 1974." She also gave the woman his address and phone number, as easily as if she'd rattled off her own. Ilka hadn't thought much about it before, but the two of them must have been almost like family from working together so long. The funeral home had been the framework of their lives. She squeezed Sister Eileen's shoulder.

"They've just brought him in," the woman informed them, "but he's not registered in the system yet."

"Where is he?" Ilka said. "Can we see him?"

"He's in the treatment area. Family isn't allowed inside." She told them to take a seat in the waiting area beside A1, which was for patients taken to the intensive care ward.

Ilka felt out of breath, as if she'd been punched. Sister Eileen led the way, and before Ilka reached the large sofas against the wall, the tiny woman had poured two cups of steaming water from a white thermos on the coffee table. She added two tea bags and handed one of the cups to Ilka.

They hadn't spoken since arriving, but now Sister Eileen cleared her throat and asked who Ilka had spotted in the foyer.

"Two of Fletcher's men. He's been keeping an eye on me since I came here. He wanted to find out what I was up to."

Sister Eileen looked startled. "What you're up to?"

Ilka nodded. She told her about what happened with Jeff when she was at Fletcher's ranch looking for Amber's horses, though she didn't mention their escapade on the boat. "The horses weren't there. But he accused me of helping Scott Davidson—being *in cahoots* with him, I think he said. So now I'm one of the enemy."

Sister Eileen's headpiece covered her forehead, as if it sud-

254

denly was too big for her. She looked frightened and confused as she stared at Ilka. "Because Davidson gave you all that money, and then left everything at the yard sale?"

Ilka shook her head. "It happened before that. Before I even met Davidson. Fletcher's people spotted a black car following me, and it sounds like they think Davidson is protecting me."

Ilka was at the end of her rope. To hell with them, she thought, and she buried her face in her hands. None of that stuff mattered anymore, with Artie fighting for his life close by.

Sister Eileen nudged her when the door to A1 opened. An Asian woman approached and informed them that they'd just put Artie Sorvino in an induced coma.

"His brain needs to rest while we determine the extent of his injuries."

"Will he survive?" Ilka immediately regretted asking when she saw the physician's expression.

"Unfortunately, it's too early to say. Right now, we're stabilizing him, and the best way to do that is to give his brain a chance to heal itself."

"But for how long?"

The physician shrugged and said it was too early to say anything about that too. "It can take days, weeks, months. It depends on the injuries to the brain."

"Isn't it risky to put him into an induced coma when he's already unconscious?" Sister Eileen said. She looked even paler now.

"It's always a risk, but it gives the brain a chance to rest and recuperate. If he wakes up now, his brain would be using energy it needs to recover."

She studied Sister Eileen a moment. "There's a chance that if his brain is severely damaged, he may never come out of the induced coma. Does he have insurance that covers this possibility?"

Ilka looked over at Sister Eileen, whose eyes were lowered. "We'll check. Is it possible to see him?"

She stood up as the physician shook her head and explained that Artie was on his way in to be scanned. "He's been placed on a respirator, and as I say, we'll be running several tests to determine the extent of his injuries. Does he have family, if it gets to the point where we should shut off the respirator? We'd need their permission."

Ilka looked away, but Sister Eileen shook her head and repeated what Ilka had said earlier, that they were the closest he had to family.

"And what should we do in case of cardiac arrest? Should he be resuscitated if brain damage is serious?"

"How serious?" Ilka was nearly shouting. Sister Eileen was holding on to Ilka's arm and biting her lip, and Ilka got ahold of herself before asking again, "How serious is it?"

The physician hesitated; then she sat down and looked at them solemnly. "We can't say yet. We found a significant accumulation of blood in his brain, in back, but we simply don't know how bad it is until the swelling subsides."

Ilka struggled to control her voice. "Can he recover and be normal again?"

The physician nodded. "Yes. But it could go the other way too."

"Can we see him when he returns from the scanning?" Sister Eileen asked. Her hands were folded in her lap now.

The physician promised to come out for them when they

brought Artie back. "It might be late, though. Maybe you should go home and get some sleep. If his condition worsens during the night, we'll of course contact you."

Ilka's voice was almost a whisper. "It could get worse?"

"Yes, it could. You should prepare yourselves for the worst. He might not survive."

A rtie was brought back at four a.m., and Ilka and Sister Eileen were led to a room on the next floor. Ilka stopped in the doorway at the sight of him over by the window, nearly hidden behind all the machines and tubes. She approached slowly, conscious of the wheezing sound of the machine helping him to breathe.

His face had been washed and hands bandaged. They'd cut his long hair, and the sight of a rubber tube inserted into the back of his head made Ilka cry. Sister Eileen looked devastated, but she retreated when Ilka told her to sit down in the chair by the bed.

"No, please, you take it," the nun said. She sat down in an armchair over by the wall. As if she couldn't stand to be so close.

Ilka pushed the over-bed table back and collapsed in the chair. During the hours they'd been waiting, the absolute worst scenarios kept running through her head. Artie died, and it was her fault. She hadn't taken it seriously when Amber said no good ever came from taking on Raymond Fletcher. She should have stayed out of it. Minded her own business. Or maybe she should have told the police that someone was following her. That she felt threatened.

Most of the night she'd been crying. She'd also gone down into the foyer to look for Jeff; she wanted to know why Fletcher's men were at the hospital, and also what he knew about the attack on Artie. A few people were sitting around, very likely waiting for news about someone; otherwise the lobby was deserted. For a second she'd thought she'd found him when a man in a hoodie stood up, but he sat down again. It wasn't him. Jeff was gone.

Ilka dozed off occasionally, and every time she opened her eyes, Sister Eileen was sitting upright, watching Artie's face. Carrying the world on her shoulders. And her expression. Full of despair, yes, but her eyes flickered nervously at every sound out in the hall. She jumped in her chair when the door opened, and when the doctor walked in, she seemed to shrink further inside her head covering. In a nutshell, she looked terrified, and Ilka had no idea how to calm her down. She wanted to comfort her, tell her everything would be okay, but she didn't believe it herself. Someone had tried to eliminate Artie, or at least send a strong message that they intended to do so. She thought about Jeff down in the foyer; he must have arrived the same time as the ambulance.

She'd considered telling Sister Eileen about her talk with Frank Conaway, telling her that Mary Ann had been driving the car. And that Fletcher had paid to keep it a secret—but why? That she couldn't figure out. It was tragic, but accidents did happen.

"Do you think Mary Ann would have divorced my father, if she'd had the chance?"

Sister Eileen slowly looked over at her. Apparently she was lost in her own thoughts and hadn't heard Ilka's question. When Ilka repeated it, she shrugged. "I don't know anything about their relationship. Artie and I never had much to do with the family."

Ilka gazed at him, wondering why he was the one they'd targeted. She couldn't sit still. The physician had been by and asked again if Artie had insurance that covered the hospital stay and treatment. She'd had to admit she didn't know.

Fletcher was going to pay for what he'd done, even if Ilka had to wring the money out of him. She thought about Amber, in a private room in the building behind them. Artie's room wasn't half as big, though for now he had it all to himself. The doctor had promised that.

Her anger with Fletcher—could that be what was keeping her going? Once more she assured Sister Eileen that Artie's condition wouldn't have been any different, had she called for an ambulance immediately. But the nun looked down at her hands and silently shook her head.

The assault was the evil Ilka had seen that night, but what had gone on earlier revealed its intent. She was certain a car had followed her part of the way to the Conaways', but it hadn't been behind her when she'd turned into the driveway. Which led her to think someone was making sure she wasn't around when they attacked Artie. The message was for her, a clear warning to stay out of their affairs.

Ilka pressed her lips together; she felt alone. And vulnerable. And angry.

* * *

Late that morning a new physician came in to check Artie. He asked Ilka and Sister Eileen to leave the room. Ilka paced around then began studying the posters and notices about first aid and support groups for families, collections for the church and volunteer nurses who offered help to the seriously injured after they returned home from the hospital. Finally she joined Sister Eileen, who looked as if she would jump a mile if someone tapped her on the shoulder.

Artie had a new bandage around his head when they were called back in. The IV bag had also been changed. A nurse explained that the drainage tube should help lessen the accumulation of blood. "He needs rest now."

Ilka looked down at his closed eyes. "For how long, do you know?"

The nurse shook her head. "It depends—" Someone knocked on the door, and the nurse turned. The officer Ilka had spoken with at Artie's house stepped inside and stood by the doorway, but before he could say more than hello, the nurse strode toward him shaking her head. "It's too soon." She promised to contact him if Artie woke up.

If. Ilka looked out the window. She needed some fresh air.

After the officer left, she thought a moment: She should have asked his name. She jumped up and jogged after him. Steve, he said. His last name she didn't catch, something beginning with Cam, but he gave her his phone number, which she stuck in her pocket when she returned to the room.

"Maybe we should go home?" she said to Sister Eileen. "We can come back this afternoon."

The nun stood up, and they walked out to the elevator. She stared at the floor as they walked through the foyer, while Ilka checked to see if Fletcher's men were around. She relaxed when they reached the big glass doors; nobody seemed to be keeping an eye on them.

When they'd almost reached the car, a man in a hoodie yelled out, wanting to know what time it was. Frantically she searched her bag for the car keys. When she looked up, the man was staring at Sister Eileen. And not only staring; it was as if he was memorizing every detail of her face.

Ilka stepped in between them, held up her phone, and told him it was ten minutes past twelve. He stood his ground and kept staring, now at Sister Eileen's gray habit. Ilka sensed the nun behind her retreating a step, obviously aware of his interest in her.

She unlocked the car as fast as she could. Sister Eileen had pulled her headpiece forward to cover her face, and now she was enveloped in gray as Ilka shoved her inside.

The man stood a few yards away as she slid in and started the car. In the rearview mirror, she saw him turn and watch them drive out of the parking lot.

When they reached the highway, she asked, "Do you know him? He was looking at you like he did."

Sister Eileen hadn't spoken since leaving the hospital. She gazed out the passenger window. "I've never seen him before."

A while later, Ilka asked her if she knew Gregg Turner. "My father's friend, the old undertaker."

Sister Eileen nodded. "He stopped by occasionally at the funeral home."

"Do you know where he lives?"

"No, he had to move after the funeral home chain took over his business."

Instead of driving straight home, Ilka parked behind Oh Dennis! and told Sister Eileen to wait in the car while she checked to see if he was there. She ran over to the door and spotted him down at his usual table; then she turned and waved at Sister Eileen to come inside.

It wasn't because she thought the old man could do much if someone wanted to harm Sister Eileen, but a public place was safer than the funeral home.

"Would you please stay here with Sister Eileen?" she said to Turner. "And call me if you need to leave."

"I'm not going anywhere."

Sister Eileen was still pale, her skin almost opaque, and she hadn't spoken for several minutes, but now she nearly pleaded with Ilka. "I'd much rather go home."

She might be in shock, Ilka thought. Maybe she should have spoken to that doctor back at the hospital.

"You're staying here. I need to take care of something, but I'll be back soon."

I lka pressed the button at the entrance until the iron gate swung open. She roared down the driveway and hit the brakes beside the front steps, gravel flying up around her.

The immaculately clad young butler was waiting when she jumped out of the car. He stepped back to let her inside, and immediately she headed for Fletcher's office. He was sitting behind his desk.

Before she could speak, he said, "Is he going to make it?"

"What in hell is wrong with you?" she said. "You try to murder a man, in fact execute him, and you ask me if he's going to make it? What kind of a person are you?"

Fletcher had pushed his chair back from the desk as if to stand up, but he changed his mind. A frown creased his forehead below his neatly trimmed white hair. The hallway door stood open behind her, and she sensed a shadow out there. *Most likely the pretty boy*, she thought.

Fletcher spoke calmly. "You're wrong. We got to Sorvino's

place shortly after you, and whoever did that to him was already gone, like you saw."

In fact, she hadn't seen that; she'd been almost totally focused on Artie. But she winced inside at the thought that Fletcher's men had been there without her knowing. That they had seen what had happened without doing anything. "If you were there, why didn't you call for help?"

"You were already on the phone."

"I saw Jeff at the hospital." She suddenly remembered that she wasn't supposed to mention his name.

Fletcher nodded. "When I heard about the attack, I sent my people to the hospital to make sure nothing happened to any of you."

"You don't need to take care of us!" Her strength began fading, and she sat down and lowered her voice. "If it wasn't you, then who was it?"

He studied her coolly. "That's exactly what I was going to ask you."

"Does it have anything to do with Scott Davidson? I know the truth about the accident, but Artie didn't. He hasn't been involved in any of that, and he didn't know I was going out to talk to Frank Conaway either."

"We'll take good care of Artie Sorvino," he said, ignoring her question.

"We don't want your help or your sympathy!" she said. "All you're doing is moving pieces around in your little game. I'm going to pay a visit to Scott Davidson and tell him everything I know about the accident. And I know it won't make any difference, but he deserves to hear the truth."

Fletcher showed no emotion as she spoke.

"And if you're going to pressure him into sharing his inheritance with Leslie, even though her mother was too good for the Davidson family, go ahead, I can't stop you. But Scott has a right to know what happened, otherwise it's not fair."

"I want to go with you." Ilka turned; Mary Ann held a purse in her lap, with a sweater draped around her shoulders. "Ilka is right. It's time for these old family secrets to come out. Leslie has locked herself in her room and refuses to speak to me. My younger daughter is in the hospital, and her horses haven't been returned, as you promised they would be. I'm done with all this."

Mary Ann swung her wheelchair around and said she was ready to leave.

Fletcher was standing now, though he didn't move. But when Ilka followed Mary Ann out, he shouted, "It wasn't my men who attacked Artie Sorvino." His voice was less steely now. "But somebody's after all of you, and it looks like they mean business. If you go out to Scott Davidson, we're not on the same side anymore."

"You've never been on my side," Ilka said. "And I'll never be on yours."

Ilka fumbled around with the start button on Mary Ann's station wagon. She'd managed to shove the wheelchair in back, and she'd also lifted her father's wife into the car without it being too awkward. Mary Ann fastened her seat belt and touched up her hair. Ilka realized the woman's icy attitude toward her had thawed. She pointed at the start button and told Ilka to push it, that the car would start. "It takes the place of a key."

Ilka nodded and started the car.

"Does Davidson know you're coming?" Mary Ann sounded a bit uneasy. Maybe even nervous, Ilka thought. "Is he even home?"

"Yes." She explained that she'd messaged him when she left the pub, and a few moments later he'd answered and said she was welcome to come.

They drove in silence for a while, until Mary Ann cleared her throat. "Maybe I should have seen him one last time. But I couldn't."

Ilka sent her a questioning look.

"Paul, I mean, before he was cremated. It was hard to accept he was gone, that he wouldn't come home, toss the paper on the table by the door. Disappear out into the yard and start the sprinklers. Paul trimmed our bushes, I used to sit up on the porch and watch him."

She paused for a moment. "But I didn't love him. I never did. And that's why I didn't want to see him. I didn't want to force that indignity on him."

Ilka tried to concentrate on the road, but it was hard not to stare at Mary Ann.

"Do you know what I'm talking about?"

"Not really," Ilka admitted, gripping the wheel tighter now.

"After he died, he couldn't tell me not to come by and look him over. Not that I think he had anything against me doing so. But that's such an intimate situation; it's only for those who loved the deceased. It's about love."

Ilka had never thought of it that way. She'd loved Flemming, and when he died she'd sat for hours trying to memorize every last detail in his face. All his features, the small blemishes on his skin. All the beauty and unsightliness. She wanted to make sure she would always remember the man she'd loved. She wanted to store him away, so she'd be able to recall how he looked. How the small cleft in his chin created two pointed tips. She wanted it all. But Mary Ann was right: It had felt like a very private act, sitting there studying his face, because he couldn't protest. Or decide how much of himself to give her. Flemming had resembled himself, but the intimacy involved in staring into a face that can no longer look back, that she understood.

"Our relationship was more about respect," Mary Ann said. "Like I said, I never loved your father, not the way people desire each other. But I cared about him, a lot, and we respected each other. And maybe, when it comes right down to it, that's more important than desire. After all, desire fades over the years."

She seemed sad, so Ilka didn't interrupt her.

"I was very grateful for how he handled our lives. And the lives of our children. I still don't feel ready to bury his urn, that's why I kept it at home. I'd planned on burying it in the yard; he loved sitting on the bench in the evening sun there. But then everything happened with the house and Davidson."

Her father's wife was getting emotional, and Ilka thought she might even apologize for treating Ilka so badly, rejecting her. But Mary Ann had other things on her mind.

"When this is all over, I'm moving away. All my life I've dreamed of leaving and not looking back."

Ilka felt the woman's eyes on her. They reached the driveway to Hollow Ranch, where two guards stood. She wasn't sure they were the same ones as last time, but now they waved her through without stopping her. She was expected.

"I hope you don't misunderstand me," Mary Ann said, as they drove through the woods on the way to the house. "I wasn't dreaming about leaving your father. It was the life I allowed myself to be trapped in, without putting up a fight. It's mostly myself I want to run away from."

Ilka parked in front of the impressive white house. Mary Ann laid a hand on her arm and held it for a moment.

"I'm sorry it turned out this way. I really am. None of us deserved what happened. Including you."

So. An apology of sorts after all. Ilka looked her in the eye and saw no tears or regret, no sign that it meant much to her that their fates were tied together, a set of circumstances they happened to share.

Ilka got out, and right before she opened the rear door Scott Davidson appeared on the steps. She said hello and noticed him stepping back when he saw who was sitting in the passenger seat. Ilka asked him to give her a hand. He looked blank for a moment before reluctantly coming down to help.

Mary Ann was watching him. "I insisted on coming along. It's time we talked."

Ilka stood by the open car door while Mary Ann took a deep breath and let Davidson lift her out of the car.

"You can pull the wheelchair up the steps backward—"

"I'll carry you up, Ilka can bring the wheelchair along." Without waiting for her permission, he carried her up the broad stone steps.

He'd taken his guests upstairs on Ilka's first visit, but now he led them into a spacious living room with windows facing a lawn the size of a park, stretching all the way to the woods. Ilka thought about Artie and checked the time. They wouldn't get to the hospital as early as she'd hoped. She made sure her phone wasn't on silent mode, in case anyone tried to get ahold of her.

For a moment she admired the view, the deep-blue sky, the treetops slowly changing into their fall colors. When she turned to join the others, she sensed the tug-of-war inside

Davidson. He didn't speak, and his movements seemed stiff as he moved furniture to make room for Mary Ann's wheelchair beside the sofa. But he'd let them in. So far so good, Ilka thought. A maid offered them coffee, tea, or water.

"Or whiskey," Davidson added. He looked like he could use a drink. Ilka sat on the sofa and said she would like coffee; her sleepless night was dragging her down.

"Nothing for me." Mary Ann nodded at him. "I've come because I owe you an explanation of what happened the day your parents lost their lives."

Ilka lowered her eyes. Maybe she should leave them alone? Yet she felt she had a right to hear what Mary Ann was about to say.

The maid carried in a tray, and they sat silently as the cups were set out and coffee was poured.

"I was in love with another man when the accident happened," Mary Ann said.

Ilka noticed how Davidson's eyebrows shot up in surprise at her candidness.

"Very much in love. I'd only been in love once before like that, when I was young and met your father. And got pregnant. I thought we were going to get married, but my father wouldn't hear of it. I let him and his threats scare me. I was afraid I wasn't strong enough to care for a baby alone. I was still living at home with my parents, I'd never been out in the world, and I didn't dare take on that big a responsibility."

Davidson was sitting now. He ignored his coffee and seemed to have forgotten about the whiskey.

"My mother stayed home after I was born, but it would be a lie to say she took care of her children. Physically she was there in the house, but the help raised us. My younger sister is made of sturdier stuff than me—she left the family the second she finished college. Packed a suitcase and headed for Europe. And she met a man and married him. She came home for Mother's funeral, but other than that I haven't seen her much, though we phone each other a lot. She's my closest friend, I can tell her anything. But she's cut off all contact with my father. The only time we see each other is when I visit her. She lives outside Lisbon."

She gazed over at the window a moment before turning back to Davidson. "I knew my father would have made me have an abortion if I didn't obey him. And he would have had the baby taken from me if I'd stuck with your father too. So I broke up with your father without telling him I was pregnant. I was focused on the life inside me. And if I couldn't have the man I loved, it didn't matter who I married. When I was introduced to Paul Jensen, I simply said yes. I didn't consider what the consequences would be for him. Or for us."

She moistened her lips but kept her eye on him. "Once in a while I ran into your father. We were always polite to each other, but we never talked about what happened. I'd hurt him badly. A mutual friend told me he rowed out on the lake the day I married Paul, and he didn't come back until the next day. Then Leslie was born, and she became Paul's daughter."

"What about your mother, though?" Ilka said. "Didn't she support you?"

Mary Ann's shoulders hopped when she snorted. "There's no way I could have confided in my mother. She wouldn't have known what to do if I had."

"Did you know my father's story when you agreed to marry him?"

"I knew he was from Denmark, and he'd been married and had a child. I didn't hear the rest until several years later, though. He asked me once if it was okay to invite you over for a visit, but I said no. I'd made my sacrifice, and the deal was that he would too. Even though I had my little daughter, I felt like everything had been taken from me. I lost the right to decide over my life. Maybe I'm like my own mother, I can see that now, but back then it was simply the easiest solution, for everyone. We accepted it. The difference between me and my mother was that I loved Leslie. I still do. My mother never loved us."

She glanced down at her hands. "My father was different. He cared about us a lot, he spoiled us, but we absolutely had to obey him. He turned his back on my sister when she called from Portugal and said she was getting married. I sent her money every month the first few years, but she got nothing from our parents. I knew he meant it when he threatened to disown me."

Her eyes darted over to the window. Ilka had the feeling Mary Ann had never told her story to anyone, ever. It seemed almost as if Mary Ann herself were hearing it for the first time. Ilka noticed her face when she paused, how she let the words sink in.

"My father means everything he says, seriously." She laughed wryly. "So I stayed. I toed the line because of my daughter. When Amber was born, our relationship changed. She wasn't born from love like Leslie, but my father adored her. She was an accomplishment to him. At least that's how I think he saw it. He'd forced me to be with Paul, and Amber was his proof that it was working. And really, it was."

275

She glanced at Ilka. "It worked for us as a family, because Amber bound us together. The strange thing was that I gradually forgave my father. I accepted not getting the man I'd loved."

She asked for a glass of water and drank it in small sips, then wet her lips. "Paul took care of the funeral home business, I took care of the girls. Our life worked fine, until that afternoon at the wedding reception. Where I met Michael."

Ilka heard her breathing as she took another short break. Then she turned back to Davidson and spoke as if Ilka wasn't there, as if it wasn't Ilka's father Mary Ann had deceived.

"I can't explain how it happened. I felt the same way I did when I fell in love with your father. It was overwhelming, so pure and impossible to ignore. I don't remember what we talked about, but afterward I had to go outside for air. I was blushing, I was afraid everyone could see what had happened. I knew it would change my life if I didn't stop right there, but I went back inside. We sang and danced, and I'm not trying to make excuses for myself, but it was a joy to be alive. I didn't even know I could feel that way again. So when Michael called that evening and asked if we could meet, I said yes. We went down to the lake, and..."

Suddenly she seemed embarrassed. "Really, I didn't mean to tell you all of this. But it's all connected, it's part of the story of what happened that afternoon."

Davidson nodded. At some point he'd stood up and poured himself a whiskey without Ilka noticing, and now he took a long swig and laid the glass down.

"I decided at that very moment I wouldn't make the same mistake twice. I'd never forgive myself if I let love slip between my fingers again. So, Michael and I saw each other in secret, until we decided to get divorced and start a new life together. I'd put as much money aside as I could. My father was still very generous when it came to the family he put together. And I talked to a lawyer to make sure I would get money for the house, even though my father had paid for it. I had to think about the girls' future, otherwise I'd never be able to afford to send them to college. And yes, I felt bad about doing this to Paul, even though we'd agreed to have an open marriage. I knew he'd never leave me, though I didn't really understand what kept him."

Ilka knew. It was the photos Fletcher showed him of his first family. The one he'd abandoned.

"I wasn't myself back then. I barely slept at night; I was constantly worried someone would find out before we were ready, before we could say we wanted a divorce. I went to the doctor for help. Something for my nerves, nothing serious, just to make things bearable. It worked, I could think clearly again. And then they called from the racetrack."

Mary Ann looked away, clearly uncomfortable now. "Paul had lost all control. For the first time in a long time, though maybe I just didn't hear about other times. Frank sounded desperate on the phone, he said Paul was betting away our house. My house, what I needed to start a new life. And he was about to gamble it all away. I knew what his gambling fever was like. I'd seen it before."

She thought for a moment. "I was scared. I knew it could be serious for him if someone didn't stop him. Serious for both of us."

She leaned forward, held her face in her hands, and began to sob. Ilka forced herself to look over at Davidson. He sat frozen, watching the frail woman cry her heart out. Ilka walked over and laid her hand on her shoulder, kept it there until the crying stopped. She handed Mary Ann one of the cloth napkins the maid had brought in.

Mary Ann's head was shaking a bit as she turned to Davidson. "I would never ask for your forgiveness, I don't deserve it, but I want you to know how horrible I feel about the decision I made that afternoon."

She took a deep breath and explained that she hadn't seen the car coming. "I was crying while I was driving. I wasn't paying enough attention, and there was a warning on the pillbox about drowsiness, that you shouldn't drive a car. But I thought if I just drove slowly and followed all the rules, it would be okay. The pills were small, not very strong, and I hadn't been drinking. I don't think I saw the car until I heard it. Or maybe I didn't really hear the crash, maybe it's something I've imagined, playing it through my head all these years. I hear screams at night, and I wake up. I feel the pain in my legs, and fear, almost like I'm being strangled. I wasn't conscious when the ambulance arrived. I didn't hear about what happened until I woke up at the hospital."

She sniffled but didn't look away. "Everyone felt so sorry for me, even though two people in the other car were killed in the head-on collision. They said I was lucky to survive. At that point I still didn't know it was your parents who were killed."

Mary Ann laced her fingers. Ilka wondered if the woman might still be a bit confused, from back when she discovered the story about the accident had been changed.

"Everything was so chaotic the first few weeks. Seeing my girls was all that kept me going. Luckily Paul brought them to the hospital every single day. At first I couldn't remember anything about Michael and the plans we'd made. I'd simply forgotten him, and I couldn't remember what had made me so sad the day of the accident, either. When I learned I'd killed somebody, and found out who it was, I fell apart.

"I asked to see a doctor, and finally I realized everyone thought Paul had been driving the car. I said it wasn't true, that I was the one to blame. But then my father showed up and said I was still confused, in shock from being paralyzed. He told them again that Paul had been driving, and I was in the passenger seat. And I kept saying he was wrong, that Paul wasn't even in the car. By then I'd remembered why I'd driven out there. My father sat down on my bed, said he knew about my plans to leave Paul, and he also knew about my prescription for tranquilizers. Someone had told him."

"Maggie," Ilka murmured.

Mary Ann looked surprised, but she nodded. Her face was swollen and a bit distorted from crying. "Michael's wife worked in a doctor's office, she had access to my records. I could've been put away for five years, maybe even ten or more, if the police found out I'd been driving. It would have been first-degree manslaughter, because I was taking tranquilizers. But with Paul behind the wheel, it was only an accident. She'd followed me because she thought I was going to meet up with her husband. She knew about us by then, also our plans to get divorces. She's the one who called for the ambulances, and then called Paul and my father. But she left before anyone arrived."

She still couldn't meet Davidson's eyes, and now she began crying again. "I did it for my girls. I lied so I could be with them." She pointed down to her legs. "Back then I told myself I'd been punished enough. But later on, I regretted it. Many times. I should have taken responsibility for what I did, should have taken the punishment. Losing control of the car was one thing, but killing the father of my daughter, the first love of my life, I'll never forgive myself for that. And of course for killing your mother too," she added quickly. "And orphaning a ten-year-old boy."

Tears streamed down her cheeks. "I can never make up for what I've done. But I want you to know, I'll stand by you now, for whatever that's worth."

She waved her hands around, as if she wanted to stop him. "I understand if you don't want my help, completely understand, that's up to you. Yesterday I told Leslie what I just told you. I doubt she'll ever forgive me, and of course I'll respect that. The same goes for you, I'll understand if you never want to speak to me again. But I'm prepared to lay all my cards on the table."

She looked off into the distance. "I wish I'd been stronger and braver. And I wish I could do it all over again. But I can't."

For the first time that afternoon, Davidson spoke up. "And if you could, I wouldn't be sitting here."

At first Mary Ann looked confused, then she shook her head. "No, you probably wouldn't. I would've married your father, and we would've had more children. But then it wouldn't be you, would it, without your mother."

As they sat staring at each other, Ilka stood up and walked out. The mood was simply too intense.

Ilka helped Mary Ann over the step and inside the police station. She'd asked Ilka to drive her into town after leaving Davidson's place. Ilka thought about Sister Eileen, and she almost said she didn't have time; she also wanted to check on Artie. But she'd ended up taking her.

They approached the desk, and Mary Ann asked to speak to an officer. They were told to wait, but they'd barely reached the chairs and marked-up table covered with old newspapers when a woman in uniform called them over. Mary Ann had buttoned up her sweater and freshened her lipstick, and the female officer looked curiously at her; an elegant older lady in a wheelchair probably wasn't a common sight at the Racine police station. Ilka spotted Jack Doonan in the enormous open work space. He hadn't seen her, and she turned at once and followed along into a small, closed office with frosted glass that offered privacy.

Ilka sat close to the door, and the officer sat down behind her desk. Mary Ann rolled up to it and explained there'd been an accident.

"And when did the accident take place?"

"May 1998." Mary Ann explained that she wanted to change her statement.

Ilka guessed the officer was in her forties, certainly not over fifty, but she looked worn out, though she projected the type of authority that comes from seeing and hearing a little bit of everything. She leaned back in her chair in surprise.

"I know, it's a little late," Mary Ann said. "And maybe the case is past the statute of limitations, I wouldn't know. But two people were killed in the accident, and I want to change my statement. I was the one driving the car."

The officer studied her suspiciously, as if she wondered if this woman was playing with a full deck.

Mary Ann gave her Social Security number and the precise date of the accident, plus the names of the two people killed.

"Davidson," she repeated as the officer wrote all the information down. "But at the time my husband, Paul Jensen, took the blame, because I was taking Xanax and shouldn't have been driving the car."

"Are there others who can verify this information?"

Mary Ann looked bewildered for a moment, then straightened up and asked sharply if they didn't usually ask for witnesses to back up an alibi and not a confession. "Raymond Fletcher can verify I'm telling the truth," she added.

The officer went out to find the case files. Suddenly the office was very quiet. Mary Ann sat erect, but she began fidgeting and lacing her fingers again. She seemed less sure of herself than when they'd arrived. Ilka checked her phone, but there were no messages from the hospital or Sister Eileen.

Fifteen minutes later the officer finally returned empty-handed and glared at Mary Ann before sitting down. "There is no case."

She rubbed her nose and turned to Ilka. "Are you her aide?"

Ilka straightened up, irked at the annoyance in the officer's voice. "No!"

"I found the name Davidson when I searched the date. A couple was killed in a one-car accident. In other words, there were no other people or cars involved."

"That's not true!" Mary Ann said. "Can I see the files?"

"There are no case files." The officer stood up.

"Then I'd like to know how you found out it was a one-car accident."

The female officer didn't even try to hide her irritation. "I can't reveal that."

"I insist on seeing where that's written."

"Maybe we should just leave," Ilka said.

"I want to see it! It's not true. I was there." She pointed down at her legs. "How can you explain me being paralyzed in the accident?"

"There are no records of any injuries."

"Could I speak with someone who was at the scene of the accident?"

"Sorry."

The officer opened the door and held it impatiently for them.

"Come on, we're leaving," Ilka said.

Without waiting, she grabbed the handles of Mary Ann's wheelchair and pushed her out of the office. When they reached the parking lot, it occurred to her how disrespectful it was to treat her father's wife this way. When she saw Mary Ann's face, she knelt in front of her and apologized, but the woman waved her off.

"It's him. My father made the accident disappear. Just like he's done with so much else. Please drive me home."

"Are you okay?"

"No, I'm not okay, but I only have myself to thank for that."

Before leaving, Ilka found Gregg Turner's number and called him. It seemed absurd that the man couldn't afford a decent meal but had a cell phone, she thought.

He answered on the first ring, and Ilka asked him to tell Sister Eileen she'd be back soon.

"But she left right after you."

"What do you mean, she left?" Ilka yelled, scaring Mary Ann. "I asked you to call me if you two went anywhere."

"No, if *I* went anywhere. I'm sorry if I misunderstood, I thought it was a question of Sister Eileen knowing I'm here if she needed me. I promised to stay here, and I did. I'm still here."

Ilka slammed her hand against the wheel and tried to get ahold of herself by breathing deeply and closing her eyes.

"What's happening?" Mary Ann spoke quietly, as if Ilka's panic had calmed her down.

"I have to stop by the funeral home before I drive you home."

Mary Ann nodded. Ilka felt the woman's eyes on her as she backed out and drove off.

"It wasn't my father's men who attacked Artie," Mary Ann said. "I know they were keeping an eye on you. My father wondered why you were in Paul's will. None of us knew that, not until the will was opened at the lawyer's office. And he wondered about Paul changing it so soon before he died. I wondered about it too, because there was nothing valuable to inherit. Except for the funeral home, but it wasn't worth much."

Her voice sounded commanding again. It reminded Ilka of Raymond Fletcher standing up after the horses were taken at the ranch. One moment he was on his knees, the next he was standing ready to fight back.

Ilka kept her mouth shut. Now she knew that her father had wanted to make sure she came over. He'd wanted her to know his story.

"There's a chip on Paul's car," Mary Ann said. "My father wanted to keep track of him. It's still there, so they've known where you were all the time. But they did follow you quite a bit, to find out what you were doing."

Ilka gripped the wheel tighter and sped up, angry now. Sweating. She didn't understand how Mary Ann could sit there and calmly tell her all this, as if what Fletcher had done was okay. But maybe her father's wife was too used to things happening this way in Fletcher's world.

She barely slowed down when she turned into the funeral home parking lot, and she didn't apologize when Mary Ann was thrown against the passenger door. She parked in front of Sister Eileen's apartment, jumped out, ran up to the door, and threw it open so violently that she stumbled inside.

Sister Eileen was sitting straight up on the sofa, facing the door and pointing a long-slide automatic pistol directly at Ilka.

Ilka stepped back in shock, but Sister Eileen lowered the weapon at once and laid it in her lap. They stared at each other for a moment before Ilka walked over to her.

"Come on. We have to drop Mary Ann off at Fletcher's ranch before visiting Artie. The car's outside."

She avoided looking at the pistol as she held her hand out to the nun. Again, she suspected Sister Eileen was in shock. She seemed terrified, but her calm, serene expression worried Ilka.

Sister Eileen picked a bag up off the floor, unzipped it, and stuck the pistol inside. It barely fit. Then she went out into the hall for her knee-length coat.

"Is that really smart?" Ilka said. She didn't ask where the pistol came from.

"I'm ready." Sister Eileen walked out the door and nodded curtly at Mary Ann before getting in back.

Everything's falling apart, Ilka thought as she pulled out of the parking lot. Strangely enough, the pistol in the car was the only thing that made her feel safe.

They'd almost reached Fletcher's house when Ilka noticed the two police cars. The front door opened, and out came a policeman with a firm grip on the young butler, who was waving his arms around and talking to the officer.

Ilka parked, and they watched as Raymond Fletcher appeared in the doorway with his hands cuffed behind his back. An officer held his left arm as they walked to the police car nearest the steps. Several patrol cars were now filling up the gravel lot in front of the house, and Ilka saw Jeff and several other security guards walking out in handcuffs.

Ilka looked at Mary Ann. "What's happening?"

"I called them while you were getting Sister Eileen." She was pale, and her voice was small, but firm. "I told them my father was guilty of fraud, corruption, and false accusations against Frank Conaway. He made a deal with Scott Davidson's grandfather after the accident, gave him ten percent of all income in exchange for his silence. When Gerald died, my father stopped paying, but he needed a good explanation of where the money had gone."

"So you knew Frank might go to prison for something he didn't do," Ilka said.

Mary Ann looked away and nodded.

"Frank has two young daughters. He could have been sent away for life, and you knew he was innocent!"

A sudden surge of rage left Ilka speechless. Mary Ann must have known Frank all her life, and yet she'd allowed Fletcher to make him the scapegoat.

"I told the police I'm willing to make a statement about the false accusations against Frank. Like I promised Scott, I'm prepared to lay all my cards on the table."

As if that suddenly made everything right, Ilka thought. But she cooled off enough to speak again. "Did your father have Maggie killed?"

Mary Ann turned to her in surprise. "Why in the world would you think that?"

"Because she knew the truth about what happened. She was blackmailing my father. Ever since the accident he deposited money in her account every three months."

She looked puzzled. "I don't know anything about that."

Ilka dropped it. Sister Eileen opened the back door and got out, and Ilka watched in the rearview mirror as she dragged the wheelchair from the back and folded it out. Then she opened the passenger door and undid Mary Ann's seat belt.

She looked over at Ilka. "May I have the car keys?"

At first Ilka thought she wanted to drive Mary Ann's car; then she realized the nun was talking about her father's car, which was parked nearby. She found the keys in her bag and handed them over.

"Let's go." Sister Eileen headed for the Chevy.

Ilka followed and joined her in the front seat. "I didn't think you could drive a car," she said.

"I can now." She backed out.

Ilka nodded back at Mary Ann, still sitting in her car. "What about her?"

"I'm sure someone here can help her inside. We have to leave, now."

She looked tiny behind the wheel, but she floored it. Gravel shot up underneath the car.

Ilka let Sister Eileen in on everything she'd learned. "I wonder if Fletcher even thought about the consequences when he involved Leslie in his fight against Scott. He should have talked to Mary Ann first. After all, Leslie has sacrificed most of her adult life taking care of her mother."

Sister Eileen stared straight ahead. "At least Mary Ann is taking him down now."

Did she even have a driver's license? Ilka thought. But that was the least of her worries.

They parked in the lot behind the funeral home. Ilka needed a shower and a bite to eat, and the nun promised to call the hospital to hear if there was any news. When Ilka came downstairs twenty minutes later, Sister Eileen had made tea and sandwiches for them.

As they were about to eat, someone knocked on the back door. Ilka stood up, but after a moment's thought she walked to the window and peeked outside. Two men in suits stood at the door; she was getting used to seeing gangster types practically everywhere she went, but these two looked more like bankers. Sister Eileen picked up her bag and set it on her lap as Ilka opened the door.

Immediately one of the men launched into a speech that essentially was a list of grievances. The only words she really caught were undertaker, authorization, education, permit, license, forbidden, fines, and shut down. She let him finish, then she stuck her phone in her back pocket as the other man explained it his way. The Association of American Funeral

Directors, he said, had been informed that the Paul Jensen Funeral Home was being run by a person without the required training. The business lacked certification, and she also had broken current regulations by performing the duties of an undertaker. Consequently, the funeral home was now excluded from the association and had to close before the end of the month.

He gathered his hands behind his back and nodded.

"In addition," the first man said, "the hearse and the business's income in the period it operated illegally may be confiscated."

"We haven't operated illegally," Ilka protested. She pointed out that Artie Sorvino had the required training, and the business did have the necessary certification.

"We've received photographic evidence clearly showing that you…" He glanced down at his papers. "…Ilka Nichols Jensen, transported a deceased person in the hearse, that you made use of an unauthorized crematorium, and that you have arranged and held a memorial ceremony." After a moment to catch his breath, he added that they also knew she had spoken with family members and overseen the decorations.

"Flowers? That can't be illegal!"

Obviously, he considered her outburst to be a victory, but she didn't care. It dawned on her who might have been keeping an eye on her lately. But if the American Funeral Group thought they could force her out, they had another think coming.

"This funeral home must be closed by the end of the month," the man farther from her repeated.

"You're too late." She took a moment to enjoy their startled faces. "We've already closed. If you had come to the front door, you'd have seen the sign. And if the American Funeral

Group had hired decent detectives, they would know I was transporting an empty coffin in the car when I drove out to the old crematorium."

She was bluffing, but she was fed up with them.

"I'm cleaning out our stock, and Dorothy Cane is running a ceramics workshop out there. She's putting together an art exhibition, death is the theme, so I offered her a coffin. It was going to be thrown out anyway. Now, either you can go through with all this, in which case you'll be contacted by my lawyer, who will sue for false accusations. Or you can apologize to me and send me a written copy of the reprimand you send to the American Funeral Group for harassment. It's your decision."

Neither of them moved a muscle while she spoke, but when she finished they seemed to consider what she'd said.

The man who had made the accusations spoke up. "How can we know it was an empty coffin?"

Ilka shrugged. "You can't. But how can you know it wasn't empty? If the people hired to spy on me had done their job, they'd have known I haven't been out there since."

She had no idea if they'd also been watching Artie, who had driven out in his pickup for Maggie's urn, but it was a chance worth taking.

"A personal apology for making false accusations, and a copy of the warning you're giving them for harassment and unethical behavior." It took an effort to stop herself from going on and on.

The funeral home director trying to ruin her business infuriated her; after all, it was clear she was already finished. And if possible, she was even angrier at Fletcher and Mary Ann because of their lies. But the absolute peak of her rage was directed at the person who had tried to kill Artie. While she was ranting at the two men, though, she realized she might be lashing out from fear, not rage. The fear of not knowing if the people who had hurt Artie would come back, or what they were after.

"We'll be back when we've investigated further," one of the men said. The other nodded.

"No! You will not come back. If you don't give me an immediate apology, I'm contacting my lawyer. You will be sued for character assassination and personal harassment, and we'll see you in court. And I want to see the evidence the American Funeral Group gathered against us. We've done nothing to justify one of our competitors in town trying to harm us."

She was just warming up, but she was interrupted by Sister Eileen. Mary Ann had called. "They've released Raymond Fletcher. He's on his way home." She sounded worried.

"We…we apologize for the inconvenience," said the man farther from her.

"Oh, shut up!" She slammed the door, leaned against the wall, and closed her eyes.

"She asked you to come out there," Sister Eileen said.

After a moment's pause, she followed the nun back to the office. She was still trembling with anger, but she managed to wash down the food with cold tea.

"Did you talk to the hospital?" She'd much rather be with Artie than waiting around at the ranch when Fletcher arrived.

Sister Eileen nodded. Her headpiece was pulled back now, and her hair was visible. "He's in stable condition, but they're keeping him in the coma until there's less blood trapped inside his skull."

"Thank God," Ilka murmured. She slumped in relief; stable was more than she'd dared hope for.

"Mary Ann sounded frightened," Sister Eileen said.

"All right, I'll go." Ilka thought about Amber. Hopefully she didn't know what was going on.

As she put on her coat, someone began pounding on the front door. *If I hear one more word out of those idiots*, she thought, as she marched out to stick the CLOSED sign in their nose. She flung the door open, but stopped herself at the sight of an elderly man.

He wore a knee-length gray tweed jacket and a black shirt. His white tie was expertly knotted. "May I ask, is there a Lydia Rogers living here?"

Ilka's arms fell to her sides as she shook her head. "I'm sorry." She explained that she was new in town and couldn't help.

The man stood for a moment, then pulled out a card from his inside pocket. He asked her to call him if she happened to meet a woman by that name. Then he apologized for bothering her and walked away from the residential district, toward the small row of deserted factories. Toward town.

Ilka stood in the doorway and watched him.

Mary Ann hadn't given Sister Eileen a number, so Ilka couldn't call to say she was on her way. For once she drove under the speed limit. She was in no hurry to be caught in the middle of a family dispute that didn't concern her. Yet she felt she'd be representing her father by standing with Mary Ann now that the woman was ready to defy Fletcher.

The gate was open when she arrived, and she drove straight up to the house. Mary Ann's station wagon was the only vehicle there. While Ilka parked, she heard two sharp cracks from inside the house, followed by a scream and loud female voices. She froze for a moment, then ran toward the front steps.

"Hello!" she yelled when she rushed through the doorway.

Everything was quiet, but a few moments later she heard moaning and what she took to be Mary Ann's voice. "Hello," she repeated, as she reluctantly headed for Fletcher's office. The moaning turned into sobbing.

Ilka longed to turn around and run away. Her hands were stinging, and she looked down; her nails were digging into her palms. Someone spoke again. Mary Ann, she was certain now.

She stepped inside the open office door and froze. Raymond Fletcher lay on the floor in a pool of blood that covered most of the Moroccan rug in front of his desk.

Leslie was on her knees, motionless, holding a rifle in her hands while staring at her grandfather. Mary Ann sat beside her daughter, and she looked up at Ilka, but Leslie seemed oblivious to her.

Without thinking, Ilka walked over to Fletcher. He was wearing the same suit he'd had on when the police arrested him. His shirt was torn up from bullets. She thought about pressing something against the entry wounds until Mary Ann shook her head.

"He's dead. I've called the police."

Ilka couldn't take her eyes off him. He must have just gotten back, she thought. And they were alone; no young butler or security people came running in like they would have if they'd heard the shots.

Leslie still hadn't moved. Was she even breathing? She looked petrified, the way she was staring at her grandfather. Ilka took a step toward her half sister, but Mary Ann stopped her with a long look. She reached over and grabbed the rifle out of her daughter's hands and laid it in her lap, then stroked Leslie's back a minute before telling her to sit down in the armchair while they waited for the police.

Ilka watched Leslie obey her mother. "What happened?"

Mary Ann's face was white, but otherwise she seemed in control of herself. "They had an argument. The police are a bunch of cowards, he was out in an hour. They let him go without charging him with any of the crimes I told them he was responsible for."

Except for when the woman told Scott Davidson about being in love with his father and, later, Michael Graham, Ilka hadn't heard much warmth in Mary Ann's voice. And there wasn't any now either as she described how her father had barely walked in the door before calling Leslie into his office.

"She's hardly even been out of her room since we argued. I was packing my things in the room beside the office here. I couldn't stay, not after reporting him to the police. I thought I had more time, but then I heard him calling Leslie, and I followed her and saw everything."

Leslie glanced at her mother then turned back to her grandfather. She hadn't looked at Ilka, and in fact Ilka doubted Leslie even knew she was in the room.

"He was furious. Mostly at me, of course, he wanted me out of the house, and Leslie too. He humiliated her, called her worthless. Said he made the mistake of his life by letting her be born. He called her biological father the most horrible things, and finally he compared her with Amber. Who was always the apple of his eye."

Mary Ann looked over at her daughter. "Leslie ran out of the office, and I went back to finish packing. I thought I'd give her a few minutes before going in to see if I could make her feel better. But then I heard the shots."

She spoke as if her daughter wasn't sitting in the chair in front of her. It was difficult for Ilka to look at Leslie too. There was something repulsive yet also tender about how she stared at her grandfather. As if she needed to reassure herself he was really dead.

Ilka hadn't heard any cars outside, but now voices and footsteps sounded out in the hall. She was annoyed at herself for not leaving before the police arrived.

Stan Thomas was the first officer in the room. He made a beeline for Raymond Fletcher, then turned to Mary Ann. "What happened?"

Leslie straightened up and was about to say something, but her mother spoke up in a clear, firm voice. "I killed my father."

She held the stock of the rifle out to the policeman and said she was ready to be taken away.

Ilka caught Leslie's darting eyes as she struggled to her feet and joined her mother. Mary Ann held her daughter's face in both hands and kissed her cheek. Ilka heard her say she was sorry, but that was all. She turned her wheelchair and slowly rolled to the door.

Ilka stepped aside so they could leave. Thomas asked if there had been anyone else present during the shooting.

"No," Mary Ann said. "I was alone."

She twisted around to her daughter, who was right behind her wheelchair. "Go see your sister. I don't want her hearing about this from anyone else."

Leslie promised to tell Amber. She seemed listless, apathetic, and she shook her head when Ilka offered to drive her to the hospital. Slowly she walked down the hall, her arms folded across her chest as if she were holding herself together.

Ilka was alone in the room as she watched her go. She didn't even want to try to imagine the thoughts running through Leslie's bowed head.

She strode over to Fletcher's desk, pulled out the right drawer, and grabbed the envelope with the twenty thousand dollars she'd returned to him earlier. Voices echoed from out in the hall, and she quickly folded the envelope and stuck it down in her high-waisted pants. After one last look at Fletcher lying in the pool of blood, she walked out of the house with the money. It was only fair.

Ilka was exhausted when she turned into the funeral home's rear parking lot. She kept seeing the look Mary Ann had given her just before taking the rifle out of Leslie's hands, an intimation that they would be sharing a secret the rest of their lives. By not telling Stan Thomas the truth, Ilka had accepted a new lie that would tie her once and for all to her father's family.

How irritating, she thought. She shook her head. Raymond Fletcher had gotten what he deserved, though, and she really didn't care which of the two women had ended his life, which was why she'd gone along with the deception. He was dead, and that was good. She would never forgive him for what he'd done to her father. And to her.

She realized she should call Davidson to tell him the good news, but after grabbing her phone she remembered Amber's horses. Davidson seemed to be a good man, but those horses would have to be returned before Ilka could trust him. She should be calling Frank Conaway; now that Fletcher was dead, she was sure the case against him would be dropped, after what Mary Ann had said.

She held her phone to her ear and walked to the back door. Odd, she thought; it was unlocked. Alarm bells rang in her head and adrenaline shot through her body as she put the phone away. The curtains in Sister Eileen's dark apartment were pulled.

Cautiously she pushed the door open, tiptoed inside, and stopped to listen. Silence. The preparation room was closed, and though Artie hadn't used it the past few days, she could still smell the sharp chemical odor. She crept past the office and arrangement room, and when she reached the reception, Sister Eileen was sitting in a chair against the wall, where Michael Graham had waited when he arrived to plan his wife's burial. A small suitcase stood on the floor beside her.

Ilka stared. Instead of her headpiece and nun's habit, she was wearing a pair of jeans and a thin beige sweater. Her short hair was brushed back. She looked Ilka right in the eyes.

"Lydia Rogers, that woman the man was asking about this morning. It's me. The people who have been following you are looking for me."

Ilka made her way over to the desk and sat down. The look on the nun's face alarmed her. She leaned her arms on the desk and waited.

Sister Eileen sat in her familiar way, hands laced on her lap, as she held Ilka's eye. "I'm sorry you've been dragged into all of this. It wasn't my intention."

"What do you mean?"

Sister Eileen shook her head but didn't answer her. "I'm

leaving now. I can't allow what happened to Artie to happen to you. They're too close, and that's dangerous."

If she hadn't looked and sounded so serious, this sinister mood the nun was building would have annoyed Ilka. But there was something else going on that sent shivers up her spine: Sister Eileen had vanished. A different woman was sitting over by the wall.

"But what did you do?"

Suddenly Sister Eileen looked over at the door, and Ilka's eyes followed, even though she knew it was locked, with the CLOSED sign hanging in it.

"It's more what they're accusing me of."

"What?"

Sister Eileen took a deep breath. "I'm not a nun. For the past twelve years I've been living underground, on the run."

Ilka sank back in the chair. This was all way, way too much; she wasn't sure she could take any more. "But why?"

"They're accusing me of something I'm innocent of. And if they find me, I'll end up on death row. And they'll execute me."

"What? Death row? But…what is it they say you've done?"

"Murder. Multiple murders. They claim I've killed at least eight people."

Ilka shook her head. Not that it was *that* great a shock to learn this woman wasn't a nun; several things about her had made Ilka wonder. But these accusations sounded incredible. Her mouth felt dry as sandpaper. "But you didn't, right?"

Sister Eileen—Lydia Rogers—glanced over at the door again before nodding. "Yes, I did. But I had my reasons to do so, and also I didn't kill as many as they say I did."

301

Ilka's jaw dropped. "You've killed someone? Your nun's habit, that's just a disguise?"

She nodded again. They sat for a moment in silence, still looking, studying each other.

Ilka sat back up in her chair. "What do you mean, it's dangerous for me?"

"If they find me here, you could be hurt."

"*They*? Who are you talking about?"

"The man who was here this morning. The people who hurt Artie. The people who have been following you. They've been keeping an eye on you, hoping to find me. And they have. The man who approached us in the hospital parking lot, he recognized me."

"I don't get it, what do they want?"

"To have me arrested. They're after the reward. Right now, they're searching for your father too."

Ilka looked at her in disbelief. "But my father's dead! What does he have to do with it?"

Again, she ignored Ilka's question. "I have to get out of here."

"How much of this did my father know about? Did he know your nun habit was a disguise? That you're on the run?"

Lydia squirmed, but reluctantly she nodded. "He found out about it the first time they tracked me down."

Ilka was lost. "The first time?"

"Javi Rodriguez found me. He showed up one evening, but Paul heard me scream. And he came over and helped."

"But why are they looking for my father? I told the man who came by during the service that he was dead. It doesn't make any sense…"

Ilka watched as the woman's face froze. "What is it you're not telling me?"

For several seconds they stared at each other, then Lydia slowly shook her head. "Your father's not dead."

To be continued...

ACKNOWLEDGMENTS

Her Father's Secret is a work of fiction. The book refers to several places in Racine that exist, but I've allowed myself the freedom to change and move them around, as well as to dream up other locales to fit my story. Spending time in Racine has sparked my imagination, but all the characters and their names are fictional.

My heartfelt thanks goes out to Christina Gauguin, an undertaker at Elholm Mortuary. She was my first contact with the funeral home business, and during the past few years she has taken time to answer many questions. And thanks to Victor, Lone, and Marianne for your kindness and time. All of you are my inspiration for this series about an undertaker's daughter.

I also want to thank the Wilson Funeral Home and Anne Meredith from the Meredith Funeral Home in Racine for opening your doors to me and all my questions. Thank you for taking time to show me around and explain the finer points of the undertaking business that I wasn't aware of, the American traditions in the branch being so much different from those in Denmark. I'm so grateful to you.

As with all my earlier books, I'm indebted to Steen Holger Hansen, the forensic pathologist who is always there to answer my questions. You are always a great help and inspiration to me.

I could never have written this book without Benee Knauer, who helps me with research in the United States. Benee has answered tons of questions and helped me dig up information I couldn't track down. She's also the one who makes sure I'm up on gun laws, medicinal warnings, the judicial system, and everything else that can be difficult for a Dane to be aware of in the States. Thank you so much for helping make Racine and my American universe feel like a second home.

And thank you, Adam. My son has turned out to be a terrific researcher. Before I wrote the book, he plowed through everything there is to know about harness racing in Wisconsin. Thank you so much, it's such a pleasure to work with you. Concerning harness racing, I've made use of actual events and procedures, but here I've also allowed my imagination to build upon the information I've been given.

This book is dedicated to my close friend Preben Vridstoft, who introduced me to Racine. He's the one who told me about the town's large population of Danish descendants and that it's also called "Kringle-town" because of its three Danish bakeries that send Danish kringles out across America. Without Preben's extensive knowledge of the United States, Racine probably never would have showed up on my radar. And now I can't imagine my story taking place anywhere else. Thanks for always being there for me, Preben.

My publisher, People's Press, also deserves a big thank-you. It's a pleasure working with you all. A special thanks goes out to my fabulous editor, Lisbeth Møller-Madsen. She's always dedicated and knows precisely what I mean and what I want to talk about. Thank you so much, Lisbeth, we make a great team. Once again Rasmus Funder has zeroed in on the perfect mood for the book cover. *Thanks!* And thank you, Louise Thuesen, from the media department. I'm so happy to work with you.

I owe an enormous debt of gratitude to Elisa Lykke, my wonderful and talented PR agent. She keeps her sharp eye focused on what's best for me. Thank you for always being by my side when I need you, both in Denmark and in the United States. You make things happen, and working closely with you means very much to me.

I am so thankful for my agent, Victoria Sanders, and her terrific team at Victoria Sanders and Associates, Bernadette Baker-Baughman and Jessica Spivey. You have become my American family, for which I'm very grateful. Thank you for the extraordinary effort you put in on my behalf; not only do you make sure my books are published all over the world, but you're there for me whenever I need you. Thank you.

And one more time, Adam—my greatest thanks go out to you. Not only are you old enough now to help me in my work, but you're also the most important person in my life, my greatest support, my greatest happiness. Thank you.

Also, I'm sending an extra big thank-you out to those closest to me, because I'm never in doubt you're there, even though I'm far away for long periods of time. Thank you for making me feel you're much closer than the miles that separate us.

Finally, an enormous and heartfelt thank-you goes out to my fantastic readers and followers. You are my greatest source of encouragement. Thank you for your support and thank you for the warm welcome you've given to Ilka. I'm deeply grateful for your interest in reading what I write. It means everything to me!

—Sara Blaedel

ABOUT THE AUTHOR

Sara Blaedel's interest in story, writing, and especially crime fiction was nurtured from a young age, long before Scandinavian crime fiction took the world by storm. Today she is Denmark's "Queen of Crime" and is published in thirty-seven countries. Her series featuring police detective Louise Rick is adored the world over, and her new Family Secrets series has launched to great critical success.

The daughter of a renowned Danish journalist and an actress whose career included roles in theater, radio, TV, and movies, Sara grew up surrounded by a constant flow of professional writers and performers visiting the Blaedel home. Despite her struggle with dyslexia, books gave Sara a world in which to escape when her introverted nature demanded an exit from the hustle and bustle of life.

Sara tried a number of careers, from a restaurant apprenticeship to graphic design, before she started a publishing company called Sara B, where she published Danish translations of American crime fiction.

Publishing ultimately led Sara to journalism, and she covered a wide range of stories, from criminal trials to the premiere of *Star Wars: Episode I*. It was during this time—and while skiing in Norway—that Sara started brewing the ideas for her first novel. In 2004 Louise Rick and her friend Camilla Lind were introduced in *Grønt Støv* (*Green Dust*), and Sara won the Danish Academy for Crime Fiction's debut prize.

Originally from Denmark, Sara has lived in New York but now spends most of her time in Copenhagen with her family. She has always loved animals; she still enjoys horse riding and shares her home with her cat and golden retriever. When she isn't busy committing brutal murders on the page, she is an ambassador with Save the Children and serves on the jury of a documentary film competition.